Praise for Michele Bardsley's
Wizards of Nevermore Series

"Ex[...]cepts, and a compellingly dark atmosphere."
—*Publishers Weekly*

"The consistently excellent Bardsley introduces a new world with the launch of her Wizards of Nevermore series.... The opening salvo in this edgy and sexy series provides more evidence of Bardsley's supreme storytelling chops! Great stuff!"
—*Romantic Times* (top pick)

"Don't miss out on this dark, vibrant, and sexy new world."
—Fresh Fiction

"The world of the Wizards of Nevermore is refreshingly new and fully developed yet interwoven inside the fast-paced story line."
—Alternative Worlds

"Combines all the suspense and excitement of a magical tale with the sensual allure of a sweet and passionate love story. I hope there's a sequel in the works because I can't wait to visit the good folks of Nevermore again."
—Jeanne C. Stein, national bestselling author of the Anna Strong Vampire Chronicles

"High-octane urban fantasy at its sexiest. Michele Bardsley is the master!"—Mario Acevedo, author of *Werewolf Smackdown*

"Darkly superb, sinfully sexy—*Never Again* should be read over and over again!"
—Dakota Cassidy, national bestselling author of the Accidental series

"Bardsley pulls no punches, opening this new series with a book that's gritty, sexy, and absolutely captivating. I never wanted *Never Again* to end."
—Nicole Peeler, author of *Tempest's Legacy*

"Grim and whimsical, sexy and sinister, *Never Again* is a wicked paranormal triumph and a clever twisty homage to Poe with a splash of Lovecraft. I loved it!"
—Mark Henry, author of *Road Trip of the Living Dead*

continued ...

"Wow! *Never Again* is a gripping addition to the paranormal genre. I loved this tale of lost characters finding each other in a world of intriguing magical realities and eerie small-town secrets." —Carolyn Crane, author of *Double Cross*

"*Never Again* sizzles when it should but doesn't skimp on the murder, magic, or intrigue. This one deserves a spot on any romance lover's bookshelf." —J. F. Lewis, author of *Crossed*

Praise for Michele Bardsley's Broken Heart Series

Come Hell or High Water

"The sex scenes are molten, the main characters engaging yet deliciously flawed, and the story line keeps you hooked from first page to last." —Fresh Fiction

"Bardsley has brought us another amazing story. . . . Phoebe and Conner's struggle between their feelings for each other and what they must do is captured by Bardsley's endless wit and humor." —Night Owl Romance

"Bardsley is a true gift to the literary world. . . . It takes little more than a page or two to suck the reader back in and remind them why Broken Heart is one of their favorite places to visit." —Bitten by Books

Over My Dead Body

"The latest chapter in Bardsley's delightfully humorous series launches the action quickly and adds more danger to the mix." —*Romantic Times* (4½ stars)

"A great paranormal romance that I would definitely recommend to readers who enjoy a fast-paced story that will leave them guessing until the end." —Fresh Fiction

"[Bardsley's] writing inspires emotions that will have you sobbing and then laughing hysterically with just the turn of a few pages." —Bitten by Books

Wait till Your Vampire Gets Home

"Has action aplenty and a free-spirited, wittily sarcastic heroine who will delight fans." —*Booklist*

"Bardsley has one of the most entertaining series on the market. The humor and wackiness keep hitting the sweet spot. Add Bardsley to your auto-buy list!"
—*Romantic Times* (top pick, 4½ stars)

Because Your Vampire Said So

"Lively, sexy, out of this world—as well as in it—fun! Michele Bardsley's vampire stories rock!" —Carly Phillips

"Five ribbons! I laughed nonstop from beginning to end.... Michele Bardsley always creates these characters that leave readers feeling like they are our next-door neighbors."
—*Romance Junkies*

Don't Talk Back to Your Vampire

"Cutting-edge humor and a raw, seductive hero make *Don't Talk Back to Your Vampire* a yummylicious treat!"
—Dakota Cassidy

"A fabulous combination of vampire lore, parental angst, romance, and mystery. I loved this book!" —Jackie Kessler

"A winning follow-up to *I'm the Vampire, That's Why* filled with humor, supernatural romance, and truly evil villains."
—*Booklist*

I'm the Vampire, That's Why

"From the first sentence, Michele grabbed me and didn't let me go! A vampire mom? PTA meetings? A sulky teenager? Throw in a gorgeous, ridiculously hot hero and you've got the paranormal romance of the year. Get this one NOW."
—MaryJanice Davidson

"Hot, hilarious, one helluva ride.... Michele Bardsley weaves a sexily delicious tale spun from the heart." —L. A. Banks

"A fun, fun read!" —Rosemary Laurey

"Michele Bardsley has penned the funniest, quirkiest, coolest vampire tale you'll ever read. It's hot and funny and sad and wonderful, the kind of story you can't put down and won't forget. Definitely one for the keeper shelf." —Kate Douglas

NOW OR NEVER

Wizards of Nevermore

Michele Bardsley

A SIGNET ECLIPSE BOOK

SIGNET ECLIPSE
Published by New American Library, a division of
Penguin Group (USA) Inc., 375 Hudson Street,
New York, New York 10014, USA
Penguin Group (Canada), 90 Eglinton Avenue East, Suite 700, Toronto,
Ontario M4P 2Y3, Canada (a division of Pearson Penguin Canada Inc.)
Penguin Books Ltd., 80 Strand, London WC2R 0RL, England
Penguin Ireland, 25 St. Stephen's Green, Dublin 2,
Ireland (a division of Penguin Books Ltd.)
Penguin Group (Australia), 250 Camberwell Road, Camberwell, Victoria 3124,
Australia (a division of Pearson Australia Group Pty. Ltd.)
Penguin Books India Pvt. Ltd., 11 Community Centre, Panchsheel Park,
New Delhi - 110 017, India
Penguin Group (NZ), 67 Apollo Drive, Rosedale, Auckland 0632,
New Zealand (a division of Pearson New Zealand Ltd.)
Penguin Books (South Africa) (Pty.) Ltd., 24 Sturdee Avenue,
Rosebank, Johannesburg 2196, South Africa

Penguin Books Ltd., Registered Offices:
80 Strand, London WC2R 0RL, England

First published by Signet Eclipse, an imprint of New American Library,
a division of Penguin Group (USA) Inc.

First Printing, March 2012
10 9 8 7 6 5 4 3 2 1

For Steve . . .
Du fyller mitt hjerte med glede.

ACKNOWLEDGMENTS

I adore my agent, Stephanie Kip Rostan, her assistant, Monika Verma, and all the wonderful folks at the Levine Greenberg Literary Agency. I luvs you all!

Chocolate-covered, gold-embossed gratitude goes to my wonderful editor, Kerry Donovan, to the very groovy Jesse Feldman, who rules the world and all who live in it, and, of course, to Extreme Team NAL.

Heartfelt thanks to my awesome Viking, Steve Freeman, for helping me brainstorm several key elements in this novel (including the cursed gun and the absinthe bar). He's also the reason I know about Lagavulin scotch. You are my real-life romance hero. I love you!

Big smoochy-woochy lurve to my babies, Kati, Reid, and Emma, and to my grandson, Keegan. You all make my world a happier place.

I have *mucho* adoration for Renee George and Dakota Cassidy, who are brilliant, kind, loving, ass-kicking, hilarious women. Mwah!

Qwill, aka Second Supreme Overlord, could probably take over a small country if she weren't so busy running my little corner of the Internetz. You're awesome, Q!

Special thanks to Kaz, who is a spectacular friend, great listener, tequila connoisseur, and freaking genius.

Big awesome hugs, thanks, and luuuuurve to the

Acknowledgments

Book Addicts: Cid, Suzan, Linda, and I-live-in-Japan Alice. Y'all rock!

Smooches to Wendy Bocock and Amanda Fenley, who held my hand (and by "held my hand" I mean "badgered me relentlessly") about finishing this book.

I also want to acknowledge my adoration for the Jennifers (Wendy, Amanda, Mindy, and Stephanie), who were named as such because I could never remember who the hell they were. But I do now! Really!

To my Minions and to all my fans everywhere—you rock! Your continued support and enthusiasm for my books mean the world. Thank you!

*Ah, distinctly I remember it was in the bleak
    December,*
*And each separate dying ember wrought its ghost
    upon the floor.*
*Eagerly I wished the morrow;—vainly I had sought
    to borrow*
*From my books surcease of sorrow—sorrow for the
    lost Lenore*
*For the rare and radiant maiden whom the angels
    name Lenore*
Nameless here for evermore.

—From "The Raven," Edgar Allan Poe

Origins of the Magicals
and the Mundanes

Once, all humans could touch magic.

Then the world fell into terror and ruin. Magic became a weapon of cruelty, of war.

The heart of the Goddess broke.

It was She who severed the link between humans and magic. But the world did not become a better place. Humans born without the innate ability to connect to the sacred energies were even more susceptible to the Dark One's influence.

The Goddess decided to return magic through the bloodlines of six champions, pure in heart and in spirit. To keep the balance, She gave each a specific element to use and to protect. So that they would remember their responsibilities to the earth and its creatures, She asked them to choose a symbol.

Jaed, keeper of fire, chose dragon; Olin, keeper of air, picked hawk; Kry, keeper of water, took shark; Leta, keeper of earth, asked for wolf; Drun, keeper of life, wanted sun; and Ekro, keeper of death, chose raven.

The Goddess imbued each symbol with the essence of the living things that represented Her Chosen. These emblems were etched into the very flesh of the champions, that they might remember their purpose—to protect life and keep the balance.

Only their progeny could access the sacred energies, and they became known as magicals. Those who had no elemental connections became known as mundanes.

As time passed, the purity of the Chosen's lines was weakened, compromised, changed. Powers intermixed, and the line of Drun appeared to die out completely. However, every so often, a magical would be born with the ability to control life, and these rare beings became known as thaumaturges. And their opposites also existed, rarer beings still, known as thanaturges—magicals who could manipulate death, in all its forms.

Two thousand years ago, the Romans created five Houses: House of Dragons, House of Hawks, House of Wolves, House of Sharks, and House of Ravens. They also created the first Grand Court, made up of representatives from the Houses, to govern all magicals. The original building in Rome is still used today. (Not long after the American Revolution, a second Grand Court was established in Washington, D.C.) Children who showed strong connections with a particular element aligned with the appropriate House and were trained by masters in the magical arts. As a sign of loyalty to both their heritage and their House, all members were tattooed with the symbols chosen by their ancestors—a tradition still strongly adhered to.

Though governed separately, most magicals and mundanes live side by side all over the world. Some choose to live within communities created to serve only their own kind, and others align with a particular House to gain their protections.

Whether magical or mundane, there is one truth that binds all: It is the heart of human struggle to seek balance between the darkness and the light.

Prologue

Twenty-five years ago . . .
Somewhere in Washington, D.C. . . .

Millicent Dover loved children.

She would never, ever be able to have any of her own, so she funneled all that motherly tenderness to her charges at the Raven's Heart orphanage.

Raven's Heart was a repository for those darlings who were too different to succeed in their mundane families. Should an infant begin to show signs of magical heritage or be born with hex marks or, in some sad cases, otherworldly extremities—tails being the most common—the parents could drop off their newborns, or any child up to the age of four, to Raven's Heart.

No questions asked.

A death certificate would be issued, and if necessary, a coroner's report.

And the poor dears would be left in Millicent's care.

Since the House of Ravens funded the orphanage, their members received priority access to the young magicals. Even so, she worked very hard to place the children in good homes, and she worked even harder to make sure the children were well mannered, strong in mind and in body, and above all, obedient.

Millicent didn't tolerate sass.

If the children at Raven's Heart had not been adopted by the age of five, they were sent to workhouses in Mexico or gifted to European businesses that catered to a . . . well, *particular* clientele.

And then there were Millicent's angels.

Like the adorable cherub who held her hand so tightly now.

She was such a good girl—smart, pretty, duteous. There was just something about her. She had a . . . sparkle. Millicent loved her angels the best, she really did, but it seemed as though Lenore had more to offer this world.

Well, thought Millicent, perhaps that shine would serve her well on the other side. Yes. Sweet little Lenore would be the brightest of all the angels.

Millicent opened the door to the special room. Only her angels were allowed to see it. It was all pink and ruffles and lace. Cheerful. Like walking into a pile of cotton candy.

In the corner sat a white chaise lounge, the perfect

spot for an angel's repose. They always looked peaceful as they lay down to rest. It was a point of pride for her that they never suffered. She photographed their final moments and put those pictures into the scrapbooks she kept. Sometimes she would take her dinner breaks in this room and remember all the children she had loved, and who had loved her.

"It's very pretty in here, Miss Millicent."

"Thank you, dear." She patted the girl's bouncy black curls. "Go sit in the chair. We'll have cookies and tea. And while you enjoy your treats, I'll read you a story."

The tea service was already set up; so was the plate arrangement of paper-thin cookies.

Lenore took her seat and waited for Millicent to take hers.

"One lump of sugar, or two?" asked Millicent as she picked up the teapot.

"Two, please."

Oh, she was so polite. Such a treasure. Millicent smiled as she poured the fragrant liquid into the delicate china cups. "You must drink all of your tea before taking a cookie."

"Yes, ma'am."

The girl placed the edge of the cup to her lips, and for the tiniest moment, Millicent had the urge to knock it out of her hand.

No. She'd been given her directive. The girl's father himself had insisted his five-year-old daughter be put into Millicent's care; and more specifically, that Lenore be given angelic treatment. Even though it was rare for magicals to give up their own children, especially a powerful Raven like Lenore's father, it wasn't exactly unheard of, either. She'd seen the disappointment in the father's eyes as he looked at his daughter.

Mundanes gave up their children for being too magical.

Lenore's father had given her up because she was not magical enough.

Such a shame, too, because the girl was otherwise perfect. But Millicent had long ago learned that she should not question her betters. Her life was devoted to the children at Raven's Heart. And though she was experiencing unusual doubts about seeing Lenore to the other side, she would do her duty.

The girl took the barest of sips before grimacing. "Miss Millicent, this tastes funny."

Startled, Millicent stared at Lenore's light blue eyes. She'd seen a crystal like that once, such a light blue it was nearly white. Like ice.

Like judgment.

A chill stole through Millicent, but she would not be cowed by the girl. She frowned. "It's very rude to make disparaging comments about what your hostess is serving. You are a guest, Lenore."

"I apologize," she said in a soft, penitent voice. "But isn't it rude of the hostess to put death into the tea?"

Millicent blinked. The brew was her own special blend of herbs and alprazolam. She used just the right amount of jasmine and magic to disguise the taste.

"I would like to go home," said Lenore. She put down the full cup, then folded her hands in her lap. She stared unblinkingly at Millicent. Those glacier eyes seemed more tinted now, more blue, more . . . magical.

The back of Millicent's neck prickled, and sweat beaded her brow. Lenore really was the most amazing child. None of her angels had ever suspected the tea was doctored. None had ever uttered a complaint.

"I'm afraid you can't go home," said Millicent.

She nodded, then sighed. "Father does not want me."

"You really should drink the tea, dear. It's for the best."

The girl glanced at the cup. "No, thank you. May I go now?"

"Where would you go?"

Lenore considered this question, one finger perched on her chin. "Away," she said. "Far, far away."

"That's not a destination," said Millicent. She rose, smoothed out her dress, and smiled at the girl. "While you decide where you would like to go, I will get the book. Do you like the story of Cinderella?"

"Yes," said Lenore.

Millicent turned toward the bookshelf. Not only did the tall pink case house a well-stocked array of children's titles; the bejeweled box on the upper shelf held a syringe. It was her plan B. Thirty-four angels she'd sent to the other side, and she'd never had to use it.

Lenore was an amazing child, indeed.

She opened the box and withdrew the syringe, cupping the cylinder in her hand to hide it, and then she pulled the oversized pop-up book from its place on a lower shelf.

"Now," she said brightly as she turned, "let's—"

Lenore stood by the table, looking at Millicent with such a sad gaze. "You really aren't very nice," she said. She looked around the room. "They're all here. And they're mad."

Millicent swallowed the sudden, tight knot in her throat. She brought the book up to her chest, almost as though it might serve as a shield. "Who's here, Lenore?"

"The children you murdered. They told me about the tea. They told me what you did."

"I would never, ever hurt my angels," she said sharply.

Pity entered Lenore's gaze. She had such an adult look about her. And she was so eerily calm.

"Good-bye, Miss Millicent."

She turned to go. She was even so bold as to take steps toward the door. Millicent was stunned by the chit's gall. Lenore actually believed she could walk out of here? Leave the only person who would ever, *ever* love her?

Rage thrummed through Millicent. She uttered a cry, dropping the book, and raised the syringe. She'd been wrong about Lenore. She wasn't special. She wasn't amazing. She was a horrid, horrid child. She didn't deserve to be an angel. Not ever.

"Evil girl," she hissed as her arm came down. "You will burn in hell."

Lenore stopped, then turned. "Not me," she said, her voice filled with sorrow. "You."

The syringe never made contact.

Lenore's odd blue gaze blazed as hard and cold as crystal, as ice . . . as death.

Violent wind came out of nowhere. It shattered the china, knocked books off the shelves, ripped the lace curtains. Lenore stood in the middle of the chaos, watching with distant eyes as Millicent was flung backward, the syringe falling uselessly to the pink shag carpet.

She landed on the chaise, her eyes wide, her mouth open in a silent scream. Pressure from little hands crushed her chest, and tiny fingers scratched at her windpipe.

Her lungs flattened.

Her heart slowed.

Her vision grayed.

11

She saw her angels then, all around her, pushing and shoving and clawing.

And as she struggled for her life, to escape from the vengeance of those she had loved, she saw Lenore give her one last pitying look and walk out of the room.

The quiet snick of the door's closing was the last sound Millicent ever heard.

Chapter 1

Present day . . .

"She's filthy."

Norie Whyte stared dully at the man in the black robe, his tall, bulky form hidden by the layers of shining cloth. The hood covered his face, but even through the mush that was currently her mind, she recognized the man's voice. He was the one who kept showing up and bossing everyone else around. The two guys holding her up were leaning away as much as possible. She'd gotten used to the stench, just as she'd gotten used to sleeping on the floor and defecating in a bucket and being naked—and being stoned out of her mind.

"You said to make sure she couldn't escape again. You didn't say nothing about keeping her clean." This protest rang out from the bald guy on the left, the one who liked to stare at her breasts and touch himself. He knew better than to try to get his jollies with her. She used to have

13

three guards, but one had made the mistake of trying to rape her.

The man in the black robe had punched a hole in his chest with his fist and magic, and then he had coldly watched the horny bastard bleed out on the floor. Then he'd used his magic to turn the body into ash. Just . . . *poof*. No more rapist. Then he'd looked at the other two, who'd both pissed themselves, and said calmly, "Do you also require an explanation of what 'virgin sacrifice' means?"

They didn't.

She didn't know Black Robe's name, his title, his House, or his face. But she knew one thing quite well: He was an asshole.

"I won't do it." She wasn't sure if the words actually made it past her throat. Then Black Robe swung toward her, and she knew he'd heard the hoarse protest.

"It's your destiny, Norie."

"Bullshit." Her voice was stronger this time, but it still sounded like a rusted hinge.

He slapped her hard across the face. She felt the shock of that blow all the way to her toes, and she would've fallen had it not been for her captors' holding her so tightly. Her cheek bloomed with wicked pain, but she still managed to turn her head and stare at Black Robe with as much defiance as she could muster.

Gods-be-damned! She wanted to punch him. She wanted to knee his balls and claw his face and pull out his hair. But she hadn't the energy, and her anger was sliding away, into the fog of apathy, into the resignation that was nearly as familiar as all the other wretched things about the turn her life had taken. She knew then that the newest dose of magic-laced drugs was kicking in. Her tongue felt thick, and her head felt stuffed with cotton.

"Are you feeding her?" Black Robe asked.

The guards shuffled their feet. "We try to, but she won't eat."

"She can't die before the ceremony, damn it." Black Robe sighed. "Very well. It's obvious that she requires care other than yours now."

"Aw right. You want us to clean up here?" asked the bald guy. He made the sound of an explosion. "Y'know, like we did the other places?"

"I can take it from here." Black Robe grabbed Norie, sweeping her against his chest and raising one hand toward the startled men. Through her graying vision, she saw the fireball emerge, split in two, and hit each of her guards square in the chest. She wasn't exactly sorry to see the bastards burn.

They screamed and flailed, falling onto the floor and trying to roll around. But the fire was born of magic, and it wasn't like a mundane-created fire. It couldn't be doused or suffocated.

Black Robe threw her over his shoulder and walked away. She realized vaguely she'd been holed up in a warehouse. She could smell the sea air, which wasn't exactly refreshing, what with all the dead-fish and garbage stink. Nausea roiled. She almost wished she would throw up, so she could ruin His Highness's robe.

The building started to flame; in moments, it was completely on fire. Norie stared dazedly at the flames licking the wood and snaking toward the wharf. The whole dock would be on fire soon. Someone from Magic Protection Services would have to be called in to combat the spell. And the bastard holding her like a moldy old sack of potatoes probably didn't give a shit if he burned down the whole city.

Black Robe tossed her into the back of the limousine. By the time she hit the seat, Norie was nearly unconscious.

"Everyone has a destiny," said her tormentor again, "and you will fulfill yours."

Those were the last words she heard before darkness claimed her.

Sheriff Taylor Mooreland slammed shut the door to his crotchety old SUV, grimacing at the creaking sounds of rusted springs and tired metal. He ought to put in for a new vehicle, but doing so would mean yet another change. And there'd already been a lot of changes around Nevermore, Texas.

It made life unnerving, damn it.

He liked routine. Order. Knowing that what happened today would probably happen tomorrow. He took comfort in consistency.

He pulled his thick wool coat tighter, zipping it up to the neck. Then he leaned against the side of the SUV and stared up at the twinkling stars.

It wasn't even dawn, for fuck's sake.

He scrubbed his face, trying to wipe off the tired, but he still felt like a zombie. He needed more coffee, and that meant hauling his ass up to his office and wrestling with that new-fangled machine. His assistant, Arlene, had requisitioned a new coffeemaker, and Gray Calhoun, Dragon wizard and the town's current Guardian, had had one imported from Italy. Italy! The thing was huge and shiny and filled with a thousand dials and spouts. It looked like something out of a Dr. Seuss book. These days, Gray took his job as Guardian seriously, getting involved in every aspect of protecting the town and its citizens, not to mention governing as well.

The wind whipped at Taylor's coat and brought with it the ashy-sweet scent of incense—from the temple, no doubt.

He shifted and paused. The wind carried another scent, too—a wonderful smell that brought back memories of his mother in the kitchen baking. Grief sliced through him. She'd been gone almost six years now. And not a day went by that he didn't miss her.

He sniffed the air. *Well, I'll be.* It sure did smell like cookies.

Sugar cookies.

His favorite.

He looked around, but Main Street was dark and quiet. The brick buildings looked the same as ever, and so did the sidewalks and the street, and there, where Main Street ended in a large cul-de-sac, gleamed the shining brass dragon, and behind it, the Temple of Light. People showed up every week to pay homage to the Goddess and to their Dragon forebear, Jaed. The big wooden doors were always unlocked—allowing supplicants into the inner chamber with its polished oak pews and shining stained-glass windows. Magic kept the torches on the walls burning red and orange, the colors of Jaed—the colors of dragons. The temple was open to anyone, night or day.

He felt a sudden urge to walk down there, to slide into one of the pews, and to ask the Goddess for guidance. He'd always had a goal, a purpose. But lately, he'd felt unbalanced, as if the ground beneath his feet were about to shift and swallow him whole.

Damned nightmares. He hadn't had a single good night's rest in the last six days. He didn't want to admit that the nightmares were costing him physically and emotionally. All the same, he figured it wouldn't hurt to talk to Ember. She was a good friend who ran the local tea shop, and she had an herbal remedy for everything; surely she could whip up something tasty and magical to help him sleep.

For a long moment Taylor stared at the temple, a beacon of solace in the darkness, and then he turned toward the steps that led up to the sheriff's office. It wasn't that he had anything against the Goddess, or religion for that matter. He deeply respected not only the faith of believers but also the right of every individual to worship whatever deities he liked. But he wasn't a church kind of guy.

Pain throbbed in the center of his forehead, and he rubbed at the aching spot. It looked like aspirin was in order, too. After a final sweeping glance of the empty street, he headed up the stairs and unlocked the door.

The smell of sugar cookies followed him inside.

"Please describe the . . . er, creature," said Sheriff Mooreland. His pen was poised above the form his assistant, Arlene Tanner, had created specifically for this particular situation. He glanced up at the man sitting in one of the leather wingback chairs facing Taylor's oversized antique desk.

"Red," said Henry Archer. "Definitely red." His cowboy hat was perched on his knee, his fingers tapping the crown. His gaze was steady, same as his manner, but the man's expression kept wavering between disbelief and shock. "Scaly, too."

Taylor nodded, then looked down at the form with its neat rows of check boxes. His pen scratched over the crisp paper. "What else?"

"Wings," admitted Henry. "It was a big son of a bitch. Blotted out the moon, Sheriff. Startled me so badly last night, I tripped over my own two feet and went ass over teakettle into Maureen's begonias."

Taylor's lips quirked. "And how'd she take that?"

"'Bout as well as you might think," said Henry, smiling, too. "Don't suppose Ant might be willing to come over and see if they can be coaxed back to life?"

"I'm sure my brother could be talked into it," said Taylor. "Especially if it means he can get within snatching distance of one of Maureen's apple pies."

"Three were cooling in the kitchen when I left," said Henry. "The more agitated my wife gets, the more pies she makes." He chuckled. "Sometimes I rile her up just so I can get some of her blackberry cobbler."

Taylor's smile widened as he looked over the report. "All right, then, Henry. Anything else?"

Henry hesitated, and then he sighed. "I saw a dragon, Sheriff. It was almost as if the statue in our town square had come to life. You don't think one of the magicals did a spell on it or something?"

Henry was looking for an explanation—other than, yeah, he'd seen a dragon flying around Nevermore's skies. In a world where some people could talk to the dead, control the elements, or, like Taylor's little brother, grow a garden from barren soil, the idea of an honest-to-goddess dragon still freaked people out.

"The statue's protected. No one could pull a prank

like that even if they were fool enough to try," said Taylor. He studied his friend. His instincts were humming, and he knew Henry was holding something back. "What else?"

Henry grimaced. "I swear I wasn't drinking," he said. "We got into the habit of not keeping alcohol in the house because Lennie . . . Well, you know. We never was much for the hard stuff anyway." He paused, his gaze dropping.

Taylor let the man have a moment. Eight months ago, Henry and Maureen's youngest son, Lennie, had been killed. The young man's demise was one of three deaths that had been facilitated by Taylor's former deputy and half brother, Ren Banton. Ren had been killed, too, and that was just as well. Hell's bells. By the time it was all said and done, six people had gone to early graves. The whole debacle still weighed heavily on Taylor's mind, but at least life had gotten back to normal—if life in Nevermore could ever really be called *normal*.

"Anyway," said Henry, "I saw someone on its back."

Taylor blinked. "You saw a person *riding* the dragon?"

Henry nodded. "A woman. I think she was wearing . . . uh, you know—a nightie."

Oh, for the love of— Taylor stifled a groan. He dutifully added the description under "More Details," and then put the pen down. "That all?"

"Yessir." Henry stood up and plopped the cowboy

21

hat onto his head. "Thanks for taking the time to hear me out."

"I appreciate your coming in," said Taylor. He stood up, too, and rounded the desk to shake Henry's hand. Then he walked the man out of his office and into the main foyer. "You headed back to the store?"

"Yep."

"Tell Maureen I said hello."

"Will do."

Taylor watched the man leave and then glanced at Arlene's desk, just as big and old as his own. It gave him a sense of satisfaction to see everything in its place. The office had been changed here and there over the years, but, like most things in Nevermore, it had stayed largely the same. He liked the continuity of it all, the way this building and all that it housed had been used by those who'd stood vigil over the town before him.

Arlene kept everything spotless and orderly, just the way he liked it. The black-and-white-checkered linoleum floor gleamed despite its age. He suspected Arlene bought magic-enhanced cleaners, which was fine by him. He didn't want to dip into the coffers to replace anything if he didn't have to.

Taylor clasped his hands behind his back and looked around. Off to the left of Arlene's desk was a locked door that led to the archives. Only Arlene ventured inside there, and not even he risked invading that domain. To the right of the foyer was the entrance to his own office, which faced Main Street. The picture window allowed him a proper view of downtown, not that there was much to watch.

A narrow hallway led to the former deputy's office, a supply closet, the bathrooms, and the break room, and the back door that opened onto the alley. Beyond the break room was the secured door that led down to the basement, and to the rarely used jail cells. One had been built especially to dampen the powers of magicals, but he'd never had cause to use it.

Satisfied that all was in order, Taylor returned to the foyer and breathed deeply. Before he could enjoy the satisfaction for very long, he caught sight of his watch and frowned. Arlene had been gone for more than half an hour. A couple times a day she'd go across the street and check on Atwood Stephens; the man, who looked like an exhausted rhinoceros, owned both the town garbage service and the weekly paper, *Nevermore News*. His health had been deteriorating rapidly, and not even Lucinda's gift of healing had been able to do much more than slow the decline. Atwood's nephew, Trent Whitefeather, had been taking over more and more of his uncle's responsibilities. He was a senior in high school, and despite the burdens of his home life, was still a straight-A student.

Taylor headed for his office, but he heard the rattle of the front door, so he turned back. He expected to see

Arlene chug inside, already complaining about Atwood's stubborn hide, but, to his surprise, he saw Gray Calhoun. The wizard still wore his hair long, but these days, he kept it neatly trimmed. His nose crooked in the middle; the angles of his face were sharp as blades, as sharp as the look in his blue eyes. A faded scar on the left side of his face twirled from his temple down his neck, hiding beneath the collar of his T-shirt.

"Gray," he said, offering a congenial nod.

"Hey, Taylor," said Gray, smiling.

He did that a lot these days. He was the happiest son of a bitch in town, and Taylor felt, well, jealous of his friend's connubial bliss. It made him feel petty, so he heartily shook Gray's hand, and said, "C'mon. Arlene finessed that damned machine into a fresh batch of coffee."

"You might want something stronger," said Gray as he followed Taylor down the hall and into the break room. "I just got word that my mother will be here in time for our Samhain celebration. With all twelve of her lictors."

"A dozen bodyguards?" Taylor gestured for his friend to sit at the table, and Gray grabbed a chair and slid into it. "I thought she traveled with only three."

"All the Consuls have been encouraged to keep their lictors close. Things are tense in political circles," said Gray. "There are rumors that the House of Ravens might secede from the Grand Court."

Shock stilled Taylor's movements. He didn't much pay attention to things outside Nevermore, but damn, that was bad news all the way around. "Can they do that?"

"There's no precedence," said Gray. "Not in two thousand years since the Houses and the first Grand Court were formed. If the Ravens withdraw from the current governing structure, it may well start a war."

"That would mean a whole lot of scrambling for the mundanes, too. Nonmagicals won't like the idea of rogue witches and wizards."

"Let's hope the current Consuls can make the Ravens see reason."

"Yeah," said Taylor. "Let's hope." He paused. "So, you got enough room in that house for your visitors?"

"Not for twelve giants and certainly not for my mother's angst. When I told her about marrying Lucinda, I think her head exploded."

"Well, you did marry the sister of your ex-wife, who sold your soul to a demon lord."

"I'm aware," said Gray drily.

Taylor handed the Guardian a mug and then took the spot across from him. "I'm surprised Leticia didn't come down long before now."

"No doubt she stayed away so she could plot in private." He shook his head. "That's not fair of me. She's upset, I know, but once she meets Lucy, she'll be fine with it."

Taylor wasn't so sure. Leticia was a spectacular woman, but she was also as stubborn as the day was long. "How long is your mother staying?"

Gray blinked. "Ah. Well, through the winter solstice festival."

"So, she'll be here for . . ." Taylor narrowed his gaze. "Oh, crap. You haven't told her?"

"No. Other than you, Ember, and Rilton, we haven't told anyone."

"Well, you don't have to," said Taylor, rolling his eyes. "Not with all the reports I've been getting."

"Sorry. We try to be discreet, but it's not easy."

"Shifting into a dragon is no small feat." He sent Gray a level gaze. "And neither is flying around with Lucy on your back."

"Oops."

"Yeah, *oops*," said Taylor. "All those stories about the magical ancestors being shifters . . . Well, people think they're myths. And you're gonna go prove 'em wrong. Everyone will know you're Jaed's champion."

"You're worried people will figure out that Nevermore is a magical hot spot."

"Bound to come out eventually."

"We have to trust the Goddess, Taylor."

Taylor nodded, but he looked away. He wasn't a magical. He lived with them, was related to them, and worked for them, but he was a mundane. And he didn't like Gray's suggestion of a magical war. All because the Ravens dropped out of the governing structure? Magical hot spots like Nevermore would be prime real estate in a wizard war. Yeah. It would be bad—for everyone, but especially for those without magic.

Gray drained his coffee mug. "I gotta get back to Lucy. The Halloween party is more than two weeks away, but she's already futzing over the decorations. You'll be there, right?"

"Wouldn't miss it," said Taylor. "I'm gonna win that pumpkin-carving contest."

Gray laughed, smacked Taylor on the shoulder, and then left, giving Taylor one last wave before he headed out.

Taylor took their mugs to the sink and rinsed them.

Pain shot from his temples to the center of his forehead, throbbing in a circle of agony. He dropped the mug, barely hearing its protesting clatter. He staggered forward, pressing his palm against his head. Gods-bedamned! Bright light danced behind his eyes, and he groaned. Then he heard a swooshing sound, like wings.

Accept what belongs to you, Taylor.

Then the pain disappeared.

He slowly straightened, wiping the sweat beading his brow, and tried to get back his equilibrium.

What the hell!?

He took a few deep breaths, clenching and unclenching his fists. With some effort, he pushed away the dread squeezing him as tightly as a constricting python.

"Taylor!"

Arlene's panicked voice had him shaking off the fear, the ghosts of pain, and rushing out of the break room, down the hall, and into the main office. He found her in the lobby, chest heaving and a quivering hand pressed against her throat. Her eyes were as wide as saucers.

"It's Atwood!" she cried. "The dumb son of a bitch went and killed himself!"

Taylor managed to snag Gray before he had gotten too far down Main Street. Together, they walked the short distance to the narrow brick building that housed the offices and home of Atwood. Arlene wanted to come with them, but Ember had arrived with tea and comfort, managing to talk his shaken assistant into staying put.

"Where's Trent?" asked Gray.

"Still in school. He usually comes over at lunchtime and checks on his uncle. Arlene passed him on the sidewalk and chatted with him for a minute. Then she went inside to harangue Atwood about his health."

"And he was still breathing?"

"Like a water buffalo in labor," said Taylor. He saw Gray's look and offered a grim smile. "Arlene's words.

He was in his upstairs apartment, lolling on the couch and watching television. She made sure he took his meds, cleaned up the lunch dishes, and was in the kitchen brewing herbal tea—and probably talking his ear off. Next thing she knew, he'd disappeared. That place isn't too big. Two bedrooms, one bathroom, the living area, and a tiny kitchen. She figured he'd lumbered downstairs to raid a stash of Twinkies or Little Debbie's. Trent told me Atwood had junk food tucked away in every nook and cranny."

"Stubborn bastard." Gray shook his head. "He left the apartment and got down the stairs without Arlene hearing him?"

"Apparently. When she realized he was gone, she went hunting for him. Found him in the newspaper archives. Said he shot himself, and she never heard a thing." Taylor sighed. "Well, no use standing out here and twiddling our thumbs."

Suicide or not, they still took the usual crime scene precautions. Both he and Gray gloved up and put booties on their shoes. Then Taylor opened the door, and they entered the dreary hallway.

The linoleum floor was filthy—not to mention cracked and hole-filled. The turquoise walls were stained, and in several places paint peeled away to reveal faded flower wallpaper. It smelled like stale cigar smoke and old takeout. Some floral scent floated through the stink, but whatever attempts had been made to cover *eau de Atwood* failed miserably. At the end of the hallway was the staircase that led to the apartment. On the left was the single-door entrance to Nevermore Garbage Services. Taylor knew the small office held a desk, two chairs, and a worn-out coffee-maker, along with two large file cabinets that didn't shut anymore due to Atwood's lousy filing system (shoving receipts and written complaints into the near-est open drawer, for example).

On the right was the door to the newspaper offices. It was slightly open, and Taylor pushed on the frosted glass etched with the faded gold words NEVERMORE NEWS. The door swung wider, and he stepped inside. Gray followed, and they both took a minute to assess the office. Two large desks—one antique and the other metal and Formica—were pushed together. A com-puter circa 1998 sat gathering dust on the metal desk, which held numerous piles of papers, files, thick dust, and Goddess knew what else—maybe the source of the bad smells. On the other desk, the typewriter looked as though it got more use than the computer, even though it was surrounded by the same amount of crap. The front windows were large, and had they not been filmed over with thick layers of grime, might have of-fered some light into the otherwise cavelike interior.

"He really let the place go to hell," said Gray mildly.

"Ramona was the one who kept everything orga-nized," said Taylor, referring to Atwood's deceased wife. A decade ago, she'd gotten on a ladder to hang up Christmas decorations, fallen off, and broken her neck. The tragic accident had devastated Atwood. He'd always been a prickly sort, but without the steadying influence of his wife, he turned into a true curmudgeon.

Everyone had been surprised when Atwood agreed to take in his orphaned nephew the previous year. Trent's parents had died in a car accident, leaving the teenager without a home, and with only one living relative. So Trent moved to Nevermore and started working for his uncle. With Atwood's health problems, the poor kid was actually running both shows. It was a lot of responsibility for a guy who'd just turned eighteen, especially one who was a necromancer, too. Trent was a talented wizard, but he refused to join a House. His father had been of Cherokee descent, so his views about magic tended to follow different paths.

"I don't think it's possible to figure out if anything was disturbed," said Gray. "I could do some spells, but I don't think it would help much."

"We don't know that we're looking for anything," said Taylor. "Not until we take a gander at ol' Atwood." To the left was another door, wide open, and he entered the small break room. It smelled rank, as if the refrigerator had been turned off and all the contents gone to rot. The sink was piled with crusty dishes and chipped mugs, and the small table held more dishes and papers.

Two rickety chairs were tucked under the table, which looked as if it might collapse at any moment. Taylor shook his head in disgust, feeling bad for Trent, who had to put up with this chaos and his surly uncle every day. The next door led into the newspaper archives, and it was a bigger mess than anything else they'd seen.

"Shit," said Gray, staring at the towering file cabinets that filled the room. A single light in the middle of the ceiling was still on, but its yellowed bulb didn't do much to disperse the shadows. It was a fairly large space, and the big metal monstrosities had been laid out in rows that created crepuscular passageways. Drawers burst with papers, and more stuff teetered on the tops. Some piles had fallen off, sliding down to clump on the floor like dirty snow. The only upside was that the stench had not penetrated in here. It only smelled musty, like an abandoned attic, which meant the door to the archives had probably been closed most of the time.

"I don't know how the hell Arlene managed to find him," said Taylor as he stepped over papers and wound through the cabinets.

"She's persistent," said Gray. He followed, cursing when he banged his knee against an open drawer. "It seems strange for a man to come all the way down here to put a bullet in his temple."

"Atwood wasn't without his quirks." Taylor paused. The musty scent of disuse gave way to the foulness of urine and feces. Poor Atwood. His bladder and bowels had evacuated. The awful stench had probably led Arlene to find him, too. She had a nose like a bloodhound.

"Over here," he called to Gray, taking the corner and nearly stepping on the body. Atwood wasn't a tall man, maybe six or seven inches over five feet. He weighed at least four hundred pounds, and he was wedged between the two rows of file cabinets. On the left were the smooth metal backs of the previous row, and on the right, a series of seemingly endless drawers, several lurching out and vomiting files. One of Atwood's arms had lodged on top of an opened drawer on the bottom, which meant the other arm was probably underneath him. On the lower-left side, where the gray metal shone dingily in the insufficient light, he spotted an Atwood-sized dent and a spray of blood and brain matter.

"He was on his knees," murmured Taylor.

"How do you know that?"

"It had to be a short fall to the floor. Otherwise, he would've made a lot more noise going down. Might've even knocked over a cabinet or two." He pointed to the gory dent, grimacing. If Atwood had taken a gun to his right temple, the force of the shot would've knocked him forcibly to the left, and then he would've fallen forward. Still, the back of Taylor's neck tingled. Something didn't feel right.

"We'll have to go around," he said. "There's no room to get by him."

"All right." Gray turned and made his way down the other side of the cabinets. Taylor followed, and moments later, they were crouched down about a foot away from Atwood, trying to study his body in the dim light.

Taylor grabbed his flashlight from his weapons belt, flicked it on, and aimed it at Atwood's head. The beam highlighted the black burn pattern around the large entry wound, which meant the gun was pressed against his right temple when it fired. *Holy Goddess.* The rest of his skull looked like hamburger meat. He was sure Atwood's right hand would test positive for gunshot residue. Taylor felt sick. It wasn't that he was sensitive to the atrocities of a crime scene, but it took him a second to tuck away the fact that Atwood, for all his faults, had been his friend. And the damned fool had killed himself. He sucked in a breath, put away his regrets, his anger, and got down to doing his job.

"Taylor," said Gray. "The gun."

Taylor shifted the flashlight, and he saw the gleam of a pistol. "Gods-be-damned," he whispered. "That's . . . It can't be." He looked over his shoulder at Gray and saw the Guardian's stunned expression.

"Harley Banton's Colt," said Gray.

"How'd it get here? It was locked up in evidence. Has been ever since the old boy killed himself a few months ago." The gun had seen its fair share of crimes. After all, the man had used that very gun to kill Taylor's father nearly twenty years before.

"You think Atwood stole it?" asked Gray.

"Don't know how he would," muttered Taylor. But how else would he have gotten his hands on the Peacemaker?

The gun was an antique, a family heirloom that was a prize possession in Harley Banton's gun collection. He'd always been proud of his grandfather's 1873 Colt SAA. It was highly collectible, one of the rare guns inspected by Orville W. Ainsworth, with an engraved silver barrel and a mother-of-pearl handle. As a law enforcement officer, Taylor was issued certain magical items for use in his job. These items could be triggered by mundanes, though true magic was always the realm of wizards and witches. He extracted a clear pellet from one of the pouches on his weapons belt. He held it over the gun and enacted the spell by saying, "Contain evidence." He dropped the little ball onto the gun. When it landed on the barrel, it broke open, and clear liquid coated the entire gun in a magical wrapping, sort of like dipping the weapon in rubber. Everything on the gun would be protected, though he doubted he'd find anything more than Atwood's prints and that the Colt had been fired recently.

After they processed the rest of the scene, Gray used his magic to transport Atwood's body to the old medical clinic, which was in the building next to the sheriff's office, and still had working cold storage and a surgery. Once upon a time, Nevermore had a doctor who'd also served as a coroner. Now they relied on Dr. Green, who rotated among the smaller towns. He made it into Nevermore once a month to do checkups, or to see to the dead. For the most part, the residents relied on themselves to fix ailments. Their only mage healer, Miss Natalie, had officially retired. People died of natural causes or farming accidents, and yeah, there was the occasional suicide. Murder—hell, crime of any kind—was rare in such a small town. Or, at least, it had been.

The so-called morgue didn't have fancy metal drawers for body storage. It had a walk-in freezer with sturdy, wide shelves. All the same, Atwood barely fit on a lower tier. He was still in his pajamas, barefoot, his skull bloodied and damaged.

"Not much else we can do," said Taylor. He cast one last pitying glance at the man, and then followed Gray out of the freezer. He shut the door and snapped the lock on it. The minute it snicked closed, a spell engaged. Anyone who touched the lock—*zzzzzt!*—would find himself zapped into unconsciousness.

"You think that's necessary?" asked Gray. "Who'd steal Atwood?"

"It might be overkill. But you know what Ren did."

"Yes," said Gray, his expression grim at the mention of Taylor's former deputy. "I know."

"I'll give Dr. Green a call and see when he can do the autopsy."

"All right. Helluva way to end the day," he said.

"Yeah," said Taylor. "Damned sure is."

"Let's go check on Banton's gun," said Gray.

Taylor had tucked the gun they found near Atwood into an empty holster on his weapons belt. Grimly, they exited the old clinic and walked next door to the sheriff's office. Ember had taken Arlene home earlier, and the place was quiet. To Taylor, ghosts seemed to hover in the corners, waiting, watching. The evidence "room" was a repurposed janitorial closet, and it hosted few items. The gun with which Harley Banton had committed suicide had been locked in a case.

Taylor opened the case and found it . . . empty.

"Shit." He pulled it off the shelf and showed it to Gray.

"The door was locked, and the case, too," said Gray. "I don't sense any magic. Someone had to take it."

"There's no way Atwood would've gotten in here without someone noticing. And I've tripled the protections on this place. Anyone who tried to break in after hours would get some nasty surprises."

They both considered the case silently. Then Taylor slid it back onto the shelf. "Maybe you should take the gun and keep it protected at your place."

"All right." Gray accepted the Peacemaker. "I'll take it home now. You let me know if you find out anything else."

"Will do."

Gray nodded his good-bye, and Taylor watched the Guardian leave. As soon as Gray shut the door, Taylor let out an unsteady breath.

What the hell was going on? He couldn't begin to fathom how the gun had gone missing and ended up in Atwood's hand. Or what had caused Atwood to end his life. He never figured Atwood for the kind of guy who'd kill himself. He was too stubborn a cuss to give up like that.

Taylor's neck prickled uncomfortably, and he tried to rub away the tingles knotting his shoulders. He leaned against a counter, still feeling the chill of that freezer—or maybe it was the chill of foreboding. He didn't want to believe that Atwood committed suicide, but it was almost better than the alternative. Still, who would murder the man? He didn't have a lot of friends, but everyone knew him and tolerated him.

No, sometimes the obvious answer was the true one. Atwood, for reasons unknown, had put the .45 to his temple and pulled the trigger. And stealing Banton's gun to do the deed added a whole new twist to the tragedy.

Yeah, Taylor felt itchy about the whole thing. Atwood was a writer. He would've left a note, or more likely, a set of instructions for his nephew. *Shit.* His stomach dropped to his toes. Taylor still had to give the bad news to Trent.

He took off his cowboy hat and slapped it against his thigh. Then, putting the hat back on his head, he tugged down the brim and strode out of the room.

Duty was duty.

Even if it broke someone's heart.

Norie Whyte awoke in the crook of a tree. It was huge, its branches thick and gnarled, and its leaves shimmered gold. Contentment stole through her, and she felt right at home.

She was clean, her skin feeling as though she'd been freshly bathed, and she wore a white robe that felt as cozy and warm as a beloved quilt. She looked out over the horizon and saw endless rolling hills of emerald green. The air was crisp, with just a bit of chill in it, and it smelled like apple blossoms.

"They're afraid you're going to die."

She looked at the big white raven sitting on the wide branch that crooked to her right. It was speaking to her. "Maybe I am."

"They're trying the ritual earlier than planned."

"Oh." *She returned her gaze to the horizon, to the jeweled blue of the sky, and the glowing gold knot of the sun.* "I love this dream."

"I'm not a dream," *sniffed the bird.* "I'm your familiar."

"That's just silly. I'm not a witch. And even if I was, familiars are . . . well, fictitious."

"We are not." *The bird flapped his wings in reproach. He cocked his head and chirped.* "You need to remember, Norie. It's time."

"You think the key to why they want me is locked inside my forgotten childhood?" *Norie sighed.* "I don't care about that. I was happy just as I was."

"Happy? You were a lonely waitress in Los Angeles."

His derogatory tone made her flinch. "My life wasn't so bad."

"You have a bigger destiny."

"I don't want a bigger destiny." He was stealing her contentment, scraping away at it with his words, and his urgency.

"You have been called."

"Called?" She zeroed in on the bird. "By who?"

"The Goddess."

She stared at him a long moment and then snorted a laugh. "Right. The Goddess. Where was She when I needed Her? I spent my entire childhood being dragged from one place to another with a mother who couldn't settle down. I've spent my entire adulthood toiling and saving for the day I could live life the way I really wanted. I'm nobody, Raven. And I don't mind that. I just want some breathing room. Some freedom to explore. To just *be*."

"Trust the Goddess. Have faith," said the raven. "And you will see the fruition of dreams greater than you imagine now."

"Trust the Goddess," she whispered. "Just like that, huh?"

"Even an ounce of faith will buoy you through the coming storm," he said kindly. He looked up. "You will awaken soon."

Fear dropped like a block of ice into her stomach. Frissons stole up to her throat. "They're going to make me suffer."

"Yes," he said. "Have courage, Lenore."

Have faith. Have courage. *It was easy for the bird to toss out those phrases. He wasn't getting sacrificed.*

"Courage," he said once more.

"Courage," *she whispered back, and then the dream faded away, and she spun through the darkness of unconsciousness, dropping down, down, down, until . . .*

She woke up chained to a stone altar. Still naked, her body shivered in the cold air. She groggily noted she was at least clean. Her skin felt scrubbed and her hair washed. The faint scent of apple blossoms tickled her nose. They were outside, in a place she didn't recognize, but it felt ancient. Large blue-gray stones enclosed the altar; above her was the star-specked night sky. There was something wrong . . . something about the place that felt as though it were grieving.

Six black-robed figures surrounded the altar, all with gleaming daggers raised. Their hoods hid their faces, but their intent was obvious. *Evil.* All of them were drenched with the stink of their malevolence.

"Begin the spell," uttered the voice she hated above all others.

When the six blades cut her all at once, she swallowed her cries. She didn't want to give them the satisfaction of witnessing her final humiliation.

Then the real agony began.

The first electric tendril of dark magic wiggled underneath her skin. It felt as though acid were winding through her veins. The magic ate away at her, and the blades nicked her, offering her blood and pain to the Dark One. Goddess, oh Goddess, it hurt! She sobbed, and the wails dammed in her throat broke free.

She screamed.

And screamed.

Until she couldn't anymore.

Chapter 2

"Taylor Edward Mooreland! You wake up right now, y'hear?"

His mother's no-nonsense voice, crackling with impatience, dragged Taylor from the dark depths of his nightmare. He awoke in his bed, sucking in oxygen like a drowning man who'd just broken the surface of the water.

"Mom?" But no, she was dead. She had been for the last six years. He'd heard her voice, though. Hadn't he? Cold perspiration dribbled down his spine, and he felt as if he were having a heart attack. He snapped on the bedside lamp and shoved off the covers.

Son of a bitch.

He rubbed his hands through his hair. He never recollected anything solid from the recurring nightmare, just wispy fragments tainted with dread. Moonless night. Incense-tainted air. Heart-wrenching screams.

He remembered only the woman in detail.

Her black hair gleamed like a raven's wing, and she had pale, delicate features—a heart-shaped face and a cute pointed chin. When she smiled, the left side of her mouth dimpled. And she had the most amazing eyes— a color of blue so light that he was reminded of the dainty flowers etched on his mother's favorite dishes, the ones he'd packed away after she died.

"Get going, boy. She needs you."

Taylor's head snapped up, and he stared into the shadows of his room. "Mom?"

He waited, his heart stuttering, his chest heavy. Seconds ticked by, but he heard nothing else. Slowly, he let out a breath. Goddess above! He was losing his damned mind. It had been almost six years since she'd died, and though he thought of his mother every day, he hadn't dreamed about her in a long while.

And he'd never heard her voice outside the dreamscape.

The room felt empty.

And so did he.

He looked at the clock on the nightstand. It was almost three a.m.; it would be hours yet before the roosters crowed and the farmers crawled out from their warm beds. He used to keep those hours, back when he was working this land with Ol' Joe. The old man had owned this farm, and Taylor had worked for him. When Ol' Joe passed away, he'd left the farm and everything on it to Taylor. It had been a good thing for his family—he and Mom and his siblings had all moved in and started over. Memories hung around like friendly ghosts. Still. The place was kinda lonely with just him and Ant, his younger brother, living there. Now all that remained were a hundred acres or so, a house that needed repair, and a barn that needed demolition. Taylor wasn't a farmer anymore.

He was proud to be the sheriff, glad to have real purpose—even though he'd been feeling somewhat restless lately—probably a side effect of the nightmares. It was his job to serve and protect, and knowing that he couldn't save someone, even in a dream, was no doubt digging at his ego.

No use trying to sleep now. He needed a workout, a shower, and a vat of coffee.

Taylor rolled his shoulders, and then he popped his neck. He'd go for a run first to shake off the exhaustion and the lingering foreboding. *Just a bad dream,* he reminded himself. *It isn't real.*

Still, he couldn't help but think that in a world filled with magic—anything at all was possible.

Nightmares could sure as hell be real.

And with that final cheerful thought, Taylor dragged himself out of bed and into a pair of clean sweats and his Nikes.

Ant was asleep; the proof was in the snores that drifted down the hallway. The kid had been working himself into exhaustion every day. The House of

Wolves had responded to his brother's petition to join; they were sending out someone to gauge his abilities. To Taylor's mind, it was more along the lines of judging Ant's worthiness to be called a magical at all, and he didn't cotton to that. But Ant was twenty years old, and he could do what he wanted. His younger brother had always been good with plants, but eight months ago, he'd become a full-blown wizard, able to wield earth magic. He'd also fallen head over heels for a girl who was his match in every way, except that she was three years younger, and one year away from being considered a legal adult. His brother maintained the friendship because his moral code would not let him do anything else.

The light of Ant's life, and the bane of his existence, was named Happy. She lived with Gray and his wife, attended high school, and on the weekends, she worked at Ember's tea shop. She honored Ant's choice to keep romance off the menu. But she wasn't that great at controlling those yearning moon-eyed stares or sighs of longing. Taylor suspected that his brother trained hard and kept busy so he'd keep his hands off the girl.

Taylor figured that Ant needed to get away from Nevermore, and from Happy, so he could get some perspective. If Ant tested well, he'd be given the opportunity to go do the traditional year of training with other Wolf novices at a facility in Canada. Truth be told, Happy needed to see the world without Ant in it, too.

They were just kids. All that goo-goo love stuff was raging hormones and lack of dating choices. After all, who could find true love in a town with a little more than five hundred citizens?

Taylor shut the front door. The weathered boards of the porch protested as he walked across it, and guilt stabbed him. As he bounded down the old wooden steps, he admitted that he really needed to work on the house. Maybe next weekend he'd do some fixing up.

It was mid-October, and in the predawn hours, it was a mite chilly. Still, it was Texas, and no doubt by noon, temps would be in the seventies. Texas held on to the heat the same stubborn way a desperate lover might cling to his ex—with passionate disregard for anyone else's feelings or opinions.

In the night sky, a multitude of shimmering stars surrounded the gleaming half-moon. He did a few stretches in the front yard while his eyes adjusted to the dark. He sucked in a deep, full breath of crisp air; then he took off, around the house, through the first of several artsy-fartsy gardens created by his brother until he hit the gravel path that took him into the woods—a few acres of densely packed, ancient trees that Ol' Joe hadn't cleared. He'd told Taylor once that the little forest was sacred, and none of the foliage should ever be cut down. That was a condition he'd even put in his will, and Taylor honored it. Ant tended to avoid the area, though he'd never really said why.

Taylor liked it.

It felt like a sanctuary. And it seemed to treat him like a favorite aunt: He got the hug, and everyone else got the pinched cheeks.

He followed the narrow, well-worn path, which he'd discovered years ago during some of his first explorations of the area. For whatever reason, it had never been swallowed up by the forest. Hell, it wasn't overgrown at all, and there was no debris on it, either. No decaying logs. No stray rocks. Not even fallen leaves. Only earth magic could keep a path that maintenance free, and Taylor wondered if in Nevermore's distant past the magicals had either created the forest, or magicked it. And if so . . . why?

For a few blessed moments, the only noise was the *shuff-shuff-shuff* of Taylor's sneakers on the dirt.

A sharp, long moan sliced right through the quiet.

Taylor stopped short, panting and feeling the adrenaline-laced beats of his heart. He did a full circle, studying the area. His staccato breaths were muffled by the sudden, eerie stillness. There were no animals scurrying, no birds twittering, no wind rattling. The back of his neck prickled. He reached toward his right hip before he remembered he wasn't in uniform, and he hadn't brought his pistol.

Caw. Caw. Caw.

"Damn it!" Taylor swiveled and looked up into the branches of a pine tree with scarred and twisted limbs. It looked half dead, at least on the side facing the path.

A raven sat on the gnarled wood less than a foot above his head. It wasn't a common crow. It was three times the size, for one thing, and for another, it was white. If it hadn't had blue eyes the size of marbles, it could've been mistaken for a big blob of snow.

The bird cocked its head and opened its beak. "Lenore," it said in a mournful tone. "Lenore."

Taylor's mouth dropped open.

Animals didn't talk. Sometimes magicals whipped up spells that gave the illusion, mostly as entertainment or as practical jokes. But who the hell would be out here at this time of night with the intention of annoying him? No one liked these woods. And he was doing his run hours earlier than usual—so who could possibly know he was out here?

Caw. Caw. Caw.

Taylor frowned. Yeah. He was definitely losing his damned mind. First there had been the nightmares, then his mother's voice, and now a mutant bird with a sense of humor.

The prickles irritating his neck paraded down his spine like tiny spiders.

"Lenore," said the raven again. Then it launched from the branch, circled once, and took off to the left. A few seconds later, it returned, circled again, and flew off in the same direction.

"You've got to be shitting me." Taylor peered into the dark recesses. Was he really gonna follow a talking raven into that mess?

The bird came back a third time and cawed.

"All right," he muttered. "But if you're fucking with me, you're dinner."

The moonlight didn't filter through the thick canopy, and the deeper they went, the darker and more foreboding his surroundings. Keeping track of the raven and his own two feet took a lot of effort. He had to follow the damned bird more by its cawing than by watching it swoop overhead. More times than he could count he was either getting whacked in the face by branches or tripping over forest detritus.

Then he stumbled into a clearing, and he stopped.

Holy Mother Goddess.

The area was ringed with southern red oaks so tightly packed that their limbs had intertwined to form a broad, leafy edge that framed the night sky. Above, the half-moon glittered like a whore's wink. In the middle of the field was a circle of six gray-blue stones. He gauged their height to be at least ten feet, and their width was six feet or more.

"Nemeton," he whispered.

He had discovered a sacred grove—what the magicals called a *nemeton*—hidden on *his* land. It was damned old from the look of it—older even than the town itself, he'd bet, which had been founded in 1845.

He knew right then this was the key to the Goddess fountain, the magical portal that Nevermore had been built to protect. Most folks didn't know anything about it—most magicals and mundanes believed Goddess fountains to be myths. And it was best to keep it that way, which was why only a very few in Nevermore knew the truth.

He walked to the nearest stone, his whole body tingling from the humming magic. It was thick here, buzzing and snapping, and it seemed to him, waiting.

But for what?

The stones were placed about two feet apart, which was plenty of room to angle through into the inner sanctum. He hesitated, wondering if a mundane could—or should—enter what was meant for magicals. He probably should call Gray. The Guardian should be the one to enter, to gauge the meaning of this place, and its purpose.

Taylor stepped back, feeling a hushed sense of expectation. It was as if the whole place were alive and holding its breath, anticipation as thick as the trees protecting it.

Caw. Caw. Caw.

The white raven dove through the gap, its guttural cries turning into a long, low moan.

Damn it. He really didn't want to enter that circle. He had a deep respect for the Goddess. Sacred was sacred, no matter whose beliefs made it that way.

51

The mournful sound came again, and this time, it sounded more human than raven. Had that creepy bird gotten hurt?

Or led him to someone who was?

The idea of a person trapped or suffering inside the sacred space was enough motivation to overcome his reluctance. He slipped through the gap and felt his whole body go electric. The hair stood up on every inch of his body, and he felt galvanized. He paused, gauging his surroundings.

There was a huge stone altar in the center.

He swept his gaze around the stones again but saw no one else—nothing else; not even the stupid bird. Taylor had the sense of being watched, even though he couldn't pinpoint a source. Completely unsettled, Taylor approached the altar and stared at its surface. Some sort of swirly-gig was carved in the middle, and more lines and swirls sprouted from it—like a mutant, tattooed octopus.

Something dark and wet smeared the stone. The unmistakable rusty scent of fresh blood edged the air. What the hell had happened here?

The moan came again. It was definitely human. Heart thumping, he followed the sound to the other side of the altar.

A woman lay on her side. She was naked, her thin, pale body spattered red. Her long dark hair fell in a wave of curls that loosely draped her waist and lay on the ground like carelessly tossed ribbons.

Taylor hunkered down, gently moving her hair so he could check the pulse of her carotid artery.

She rolled away from him and staggered to her feet. She bared her teeth, her ice-blue eyes shadowed with pain.

A silver dagger quivered in her blood-streaked hand.

Taylor's heart stopped beating.

It's her.

The woman he'd spent too many nights dreaming about—the one he couldn't save.

He fell to his knees, accidentally assuming a penitent pose. He swayed forward, arms at his side, and just stared at her. Her presence stripped him bare. He couldn't get air into his lungs. Nightmare and dream come to life—right fucking there in the wounded flesh.

The magic of the *nemeton* pulsed around them, living and breathing and anticipating.

She seemed disconcerted by his reaction. Hell, she wasn't the only one. She studied him, those diamond eyes snapping with intelligence and resolve and agony. Her curly black hair swung in an arc, giving it the appearance of a ruffled cape. She was no more than five feet tall, lithe and graceful despite how thin she was— starved really, and obviously weak. The strain of her holding the knife in a proper attack position made her arm shake. Plus, she had cuts on her from head to toe, most of them still bleeding.

"I'm Sheriff Taylor Mooreland," he said. "Tell me your name. Tell me what happened."

She bared her teeth again and moved backward, her gaze darting around the stones before returning to him. She wasn't about to let her guard down. He didn't blame her, but he couldn't let her stand there and bleed to death, either.

"You're a magical, right?" he said. "You sent that raven. He brought me to you. These are my woods, and my home's not too far."

She kept the knife at the ready but cocked her head in the same manner the raven had, studying him intensely.

"I won't hurt you," he said.

She was swaying now, too, her face going gray, but she wasn't going to give him an inch. Her frown deepened, and she scooted back a few more steps, as though thinking about running. She wouldn't get far, not before she either collapsed or he caught her.

And he would catch her.

"I won't hurt you," he repeated as he slowly, carefully rose to his feet. "But I'm coming over there. I'm taking you somewhere safe, I swear."

She shook her head violently and scurried backward until she hit the broad base of the nearest stone. Her eyes went wild then, and she opened her mouth as though she might scream.

He rushed her, and within seconds, he'd divested her of the dagger and scooped her against his chest, banding his arms around her. She struggled violently, and he was surprised at the vehemence she managed to muster. He could feel how frail she was, how her body quivered with pain and exhaustion even as she kicked and wiggled and slammed her head against his breastbone. He grunted and hissed as she connected again and again. The worst thing about the whole experience was the silence. She didn't make a sound as she tried to claw her way out of his arms.

"My mama used to say that any man who told a woman to calm down deserved whatever came next," he said quietly. "But I would kindly appreciate it if you would let me help you. Please."

She shuddered and went still. She was stiff in his arms, her body shaking so badly, her teeth rattled. Then she tilted back her head to look at him. Tears streamed from her eyes, and he saw her frustration, her terror, her surrender.

She wept without making a single sound of distress. She stared at him, refusing to spare herself the humiliation. She was exposed, not only in body, but in soul, too.

She broke his heart.

Taylor swallowed the sudden knot that clogged his

throat. He dared to loosen one arm so that he could wipe away the tears. Her skin felt fragile, like thin parchment underneath his calloused fingers. "I swear to the Goddess, I will protect you."

He felt a quick, electric jolt. He shuddered, suddenly breathless, his focus riveted on the girl. *So shall you say, so mote it be.* It was what Ember said sometimes when she was making up her bespelled teas for customers. Still. Maybe it was his promise, or maybe it was her injured, exhausted body finally giving out, but her lids fluttered as her eyes rolled back in her head. She went limp in his arms.

He laid her on the ground; then he pulled off his sweatshirt and wrapped it around her. With as much care as possible, he picked her up, cradling her against his bare chest, and took his precious bundle home.

Getting to the house involved the longest walk of Taylor's life, especially since the woman's breathing seemed to go shallow. She was as soft and light as a bag of feathers, her skin so pale it was nearly translucent.

When he managed to get through the back door and stumble through the mudroom and into the kitchen, he saw Ant leaning against the counter, still in his boxers and with a raging case of bed head. He almost dropped the mug of coffee he'd brought to his lips. Coffee splattered, and he cursed, putting the cup on the counter.

He eyed the girl and then Taylor. "Rough morning?"

"I've had better," he said. "Call Gray and Lucy, will you? We'll need Ember, too."

"Done," said Ant. "Which bedroom upstairs?

"Mom's."

Ant nodded. After their mother passed away, the kids had cleaned out her room. Clothes went to charity, pictures and decorations were packed, and knick-knacks were divided. The antique furniture remained. Taylor had replaced the mattress and the pillows. Every other week, either he or Ant laundered the sheets and quilts—quilts his mother and his grandmother had sewn with their own hands—and remade the bed.

But no matter how clean they kept it, or how blank the walls and empty the dressers, the memories stayed the same. It was their mother's bedroom, whether or not she was still around to occupy it. It was also the only other room upstairs with a suitable bed.

It took some effort to pull down the covers, especially with a lax, injured woman in his arms, but he managed. He tucked her in, and then he went into the little bathroom, which still smelled like the roses his mother had loved so much, and wet a washcloth. By the time he placed it on her forehead, Gray, Lucinda, and Ember were walking through the door.

Relief shuddered through Taylor. What was going on with this woman was way outside his comfort zone. All the same, she was his responsibility.

At least until he figured out who she was—and why the hell he'd been dreaming about her.

His friends had gotten here fast, which meant they'd used the magical portals that the first Dragon Guardians had created for the convenience of Nevermore's populace. Many of the locations had been forgotten over the years, but Gray and Lucinda had been finding and mapping them, and the portals were more in use nowadays. He'd been surprised to find out that his farm had one; Joe had never mentioned it—maybe he hadn't known about it. But the man had kept some secrets. Taylor had no doubt the old man had been protecting the location of the *nemeton*.

As usual, Ember wore her special glasses: One side was purple tinted, and the other was blacked out completely. She was a prophet of the Goddess, and she had been given the ability to see the spiritual soul of humans—not always a pretty picture; thus the need for her protective eyewear. She was over six feet tall and wore a violet-striped dress that clung to her curvaceous form, and a pair of gray high-heeled boots. Her long hair was a mass of tiny black and purple braids.

Lucy was shorter and leaner. Her feet were in sneakers, and she was dressed in jeans and a T-shirt too big for her. A brunette with moss green eyes, she had an inner glow that had a little to do with her magical powers and a lot to do with the man standing at her side, her husband, Gray.

"Who is she?" asked Lucy as she leaned over and peered at the woman's face.

"I don't know," said Taylor. "I found her in the woods. She was naked as a jaybird and cut all to hell. Damned near took my head off before she fainted."

"She say anyting?" Ember's Jamaican accent faded in and out like a badly tuned radio. The stronger her emotions, the stronger her accent—and it was thick as mud right now.

"Nothing," said Taylor. "It's almost as if she can't."

That statement got Gray's and Lucy's attention, too.

"What do you mean?" asked Gray.

"She didn't say a word. She cried without making a sound. It was as though her voice were turned off."

Ember nodded. "Dat's what I thought. Somebody don' wan' her to talk, so dey bound her voice."

"That kind of spell would be strong," mused Gray, "but limited. Probably a few days at most."

"Unless it was demon magic," said Lucy softly. She'd been cursed with Pit magic and had barely survived. Taylor knew how badly she had suffered—and how difficult it had been to get free of that evil. His stomach clenched as he gazed at the pale face of his mystery woman. He sent a quick prayer to the Goddess that she was not suffering from demon-wrought spellwork.

"Not demon," said Ember, shaking her head. "Dis magic Raven."

"Well, that's not much better," said Gray. "Why would the Ravens want to hurt her?"

"How'd they get into Nevermore?" asked Taylor. "Into *my* forest? And into the *nemeton*?"

Three pairs of eyes zeroed in on him.

"What?" Gray frowned. "There's a *nemeton* in your woods?"

Even Gray, who basically protected and governed all of Nevermore, understood that Taylor's land, and those mysterious woods, belonged to the sheriff. Taylor rubbed his face. What was wrong with him? He was doing this whole thing ass-backward. He couldn't keep his eyes away from *her*, and he couldn't keep his thoughts straight, either. He sucked in a steady breath. Then he told the story—skipping the part about his nightmares and hearing his mother's voice.

After he was finished, silence blanketed the room.

"The raven was white," repeated Gray incredulously. "And it actually said Lenore?"

Taylor nodded toward the girl. "I think it might be her name."

"Well," said Lucy, "that's just . . . weird."

"Raven magic, raven bird, raven poem," said Ember. Her gaze drifted over the prone female. "Raven girl."

Taylor stared at Ember. What the hell did all that mean?

"Let Lucy and Ember heal her," said Gray. "You show me the *nemeton*. Then we'll figure out how the bastards got in, and we'll seal the gaps."

"All right," said Taylor.

Gray kissed his wife and then clapped Taylor on the shoulder. "C'mon."

Taylor cast a final look at the woman tucked underneath his mother's quilt, his heart clenching, and then he followed his friend and boss out the door.

After Taylor put on a clean shirt, he grabbed his pistol, even though having Gray along was like carrying a magical bazooka. He was a very powerful wizard and the only shape-shifter in the world—probably. Who knew what secrets other magicals held? Gray had only figured out the ability a few months ago, and Taylor still didn't quite understand how it all worked. But he'd seen Gray as the dragon, and it was damned impressive. There were plenty of myths about magicals who could shift into animals—tales as bold and unbelievable as any of the ancient stories archived in the Great Library. It seemed those legends had grown from seeds of truth.

He'd grabbed his flashlight, too, but as he, Gray, and Ant made their way into the forest, Gray whispered a spell that created a basketball-sized orb of light. It bobbed on the path ahead of them. When they got to the half-dead tree, Taylor sucked in a steadying breath and dove once again into the dark, tangled forest.

He had no idea how he managed to lead the other men to the *nemeton*. But he was able to get them there, and his skin started to prickle again as they reached the entrance. He realized now that it was an actual entryway; a stone arch covered with moss that was tightly wedged between two oaks. He hadn't even noticed before—he'd been too distracted by the unexpected discovery of the *nemeton*.

Gray went first, and then Taylor. Ant followed. They all stopped to admire the massive ring of blue-gray stones.

"Holy shit," said Ant.

Gray flicked a look at him. "You didn't sense it at all?"

Ant shook his head. "It's as if a big Do Not Disturb sign hovers over this place. It repels people on purpose. Except Taylor, apparently."

"He's the deed holder to the land," said Gray. "Ol' Joe gifted him more than just a farm. He's been the unknowing guardian of it."

"Terrific," muttered Taylor. Why hadn't the old man ever said anything?

Gray started forward, the magic light pushing through the gap between the stones. Taylor followed, and his little brother entered last.

Ant whistled.

"Six stones," said Gray. The orb rose into the air and made a slow circuit. "Look. Symbols of the Houses."

"No," said Ant as the light reflected an etching of the

sun. "Symbols of the first magicals. There is no House of Sun. Hell, there are no Sun magicals."

"Unless you count Lucy," said Gray. "Thaumaturges are as close as you can get to the line of Drun these days."

They watched the light brush the other carved symbols.

"We can assume that the *nemeton* was built at the same time as the town," said Ant. "Right? But these stones and that altar"—he paused to gather himself, his horrified gaze on the bloodstained rock—"are much older."

"Ancient," agreed Gray.

"Maybe carved even before the Romans reorganized the magicals and created the Houses," said Ant.

They shared a look, and Taylor felt a shiver go up his spine. Shit. He had a feeling his life was about to get a lot more complicated. The image of Lenore, standing like a wounded goddess on the other side of the altar put a hitch in his step. *Stop it. She's a—a victim. That's all. Now start acting like the sheriff, moron.*

"It's been desecrated," said Gray tightly. Now they were all looking at the dark stains on the altar. "Someone tried to commit evil here. We'll need to cleanse everything." He peered closer and grimaced. "It seems your new friend was bound here. I can still see the remnants of the magic that kept her lashed to the stone.

"Let's look around," Gray continued. "Maybe we'll be able to piece together some useful information."

While Gray and Ant examined the stones for further clues, Taylor rounded the altar, studying the place where Lenore had lain. His stomach clenched at the blood that splattered the stone base and the grass. He clicked on his flashlight and swept the beam across the dewy grass. What had she been doing here? How had she gotten in? Surely she hadn't been alone, or inflicted those wounds on her own body. *You can't save her.*

He was desperately trying not to focus on the nightmare, but it clung to his thoughts like a fungus. Dreams weren't reality, damn it. He needed to keep his mind on the current situation. *So.* If someone had forcibly brought her to this location, how had he gotten through the town's magic-protected perimeters without setting off any alarms? And how had he known about this place?

The flashlight's beam caught the glint of Lenore's silver dagger that he'd managed to wrest from her. It had landed flat in the grass. He carefully stepped to it and crouched, studying the bloodied blade. The hilt was ornately carved with a bunch of fancy swirls that surrounded the engraving of a raven.

Was Lenore a Raven witch?

If so, why would members of her own House bespell her? Or had other wizards done the deed, and if so, why? It always boiled down to why. Figure out the why, and everything else would fall into place. But right now, he didn't know if Lenore was one of the good guys. He'd learned a valuable lesson about trusting appearances. Sometimes, what was visible was a carefully constructed lie that gleamed like truth.

He stared at the blade, his thoughts whirling. What did she know that was so important her voice had to be taken? Why not just kill her and ensure permanent silence? Or maybe that was what they—whoever they were—had been trying to do.

The back of his neck was tingling again.

"What is that?" asked Ant as he crouched next to Taylor.

"Some kind of ritual dagger. She was holding it when I found her."

Gray knelt across from them and examined the blade. "Raven," he muttered. "Not too subtle." He pointed at the hilt. "See that symbol under the raven? It's the sign of rank in the House of Ravens."

"So either someone high up in the Raven ranks was here," offered Taylor, "or someone was ballsy enough to steal it to use here."

"Sooooo . . . the Ravens were trying to sacrifice her?" asked Ant. "Why did she—or whoever—send a raven for help? I mean, isn't it weird that she can wield the symbol of their House?"

"We don't know anything yet," said Taylor. "The only person who knows what went on here is unconscious."

"And mute," added Ant.

"We don't really know that, either," said Taylor. "Where are the signs of struggle? Or pursuit? Something about this situation is all wrong. If she came all this way by herself, then that means she crawled up on that altar and cut herself."

"I don't buy that," said Ant.

"Me, either," said Taylor. "She was terrified."

"So, she's connected to the Ravens," said Gray.

"If by connected, you mean imprisoned," said Ant.

"That's a leap." Taylor cocked an eyebrow at his brother. "Unless you've been talking to trees again?"

"As a matter of fact, I heard the stones whispering."

Both Gray and Taylor gave Ant startled looks.

"You can talk to rocks?" asked Taylor.

"I don't know. But I can hear them. It's as if . . . well, as if they're alive."

Taylor glanced at Gray's expression. Even the guy who could turn into a dragon seemed daunted by Ant's abilities. "I can't believe I'm gonna say this, but maybe you could go ask 'em a few questions?"

"See if they know the girl, who else might've been here, and confirm if we've got any lurkers to worry about."

"That's a start," said Taylor.

"I'll try the one with the wolf symbol," said Ant. "Kindred magic an' all." He stood up and walked toward the right of the enclosure.

Taylor looked at Gray. "Can you hear them?"

"No. But I can feel the pulse of ancient magic. And I feel the recent presence of other magicals, but the imprints are too faint to get a real read."

"Perfect," muttered Taylor. He'd brought his gun but not his weapons belt. Without access to his gear, he couldn't secure the dagger. "You got any spells that will seal the blade?"

"Yes. And I'll transport it to your office." Gray stood up, too, and started working the spells needed to protect the dagger—and whatever evidence clinging to it. Taylor got to his own feet and did another perimeter search. When he reached Ant, his brother stepped back and shook his head in puzzlement.

"We're talking two different languages."

"Maybe they got a Rosetta stone program for speaking rock," said Taylor with a small grin.

"Har, har, bro." Ant shook his head. "We might not be able to connect enough to really communicate, but I understand one thing. They're Guardians." He looked at Gray. "I think this is the Goddess fountain, Gray."

"The Goddess fountain is all of Nevermore," said Gray. "That much we've figured out. At least, the powerful magic is sealed within the town's borders as far as we can tell. Ember and I have been looking for its access point, but . . . no wonder we couldn't find it."

"Well, how the hell did the Ravens find it?" asked Taylor. "And how did they know about the Goddess fountain?"

"Maybe they don't," offered Gray. "Maybe they just knew about the *nemeton*. They used to be all over the place in ancient times. Magicals used them to gather and strengthen their magic for rituals."

"Or for war," said Ant. "So they bring a girl here to be sacrificed—why?"

"Too many damned questions and not enough answers," groused Taylor. "How do we find out if this is the Goddess fountain doorway, or whatever?"

Ant reached out and put a hand on the rock in front of him. Seconds ticked by, but Ant pulled back, shaking his head. "I can't get a straight answer. They keep sorta muttering 'stars'—I think."

"Nice of Ol' Joe to tell me about this place," said Taylor. Not even the Guardian of Nevermore had known about the *nemeton*. Taylor rubbed a hand across his hair. "Why didn't the previous Guardians leave some damned instructions?"

Ant rubbed the stone, almost as if smoothing it. "Well, whatever the Ravens—or whoever—were doing here, it was bad juju." He grimaced. "They seem to be . . . waiting."

Taylor felt his gut clench. He'd had the same kind of feeling, and he wasn't even a magical. He didn't want to be one, either. Look at the kinds of things you got sucked into. "For what?"

"I don't know," said Ant. His eyes filled with worry. "But whatever it is, it's certainly not good."

*　　*　　*

Trent Whitefeather pulled his motorcycle onto the paved road that led to the Elysian Fields Cemetery and cut the engine. It was barely six a.m., but he hadn't been able to sleep. Being at the apartment felt too strange. His uncle hadn't been an easy man, but he'd loved Trent in his way. The idea that the old man would just take his own life—just fucking kill himself—well, it was unbelievable.

After Sheriff Mooreland had broken the news, he'd gotten a pass to leave school. He went to his uncle's office with its mess and its stench, and he wept like a little kid. He couldn't bear to go into the archives where his uncle had been found. It didn't matter, anyway. Taylor had told him not to go in there because that area was a crime scene. Was suicide a crime? He wondered. It wasn't as if anyone could be convicted of it. There was no justice, no answer to the question why, when someone took his life. Damn it all. Atwood murdered himself. It was crime and punishment all in one terrible act.

Trent wasn't done with grief—not by a long shot. His unc's death had also refreshed the loss of his parents. His whole family was gone. For a moment, the loneliness cut at him like a blade, but he pushed it away; he pushed it back. He wasn't a quitter. He had friends. A life. Goals. He'd continue on, head down, teeth gritted, heartsick, because he wasn't a gods-be-damned quitter.

Not like you, Uncle Atwood. Bastard.

Trent stared up at the huge wrought-iron gates. They were always open because Mordi said the dead didn't have regular business hours. Mordecai "Mordi" Elizabeth Jones was the undertaker of Nevermore's only cemetery. She'd told him that every first child in the Jones family was named Mordecai, boy or girl, because that was the tradition—as was training that first child to take over the family business. A Jones had been in charge of Elysian Fields since the day Nevermore became a town. Mordi was proud of her heritage, and to his mind, the best undertaker there ever was. He was a necromancer, so he'd know.

He got off the bike, put it in neutral, and walked it forward. Just a few feet down the road there was a small whitewashed cottage. The porch and shutters were painted a sky blue, and wind chimes shaped like stars dangled from the entryway. In the sharp October wind, they jangled wildly. The postage-stamp-sized front yard was well tended, and a concrete path led from the drive to the porch steps. On the far side of the yard was a gazebo with a big white swing. All kinds of plants and trees thrived, even in October. That was part of the mystery—and the charm—of Nevermore.

He parked the motorcycle and trudged up to the porch. He stared at the screen door, wanting to knock on it—and wanting to run away, all at the same time. He liked Mordi. Well, it was more than that. He was drawn to her. They were only a couple years apart; he was eighteen, and she was twenty. But she always seemed so much older, more sophisticated, more worldly. He wasn't a wuss. He'd done his fair share of dating girls. That was the problem. Mordi wasn't a girl. She was a woman.

His palms started to sweat.

Fuck it.

He turned on his booted heel, ready to leap off the porch and get the hell away. Then he heard the front door snick, and the outer screen door whispered open.

"Trent."

Her voice flowed over him with sweetness and sympathy, and he felt the backs of his eyes ache. She knew. Damn it. She always knew. She wasn't a magical, but she had this kinship with the dying and the dead.

And the grief-stricken.

He turned back, wound so tightly, he was afraid to speak, to move. He was scared. On top of everything else, at this moment, fear slashed at him like shards of ice.

Goddess, she was beautiful. She was slim, nearly as tall as his own six-foot frame. She wore a pale pink nightdress that swirled at her ankles. Her feet were bare, her toenails painted lavender. She liked Easter egg colors, the soft palette of pinks, purples, yellows, greens. He'd noticed that about her, just as he'd noticed a million other things.

71

Mordi's auburn hair fell around her shoulders in thick waves. He blinked. He'd never seen her with her hair down like that. She always wore it in a French braid or neatly pinned up. Her gray gaze was on his face, her smile slight but welcoming. She seemed to emit peace and calm, and he suddenly felt angry. He wasn't one of her wimp-assed clients. He hadn't come here to be . . . consoled, to be treated like a fragile soul who'd lost his whole world.

She seemed to recognize his anger. That she'd somehow pegged him so easily made him madder still. Confusion ribboned through his fury, through his anguish. He wasn't special, not to her.

He whipped around, feeling as if he were burning from the inside out. He needed to get away. He needed to get somewhere dark and quiet and alone—somewhere he could scream and weep and punch stuff.

But even as his foot came down on the first step, Mordi glided across the porch and grasped his hand.

Just like that, she'd trapped him. Her solace covered him like a fuzzy blanket, and he choked on the grief barbing his throat.

She didn't make him turn around again. No, she came around instead and faced him, her gray gaze luminous.

"Don't," he managed in a hoarse voice. He couldn't imagine what he was asking her not to do, but there was something in her eyes, something that flitted like a ghost across her face. She wasn't just some ghoul who ran the cemetery. She was its keeper. The watcher. The very bridge between the living and the dead. And still, he didn't want her to treat him like all the others she'd helped.

She kept her hand in his, then lifted her other hand to his face. Then she drew him down toward her and brushed her mouth over his.

His heart stuttered, and his breathing hitched, and the fucking tears spilled.

"I'm sorry about your uncle," she said. She kissed each corner of his mouth, tasting the wet trails that bracketed his lips. "I'm sorry you're in pain."

"You can't help me." He tried to pull back, but she stayed him easily by looping his wrists with her fingers. "I don't want you to . . . do this." He sucked in an unsteady breath, trying to get back some of his dignity. "I don't want a pity fuck."

"I don't pity you," she said. "What do you need, Trent? Do you need to get back on your bike and ride away? Or do you need to come inside with me?"

"I need . . ." He looked at her then, really looked at her, and saw the tenderness, the patience. "I need you, Elizabeth."

She smiled. "All right."

He hesitated. "It's not . . . You don't . . ." How did he ask if this was something she did for others? He felt petty and mean for even thinking it, but he couldn't help it. The world was one big bastard to him right now. Trust wasn't an easy thing for him on the best of days—with the best of people.

"Only you," she reassured him. She let him go then and walked to the screen door. She kept her gaze on his, waiting.

Suddenly, being alone with his grief and his doubts didn't seem the way to go. She was there, soft and warm and willing, and so he followed her inside.

Chapter 3

The Grand Court in Washington, D.C.
Chamber of the House of Dragons

Cullen Deshane shuffled down the massive, elegantly appointed hall, eyes forward, head held high, and shoulders back. Wizards and witches ceased their conversations to stare at him; in the sudden, awkward silence echoed the metallic ring of his ankle shackles scraping the polished marble floor.

Cullen kept his gaze on the white-robed back of the lictor in front of him, watching how the fabric crinkled as he marched forward. He felt the hulking presence of the other lictor behind him, and he had the unsettling sensation that an oak tree was about to fall upon him. It wasn't that he was a small man himself; he was six feet five and well muscled. But he was cautious. Fighting wasn't always the way, even though he was good at it.

Whispers rose and fell like crashing waves. His audience hissed and muttered—some voices hard with judgment and others soft with pity.

He couldn't blame them, not really. He was, after all, the incarcerated black-sheep son of Leopold Deshane.

For the thirty years his father had been a veteran Consul in the House of Ravens, he'd been lauded for his political policies and for his charitable work. Each House had only three Consuls—positions at the top of magical political structure, both in-house and in the Grand Court. His father had been a very powerful, and in some circles, a very feared man.

Now dear old dad was facing jail time—if they could find him. Leopold had disappeared, and no one had been able to track him down.

Cullen had laughed at the irony. He'd known his father was a hypocritical prick—he'd fooled the world into believing he was some sort of philanthropic Goody Two-shoes. Cullen had long been seen as a thorn in his side, as the widower supposedly tried everything to manage his unruly son. So no one had seemed too surprised when Cullen had been accused of—and convicted of—burning down the Raven's Heart orphanage. Children had died in the blaze that decimated the building and everything in it. Goddess! It made him sick to his guts to know others believed he was such a conscienceless bastard.

What no one had known was that Leopold had set

him up, his own fucking son, and made sure he'd ended up in prison.

Then eight months ago, a banned Raven wizard named Bernard Franco had disappeared. Despite efforts of his friends and family, he'd never been found, but one thing had become clear: He'd been murdered.

A natural death would not have enacted Bernard's little protection scheme: truth spells. Franco had been the keeper of many secrets and had worked a powerful magic to ensure no one would ever try to kill him. It appeared someone had either not known or not cared about the spells that would expose those secrets. The lifelong transgressions of many Ravens, and even the corrupt practices of the House of Ravens itself, all those terrible truths Franco had been safeguarding, were magically sent to the appropriate authorities upon his death.

Word had spread through the magical community and had even reached the ears of those sitting in prison. Whispers about Bernard's death had turned into shouts of outrage. Franco had been careful and thorough, backing up accusations with solid evidence.

Leopold Deshane had been the biggest offender.

Collusion with demons, circumventing magical law, and willful endangerment of children were among many of the charges levied against his father. Thanks to the discovery of Leopold's many and varied illegal activities, Cullen had actually gained some sympathy among the ranks. Maybe that explained why Dragon

Consul Letitia Calhoun had pulled strings for this visit to the Grand Court.

What Cullen had never figured out was why his old man hadn't just killed him already. Leo was perfectly capable of being ruthless, even against his own family members. As soon as he figured out that Cullen wasn't going to be a ruthless, soulless asshole—when he was around fourteen and had actually punched his father in his bloated face—the "accidents" began to occur. He wasn't sure when his father grew bored with his attempts to take out his son—and Cullen damned sure never figured out why he managed to survive the falls, the car accidents, the fights with unknown bullies on the streets. He always bounced back, or just bounced away. His best friend, Laurent, liked to say that Cullen was the luckiest bastard he knew.

Then Leo just made damned sure Cullen's life was ruined, shattered beyond repair. And sometimes, some days, that was fucking worse than death.

Cullen and his guards reached the imposing double doors that led into Consul Calhoun's office, and a tall, well-built gentleman stepped smoothly in front of them. Like the escorts, he wore a traditional white robe, and a blank expression. Cullen's gaze dropped to the upper-right corner of the robe, where the gold-stitched dragon was bisected with a fasces. The ancient Roman weapon of bundled sticks with an ax sticking out of the middle was still the symbol of the bodyguards of the Consul.

"Welcome to the office of Dragon Consul Calhoun," he said in a polite voice. "Please wait here while I inform the Consul of your arrival."

Cullen looked him square in the eye. "Thank you."

He inclined his head, his expression as smooth as glass. Then he opened one door and slipped through it. A moment later, both doors swung open, revealing the imposing figure of Leticia Calhoun.

The woman was tall, gorgeous, and wore confidence like a cashmere coat. Her dark hair was tamed by a single, long braid. Her sky blue eyes snapped with intelligence. Even though she was in her fifties, her face was pale perfection. Then again, magicals aged much more slowly than mundanes (and conversely, emotionally matured much faster) and often lived two centuries or more. Dressed in the black-trimmed red robe that denoted her rank, Leticia Calhoun was a confident, terrifying package.

The Consul stepped out, smiling as she held out her hands. "Welcome to the House of Dragons." She spoke loudly enough for everyone to hear. "So long as you are within our walls, I offer you both our hospitality and our protection."

Cullen's jaw dropped. He hadn't expected an out-and-out display of support. Why the hell would the woman do such a thing?

"Close your mouth, dear; you'll catch flies."

He pressed his lips together. Then he carefully took

the Consul's slim, cool hands. She squeezed lightly, then let go. "Let the man through."

The guards moved aside, and Cullen scuffled forward.

"For the love of the Goddess!" scolded the Consul. "Take off the manacles!"

The door guard looked as though he wanted to protest, but one sharp look from the Dragon witch had him snapping his mouth shut and gesturing at the other lictors.

Cullen's chained hands and feet were relieved of the shackles. He rubbed his tingling wrists and shook each foot. "Thank you," he said to the guard who'd removed them. Then he lifted his gaze to the Consul. "And thank you, Consul."

Cullen saw sadness flicker in the woman's eyes. Then her gaze cleared, and she smiled warmly. "Come. We have much to discuss."

They walked through a series of lushly appointed rooms until they reached a charming parlor. A tea service had been set up at a small table framed by two needlepoint-upholstered chairs. It was cozy, especially with the sunlight streaming in through the nearby lace-curtained window. It really was not his kind of scene, though. He'd much prefer a dark, smoke-filled bar with a selection of good beers and cheap women.

"Please," said the Consul, gesturing toward one of the chairs before taking her own seat. Cullen sat and watched the woman pick up the teapot. "Sugar? Cream?"

"I don't drink tea."

"Ah. Perhaps some coffee? Or lemonade?"

"No, thank you, Consul."

"Very well. And please, call me Leticia." She added sugar and cream to her cup. Then she sipped her tea and took her tablemate's measure. "How are you feeling?"

"Confused," said Cullen. "Why am I here?"

Leticia set the cup on its matching saucer, and then she delicately pressed a napkin to her mouth. The pink cloth fluttered as she dropped it onto the table. "It's become clear to me that your father had you jailed to keep you under control."

"And? You're wondering why he didn't just kill me." He shrugged. "I've had the same thoughts over the years. And no answer."

Leticia looked taken aback. "Surely, he wouldn't . . . You are his son."

"That doesn't count for much," said Cullen matter-of-factly.

"Rumors say"—Leticia paused and waved her hand as though dispelling the wispy nature of rumors—"that he's afraid of you."

Cullen snorted. Maybe Leopold was scared of him, but he doubted it. And he couldn't fathom why his father, a powerful Raven in magic and political power, would give a damn about a son who had few abilities. He'd known his father didn't like him, and he had known that since he was five. He could pinpoint it exactly to the night Father had found him in the living room, sitting next to the hearth where his mother's body lay. Mary Deshane's throat had been cut. The pool of blood gleamed wetly in the flickering firelight. Cullen remembered that singular moment from his childhood—his father had rushed in, his Italian leather shoes slapping against the marble floor, his breath harsh and uneven and his face contorted with rage.

He stumbled past the huge Christmas tree with its bounty of gaily wrapped gifts and crouched next to him. He grabbed Cullen's face, his fingers digging cruelly into his son's cheeks. "What the fuck did you do?" he screamed.

Cullen remembered nothing else, nothing before he was five, before that terrible night, and after that . . . Well, his father had sent him away.

From the speculative look on her face, it seemed the Consul was following his thoughts. Usually he was better at controlling his expressions.

"He sent you into private care when you were very young," she said, her voice soft with empathy.

Such a diplomatic way of saying it, thought Cullen. The family vacation home in upper New York had been turned into a state-of-the-art clinic, and he'd been the only patient. It was a luxurious prison filled with people whose daily jobs were to make sure he was comfortable and to remind him that he was, indeed, deranged.

"It was an old farm, very isolated. I stayed there until I was ten, when I was deemed mentally sound, and then my father shipped me off to boarding school." It had been a special boarding school for fuckups like him. His whole life he'd been in prison in one form or another. Getting put away in the Institute for Magical Reform, especially since he had little magic at all, hadn't been much different from all the institutions he'd been in.

"You deserved so much better."

"Did I?" He snorted a laugh. The Consul thought she knew him? He schooled his features. Life had turned him into a cynical bastard. She wanted something, and all the tea and sympathy in the world wouldn't cover up that single fact.

Leticia resumed sipping from her delicate cup, watching Cullen with a careful expression. "Do you remember very much about your mother?"

"No," he lied. "I hardly remember her at all." After she died, his father had taken down every picture, put away every reminder. On the few visits Cullen made to the family estate over the years, he noticed how empty and cold the house was without his mother in it. She'd been the soft one, the one ready with a smile or a hug, the one who took away the fear his father had been so good at instilling. His jaw tightened. Yes, he remembered his mother, but those faint memories belonged to him, and to him alone.

"I went to high school with Mary in Nevermore, Texas," said Leticia. "I was a senior, and she was a freshman. We knew each other, of course—it's impossible to be a stranger in Nevermore. Still, I wouldn't say we were friends. Mary left town right after graduation. She wanted to be an actress. The last anyone heard, she'd moved to Los Angeles. I didn't know that she'd married Leopold and moved to Washington. Of course, Ravens and Dragons rarely mix socially, which may be why I never ran into her before she died." She paused, gauging his reaction. Everyone believed that Mary Clark Deshane had committed suicide. He wasn't at all sure about the details of that night, but he remembered quite clearly the blood. He'd often wondered if his father believed that Cullen had killed Mother. Maybe Leo had been afraid of his son on some level, after all. Well, maybe Cullen didn't remember the events of that night, but he was damned sure he hadn't slit his own mother's throat.

"Do I have any other relatives?" he asked.

Leticia's eye flickered with sorrow. "The last living Clark passed away almost two years ago. Your grandmother—Thelma."

"Oh." Disappointment flickered, but he tamped it down. His grandmother might be dead, but the connection his mother had to her and to Nevermore still existed. That was something, at least.

"That was why I invited you to visit with me," said Leticia. "You're the Clark heir. You can claim your grandmother's home and business. It appears that your father made sure the bills were paid on both, so they were never returned to the town Guardian." Leticia offered a delicate cough. "Of course, if you choose to live there, you will have to swear fealty to the Dragons. Since you are the son of a Raven, that might not be . . . politically correct."

"I'm not a Raven," said Cullen. "Nor am I a Dragon." An inheritance in Nevermore. Goddess above! He felt as if someone had just knifed him in the belly. "Did you forget I was in jail? I can't claim anything, lady."

One single eyebrow lifted at his crude manner, and he felt properly chastised. He knew how to be polite, but he'd been sideswiped, and, damn it, he was tired of his chain being yanked. Hope was dangerous. It made a person want what he couldn't have.

"That's the good news, Cullen. Given the evidence that your father committed the crime you were incarcerated for, you're being released."

And the blows kept coming. He took a moment to absorb the news. "There was evidence that my father framed me for burning down Raven's Heart?"

"Yes." She grimaced. "That was a terrible tragedy in many ways, not the least of which was finding out the place's true purpose. It's the magical community's great shame we weren't better protectors of our young.

It's horrible that the Ravens were . . . securing children for various illegal purposes."

Horrible wasn't a bad enough description in Cullen's opinion. Reprehensible was closer, but even that word couldn't give voice to the heinousness of Raven's Heart.

"Eight children and two caretakers had died in the blaze," he said.

"Yes," said Leticia. "Did you know that bodies of other children had been found buried in the basement? All of them poisoned."

Cullen's throat went dry. "No, I didn't know."

"Such a tragedy," Leticia repeated, shaking her head. "After Bernard Franco's truth spells released his secrets, the Ravens did all they could to separate themselves from the more unseemly of their members. They claimed Leopold was part of a fanatical faction of their Order, and he and his so-called followers were responsible for what went on at Raven's Heart. They made quite a show of discovering the offenders, banning them from the House and then prosecuting them." She grimaced. "Your father set that fire to destroy the evidence of the true purpose of Raven's Heart. Perhaps he was a fanatic, but it's more likely the Ravens, who are not known for their altruism, knew full well what was going on there."

"My father framed me," said Cullen tightly. "People believed I was capable of burning children alive." He drew in a shaky breath; he knew he was close to just freaking losing it. "When did this evidence that he had committed the crime come to light?" he asked. She didn't answer right away, and his stomach dropped.

"Franco died in March," she said carefully. "It took the Grand Court committees months to cull through all the information received and determine validity."

"So, my innocence has been known since March?" he asked. Anger twisted inside him.

"Ah. Well." She paused for tea. "Franco's truth spells have altered—or destroyed—many lives," she said.

Well, that wasn't exactly an apology, was it?

"He could only destroy the lives of those who deserved it," he said.

"Debatable, in some cases." She cast a look at him, one he couldn't interpret.

Cullen decided to hold his tongue. He wanted to rail against the unfairness of sitting in jail for a crime he hadn't committed . . . but he had other sins staining his soul—sins that no amount of prison time would erase, or make easier to bear.

"You will receive compensation from the Grand Court for your suffering."

His anger receded, a little. He supposed compensation would soothe some of his wounds—but not all. And he would never get back the time he'd spent paying for a crime he hadn't committed. Damn. He wished the Consul had offered something stronger than tea. He could use a good slug of scotch right about now. Holy Goddess.

He was about to be set free. And he was getting a settlement. His father had long since cut him off from the family money. With whatever the Grand Court gave him, he could do anything and go anywhere. He flicked a glance at the woman studying him. "I take it you think I should accept my inheritance. Move to Nevermore."

"The Goddess," said Leticia, "or rather, the Goddess speaking through Her prophet thinks you should."

"The Goddess?" he asked, cynicism lacing his tone.

"Yes," said Leticia softly. She shook her head, bemused. "I admit that I had my doubts about your situation. And I am sorry for that. I know you have less reason than most to trust Her wisdom, but I would like to ask you to at least go to Nevermore. Check out the property, the house. You might find you like the town."

He doubted it. But he was curious about his mother's past, about the grandmother he'd never known. He didn't really think small-town life was for him. And he wasn't the type to settle down, not after spending most of his life being manipulated by his father. For the first time in forever, though, he could be his own man, make his own choices—and just days away from his thirtieth birthday, too.

"All right," said Cullen. "I'll go. I make no promises about staying, though."

"Of course," said Leticia. "You can travel with me. I'm leaving for Nevermore in a couple of days. My son is the town Guardian, and he can help you get settled in."

"Gray Calhoun." Cullen remembered the scandal of the man being sacrificed by his own wife to a demon, and how he'd given up his career, hell, his whole life. Cullen knew too well what it was like to be betrayed by someone who was supposed to love you.

"Yes," she said, "it's time I met his new wife."

She didn't sound exactly thrilled about the prospect. Interesting. He reached across the table and offered his hand. "To new beginnings, Consul."

She shook his hand and smiled. "Yes. New beginnings."

He pretended not to notice the calculation edging her smile, or the cunning that ghosted across her expression. Leticia Calhoun wanted something from him—obviously. If she tried to drag him into any drama, she'd be sorely disappointed.

"This calls for something stronger, then," she said. "To celebrate."

"Now you're talking." Cullen rose from the table and followed the Consul to the fully stocked bar in the room beyond the parlor. And as he took his first sip of fine scotch—Lagavulin, no less—he grinned.

Leticia Calhoun wasn't the only one with an agenda.

It was creeping toward nine a.m., long past the time by which Taylor had usually left for the office, and he was feeling . . . off. He hadn't slept well, mostly because he'd been trying to keep an eye on his new charge. He

leaned against the doorjamb and stared at the unconscious woman tucked into bed. She looked so fragile,
like one of Ant's delicate flowers. But he'd seen the
steel in her. She was no drooping daisy, waiting for
someone to pluck off her petals. She was too strong for
that. The sleep spell had been woven by Ember and
reinforced by Gray, who could actually enter—even
manipulate—someone else's dreams. He hadn't tried,
though, with Lenore—if that was really her name. Oh,
Gray had suggested it, and then he dropped the subject
after taking one look at Taylor's grim expression. This
woman had a hold on him, and he didn't want anyone
else, not even the Guardian, messing with her.

It wasn't something he could put into words, or hell,
even into thoughts. It was a primal feeling of protection. He'd made a promise to her in that ancient place
of magic, and by the Goddess, he would keep it.

"Still not awake?" asked Ant. He paused next to the
door and surveyed the sleeping woman.

"Won't be for another day, maybe two. It's a healing
sleep," said Taylor. "Supposed to take care of all those
cuts and bruises."

"Good. Doesn't look like she's had a decent meal in
a while," said Ant.

"She's too thin," agreed Taylor.

"What the hell do you think happened to her?"

"Don't know. As soon as Ember and Lucy arrive to
watch over her, I'll go out and do another survey of the

nemeton. Maybe the light of day will reveal something to help us figure out what happened."

"Gray going with you?"

"Yeah. He's gonna try to track down more of the magic." Taylor turned toward his brother. "The wolfie woo-woo lady comin' today?"

Ant snorted. "I dare you to call her that to her face. Yeah. Elandra should be here soon."

"Nervous?" asked Taylor with a half grin. "You never did like taking tests as I recall."

"I'm not nervous about the testing," said Ant. "But Happy . . . Well, she's not too thrilled about me leaving."

"She's seventeen."

Ant glanced at his brother and shook his head. "You don't get it, bro. Yeah, she's just a kid. Hell, I guess I am, too, but . . . there's something about her. I think . . . shit." He rubbed his hand over his hair. "I think it will always be her."

Taylor nodded, but he turned back to his vigil of Lenore so his little brother wouldn't see his expression or guess at his cynical thoughts. Aw, hell. Who was he to be telling Ant anything about how he was feeling? Taylor had been dreaming about a woman he'd then actually found naked in the woods. If that wasn't some kind of . . . well, crazy, he didn't know what was. The woman had infiltrated his subconscious before he'd even known she existed. And now that he did, she was

91

there, in his thoughts, all the time. Like a goddamned ghost. Haunted. Yeah, that was the word that described it best. Lenore haunted him.

It didn't make sense. Just like Happy and Ant didn't make sense. But his mother had once told him that the heart wants what the heart wants. But he wasn't exactly buying that. Not by much. How could the heart want what it hadn't known was real?

Lenore.

He felt his chest squeeze. There was just something about her—something that got to him.

Maybe he was magicked. Maybe she'd somehow entranced him. But how? Why? All he knew was that falling under a literal magic spell made a helluva lot more sense than this apparent random confluence of events.

"I'm heading into town," said Ant. "Elandra's meeting me at the temple."

Taylor raised an eyebrow.

"Magical stuff," his brother said. "She's making an offering to Jaed. It's sorta like when you bring a bottle of wine to someone else's dinner party."

"I get it," said Taylor drolly.

"Yeah." Ant snorted a laugh. "I'm gonna get going. You sure you won't need me at the *nemeton*?"

"Nah," said Taylor. "If anything changes, we'll call you."

Ant nodded and then took off down the hallway to his room.

Taylor turned his gaze once again to the woman sleeping so peacefully under the safety of his roof.

"Who are you?" he whispered. "What are you doing here?" He sucked in a breath. "And what the hell do you want with me?"

She stirred, appearing restless. And he watched as she struggled under the covers, her expression filled with pain, fear. He couldn't bear it. The thought of her being hurt, or suffering, killed him, so he crossed the room, sat on the edge of the bed, and put his hand on her forehead. "Ssshh," he said. "It's okay. It's all right now."

Lenore quieted. She turned her face toward him, still deeply asleep, and her cheek slid against his palm. Her soft skin felt like silk on his calloused hands. Working man's hands, he thought. She deserved better. But he wanted her.

Goddess, how he wanted her.

She took his breath away, this woman, this stranger.

Her breathing evened out, and her body relaxed. When he was sure that she was through the nightmare and that she felt safe once again, he slipped off the bed. He paused at the doorway, giving one last look over his shoulder.

In the light of day, the *nemeton* looked almost peaceful. The sense of waiting had not dissipated, and the vibes of urgency—and that taint of dark magic—made Taylor's skin prickle. While Gray wandered around, apparently seeing magical imprints all over the place, Taylor studied the altar where Lenore had been bound.

Her blood blemished the rock. Now black, it looked like sin staining an ancient soul. He could almost feel the protest of the blue stone, and its imperious outrage of being abused.

"Taylor."

"Yeah?" He turned away from the altar and joined Gray in front of the large stone that belonged to the House of Ravens, the symbol of Ekron, the keeper of death. The stone was scorched. And the shape of the mark looked . . . well, human.

"Someone was burned into ash." Gray pointed to the grass, and Taylor crouched down to look at the pile of gray powder.

Taylor got to his feet and slowly turned to examine the other stones. None bore the same burned impressions. "You think it's coincidence Ekron's stone is the one with a dead guy's outline?"

Gray shook his head. "Magic has too much symbolism, too much intent, for it to ever be accidental."

"Shit." Taylor rubbed the back of his neck. "What the hell happened?"

"Lenore is the only one who knows," said Gray. "I can't track much in this place. I sense six individuals. And I feel Lenore's presence on the altar. Whatever they were trying to do, it failed."

"You think they'd have the balls to try again?"

"The House of Ravens is not known for leaving well enough alone, especially if they hope to gain power. What I don't understand is how the hell they knew a *nemeton* was here when we didn't. Or how they got into town without us knowing about it."

"Damn it. It's likely they know about the Goddess fountain, too."

"Yeah." Gray blew out a frustrated breath. "I'll start the cleansing. When my mother gets here on Friday, I'll ask her, Ember, and Lucy to help me reinforce protections on the town and your land." He looked at Taylor. "All the same, maybe someone should keep watch out here until the protections are reinforced."

"No offense about your abilities, Gray, but the damned town has been in magical lockdown since March. If they got through all that, then some extra magic isn't going to matter much." He sighed. "Neither will some humans hanging around here."

"I'll create vigils," said Gray. "They'll keep watch and warn us if anyone unauthorized enters the *nemeton*."

"What the hell is a vigil?"

"Sorta like a magical mud doll. I'll make them from the earth around here, and they'll keep watch. They can't do magic, but they'll trigger protections and send us warning."

"Mud dolls, huh?"

"Yeah," said Gray. "Kinda creepy, I know." He looked around. "I've been thinking about Atwood's suicide. You think his taking his life is somehow related to all this?

"No coincidences," muttered Taylor. It didn't make much sense, but then a lot of strange things happened in Nevermore. Was there a connection? Hell, there wasn't much he could do about Atwood until he got Dr. Green's official coroner's report. "You okay here?"

"Yeah," said Gray. "As soon as I finish the cleansing, I'll check in with you and let you know if I found anything else."

"All right." Taylor nodded good-bye, and then he left. Damned place was so sad, he couldn't get outta there fast enough. When he got to his house, he debated about whether or not to check on Lenore. He wanted to see her again with his own eyes, make sure she was all right, and that bothered him. She wasn't exactly his, was she? Lucy and Ember would take good care of her—between Lucy's empathetic nature and Ember's mothering, the girl would be fine.

Casting a glance at the upstairs window that designated his mother's bedroom, he turned away and got into his SUV.

By the time Taylor got to work, it was nearly eleven a.m. Arlene sat at her desk, typing up reports. He should've known she wouldn't stay home like a sensible person. He stood in the foyer with its gleaming black-and-white-checkered floors, and stared at her until she looked up.

She had a determined look in her eye, the kind of look that said any fussing on his part would be met with militant resistance.

"I made coffee," she said.

"Thanks." He didn't move.

Arlene started typing again. After a few more moments, she stopped and sighed. "He was my friend as much as he was anyone's friend, stubborn old cuss. But what good would it do me to sit at home stewing about it all? At least here, I can get work done and keep my mind occupied." She waved her hand. "And Jimmy's driving me crazy. He asks me if I'm okay, if I want tea, if I gotta cry, if I need a hug . . . My husband's turned into Oprah."

Taylor laughed, and then he shook his head. "All right. But if you feel a need for any of those things—"

"I'll call Jimmy," she promised. Grief shadowed her gaze. "Did Atwood really shoot himself?"

"Looks like," he said quietly. "But we won't know for sure until Doc Green takes a look." He wondered what Arlene would think about the significance of Atwood's using Banton's Peacemaker. But reminding her of Banton—both Ren and Harley—would just be putting salt in still-fresh wounds.

"Guess I'll go get that coffee," he said. "You need another cup?"

"Just poured one, so I'm good."

He nodded and then headed back to the break room. He'd barely gotten a cup poured before he heard the front door open and close, and Arlene's startled, "May I help you?"

He brought his mug with him as he returned to the foyer.

He stopped next to Arlene's desk and eyed the newcomer. The man was dressed in formal robes—the glimmering black material with its silver raven on the upper-right shoulder denoted him of the House of Ravens. And the scroll crossed with a sword that was stitched on his left shoulder told Taylor this magical was a special investigator. He carried a black leather satchel emblazoned with the same symbol.

Taylor offered only nonchalance as he sipped his coffee, but his mind was racing. Had they followed a trail from Bernard Franco to Nevermore? Franco, Lucinda's ex-lover and the man who'd cursed her and then tried to murder her, had been killed by Gray while he was in dragon form. Rather than try to explain how the man had gotten flattened by a mythical creature, they'd disposed of the body themselves and pretended he'd never graced the borders of their town. Neither he nor Gray could've known that Franco had created protections against getting murdered—and all those dirty little secrets he'd kept for others had sprung into the oily light of day. Most of the fallout had been in Washington, among the House of Ravens, and other politicians; yet it seemed the only likely explanation for this investigator's arrival in the small town.

Gray had said there were no coincidences. And wasn't it just lucky that a special investigator arrived the day after they'd discovered a sacrificial victim with Raven connections?

The man studied him with the same keenness. He wasn't a big man; he was on the short side, maybe a few inches over five feet, on the thin side, too, and his hair was cut stylishly. His eyes, as dark as mud, didn't give much away. Taylor noted the man's manicured hands and the expensive platinum ring that glittered with a pea-sized diamond—not to mention the Quasar watch, the magical equivalent of a Rolex. The wealth was understated but not hidden. Interesting. This was a man who wanted people to notice his worth.

"Sheriff Mooreland?"

Taylor rocked back on his heels and tipped up his hat. He kept his smile congenial—nothing like the small-town-cop routine to throw off the unsuspecting. "Yep. You are?"

"Special Investigator Orley Ryerson. I'm investigating the death of Bernard Franco."

Bingo. Taylor kept his expression one of mild interest. "I heard about all that mess up in Washington." He paused. "I also heard that Franco was no longer on the membership roster of the House of Ravens."

Ryerson allowed a small tight smile. "It was merely a suspension, so technically, he was still a member, and therefore—even deceased—he merits full rights and privileges." The smile widened infinitesimally. "I'm merely informing you of my presence, Sheriff. As a courtesy."

Taylor took a long sip of coffee. "Well, then. All I need to see is your paperwork, including the *Facio* you received from the Guardian to investigate here."

The man's smile disappeared. "I don't require a *Facio*. The Grand Court has granted me *Detego Detectum*."

There wasn't much Gray could do about a Grand Court–sanctioned investigation, especially not if his own House voted for it. And Taylor knew a *Detego Detectum* required a majority vote from all the Houses to pass. Maybe the Grand Court was trying to keep the Ravens from going rogue by granting them the right to investigate Franco's death. If the House of Ravens seceded from the magicals' governing structure, it was bad news for everybody.

"So you've already informed the Guardian of your presence?" asked Taylor. He took a deliberate sip of coffee. "As a courtesy."

The man's eyes narrowed. "I assumed his offices were here as well."

Taylor quirked one eyebrow. "Didn't realize making

assumptions was an actual investigative technique." He shrugged. "But what do I know?"

Ryerson's gaze flashed with fury; then he buckled in the emotion. "Perhaps you should inform the Guardian that I'm here."

"Oh, you can do that," said Taylor in an aw-shucks voice. "Out those doors, make a left. Up the hill to the big pink house. Can't miss it."

For a moment, Ryerson seemed flabbergasted by the idea that he was expected to handle the matter himself, as though Taylor were some kind of servant who'd rebelled against his master. Taylor touched the brim of his hat. "You have a nice day, now."

He meandered to his office, effectively dismissing the odious Raven mage. The man slithered outside. Cell phones had spotty reception in Nevermore, mostly due to the magic that was so easily amplified by the Goddess fountain, not to mention the magicals themselves. Still, nearly everyone had a landline, and the minute Ryerson stomped past the picture window of Taylor's office, he picked up the receiver and dialed Gray.

The conversation took less than a minute. Gray sounded none too pleased about this newest development. The timing seemed kinda hinky to them both, especially since it had to be well-known that Leticia Calhoun was coming to town soon. And after eight months, the Ravens chose now to send out an investigator?

Oh, yeah. Something else was going on.

Taylor stared down into his empty cup.

Well, shit.

Kenneth Mooreland took on a farmer's life because that was all he'd ever known. He'd been raised on a small farm with a doting, hardworking father until . . . Well, for so long everyone believed that Edward Mooreland had abandoned his family. Now, however, everyone knew he'd been killed twenty years ago by Harley Banton. Damn. It was still difficult to wrap his brain around it.

But later, after they moved into Ol' Joe's place, he'd worked side by side with Taylor and their siblings on that farm. When he started courting Betty Mae, her parents had been right thrilled. They'd wanted to keep their farm in the family, and since Bets was their only child, and not much on farming, honestly, they'd told Kenneth he was sent from the Goddess. Soon as he and Betty Mae got married, her parents retired and moved to Boca Raton. So, here he was, thirty years old, married for the last six, and hoping to be a father soon. Betty Mae wasn't as keen on the idea of starting a family. While he worked from dawn to dusk keeping the farm going, she kept the house, took care of the bills, and cooked the meals. Then she spent half the night on the Home Shopping Network, buying all kinds of crap they didn't need—and hell, half the time, he couldn't figure out how to work.

All the same, Bets was a good wife, and they'd been happy enough.

If there was a tiny voice of discontent that occasionally piped up, he ignored it. Maybe things weren't as they'd been in the beginning. Marriage was about compromise, right? People changed, and if they wanted their relationship to remain solid, then they learned new ways to communicate and live together. And if it seemed to him that Bets might've been doing a lot more changing lately . . . Well, all he could do was try to accommodate his wife. He loved her. The sliver of something-ain't-right that tickled his gut lately—well, that didn't mean a damned thing.

Ken stamped his boots on the front porch, wiping them on the welcome mat in front of the door. He took off his hat and went inside. He could hear the TV blaring in their small living room, but it took only a second to see that his wife wasn't sitting in her usual spot. Her current crochet project had been draped on the arm of the pink recliner, which looked ridiculous in the otherwise traditionally furnished room. Still, he'd always liked that little quirky addition. It was so like Bets.

"Baby?"

He got no response, and frowned. The farmhouse was a one-story, three-bedroom ramshackle old thing, built about the time Nevermore had been founded. Betty Mae's family had taken care of this land for generations. He was proud to carry on the tradition. And he really wanted children, so they could carry it on, too. There was something sustaining about having roots, having a connection, having a legacy. He'd always be grateful for all those things, and he wanted very much to share it with his own progeny.

He didn't understand why Betty Mae kept stalling about having kids. When they were dating, they'd talked about having a family, and she seemed genuinely excited about being a mother. And it wasn't as if he didn't enjoy their time together. They had a rhythm to their lives that made them happy. But surely Bets felt as he did that something was missing. An incomplete circle, he thought. Two people weren't enough. Granted, he'd grown up one of seven children, and he missed the loving chaos of his childhood. There was always someone to play with, someone to get into mischief with . . . someone to lie for you.

He grinned. He needed to swing by and visit his brothers. Just kick back with a few beers and talk about the old days. He hadn't seen either Taylor or Ant in a dog's age.

"Betty Mae?" Ken looked around the neat-as-a-pin kitchen and frowned. Usually he could smell supper cooking, but there wasn't a pan in sight. The oven was cold, the counters gleaming, and the sink dry as a bone.

A little knot of worry formed in his stomach. He walked through the kitchen, to the back of the house where the bedrooms were located. Their door was closed, and for some reason, his fingers trembled when he reached for the knob.

He opened the door and stepped inside. He saw her on the bed, his gaze riveted to the slim, pale arm that hung off the side of the bed. "Bets? You feeling okay, honey?"

When he crossed the room and looked down, he couldn't comprehend what he was seeing. Why was there blood? And Betty Mae's pretty face was . . . *Oh Goddess.* He stumbled backward, slammed into the wall, and stood there, frozen in horror. He closed his eyes, his breath rasping, and felt chilled to his core. *No, no, no!*

He didn't know how long he stayed there, whispering prayers, eyes closed. He didn't know he was crying, until the tears dripped onto his folded hands. And he wasn't sure what finally propelled him to leave, to go rushing into the living room and grab at the phone.

When his big brother answered, he couldn't push any words past his throat. Finally, he managed to whisper, "She's dead."

Chapter 4

Elandra Garou was small and delicate, as pale and fragile looking as angel feathers. But Ant could see the steel in her. She had a reputation as one of the best, as in most hard-assed, examiners in the House of Wolves; he was honored that she'd been sent to test him.

He waited at the temple's entrance while she finished the ritual offering to Jaed and the subsequent prayers to the Goddess. Though the magicals owed allegiance to their ancestors, at the end of the day, it was the Goddess who had created them—created all.

He'd spoken to Elandra a few times, but this would be the first time he'd ever met her. Though his talents seemed to be easily accessed and used, which was not the case for all magicals, he knew he still needed a lot of training. There was so much he didn't know; so much he wanted to learn.

Ant glanced over his shoulder, his gaze moving down the clean, empty streets, to the square purple building where Happy worked as a part-time server. Rilton, the husband of Ember, the enigmatic tea mistress, was teaching Happy how to bake. Right now, though, she was in school. *High school.* Even though he'd kept to his promise of friendship and loyalty, there were days he'd wished—just for a second or two—he wasn't such an honorable man. Happy was a beautiful girl; when she entered the full bloom of womanhood she would be . . . whoa. His gut clenched—and so did parts farther south.

And that was the problem.

He wanted Happy. And despite the relatively small age difference, he knew there existed a wide chasm between them. He was more experienced, more emotionally mature, and an actual adult. With Happy, he was getting too close to giving in to temptation. And if he did that . . . then he wouldn't be the man she deserved. That was why he wanted to test for the House of Wolves. He wanted to go somewhere Happy-free so he could stop so much fucking yearning.

He suspected, though, that no matter how far away he got from Nevermore or from his girl, he would feel the same. It was as if he were tethered to her, not only through his promise, but through the absolute—and yes, he was saying it, damn it—knowledge they were meant for each other.

Patience. All he needed was to keep cultivating his patience.

"You seem distracted."

Ant whipped around at the sound of Elandra's fairy-light voice. He blushed to the roots of his hair, and she laughed at his obvious embarrassment.

"I've been standing here for at least two minutes, and you didn't even notice. What's her name?"

Ant tugged down the brim of his cowboy hat. "How'd you know it's about a girl?"

"Always is." She offered him a half smile. "It's a good way to lose your focus. You sure you're ready for the testing? It will be a very long three days. If you're not prepared—"

"I'm ready." Ant met her gaze steadily. "I won't fail."

Her smile widened, and she inclined her head. "We'll see."

Ant knew he was probably going to get his ass kicked. Most magicals were born with a strong-enough affinity to simply be assigned a House. His powers had been latent, blooming suddenly and inexplicably. So he had to do a little more work to get into the House of Wolves. It was rare for a pledge to get tested—at least to the degree that Elandra had planned for him—but the Wolves wanted to be sure he was truly a magical.

He knew he was the real deal. He sure as hell didn't need the approval of the Wolves. But he wanted the training, and he needed to go away, just for a while, just long enough for Happy to enter womanhood.

Goddess, he loved her.

And wanted her.

"You want a few more minutes to moon around?" asked Elandra.

"Hell, no."

"Good. Let's go."

Gray stared at the Colt Peacemaker that lay on the wood floor, gleaming like vengeance. Two crime scenes in one week with the same weapon.

What the hell?

He'd locked up Banton's gun in his own magic-protected safe. No way could it have been removed from that safe or his property without his knowing about it. He gathered his power and sent it toward the weapon. Nothing. Damned if he could feel even an ounce of magic in it—or on it.

If it wasn't magicked, then it made no sense about how it kept disappearing from secured locations, only to end up in the hands of people who had no reason to take their own lives. He looked at the remains of poor Betty Mae Mooreland. Now, there was a lady whose life seemed all right. She and Kenneth had made a nice couple; she was shier than her gregarious husband, and she was prone to blushing. He hadn't seen them in a while, especially since the café had been burned down. Nevermore really needed a restaurant, maybe even two. Making that happen was yet another thing on his very long Guardian to-do list. But that was neither here nor there.

Taylor was splitting his time between documenting the scene, keeping his brother going with coffee and empathy, and putting in calls to Dr. Green. He had brought Gray along for an extra set of hands.

Gray gathered his power and used it to once again seal the weapon. Then he took it carefully, put it in a special, silver-charmed box, and held on to it. This time, he was taking the damned thing to the Dragon archives in Dallas. Magic or no magic, the Peacemaker would stay put. And maybe then they'd be able to put a stop to whatever was going on in this town.

Gray couldn't help but wonder: Why Atwood? Why Betty Mae? Why would they kill themselves? And why both of them with *this* gun?

"How'd she get it?" asked Taylor.

"She didn't," said Gray. "She couldn't."

Taylor nodded, but Gray could see the worry in his friend's expression. "Ant will be here soon to get Ken. Once he's gone, we'll be able to transport Betty Mae to the morgue. Damned place is getting a lot more business these days."

"These suicides are a piece of a bigger puzzle. And I don't think we'll like the picture when it's done." Gray told him about taking the gun to Dallas for storage. Taylor agreed. "In Dallas, I'll do some digging around in the archives about the Peacemaker. If it has a magical history, then it might have documentation. Maybe there's something that will enlighten us about Banton's gun."

"Good idea. Dr. Green will be here tomorrow to do the autopsies. Can't be anything other than suicide, but if it's not . . ."

"Yeah," said Gray, running a hand through his hair. Frustration ate away at his composure. "Then we've got another murderer loose in Nevermore."

Norie Whyte awoke with a scream trapped in her throat, her arms and legs straining against the manacles on her wrists and ankles. *You won't break me*, she thought. *I won't let you.*

It took a few seconds for her to realize she was freely moving her limbs and that she was in a warm, comfortable bed. She stopped struggling against the nonexistent restraints and lay still, listening to her own rasping breaths. Her body ached, but she was so used to feeling pain that it took her a moment to realize she wasn't experiencing the usual agonies.

Gingerly, she sat up and looked around. The big room was furnished with lovely antiques. On either side of the four-poster bed was an arched window. Pale light filtered through the gaps in the shut curtains, dappling the wood floors.

She pushed off the covers and noted that a cotton nightgown covered her from neck to toes—and she wore thick black socks—men's socks.

Where was she?

And how had she gotten here?

Images flickered. Being trapped on the altar. People around her. Knives slashing. Spells poisoning. Pain flowing.

She swallowed the knot of terror clogging her throat.

They'd been trying to sacrifice her.

And then . . . what? She closed her eyes and tried to remember something solid—something real. There'd been a sudden, terrifying cold. And screeching—birds, maybe? Then a blast of light. An awful smell of burned flesh.

The faint memories wiggled away, like shadows chased out by sunlight.

Her mind was in protection mode, and given the ugly turn her life had taken and all she had endured, she shuddered to think what other horrors had occurred—an experience obviously so bad, her brain had shut off access.

Chilled, she pulled the covers up to her chin and had a childish moment of wishing someone would come in and shoo away all her monsters. But some monsters could not be defeated—especially the ones growling and clawing inside the soul.

"My son rescued you."

Norie glanced to her left and saw an older female sitting on the dresser. She was pretty, with graying brown hair tucked into a bun and kind eyes the color of spring grass. She wore a floral-print dress covered by a white apron, and a pair of pink flats.

Then Norie realized she wasn't exactly sitting on the dresser—she was sorta drifting above it.

"Yes, sweetie, I'm dead." She smiled, and the left side of her mouth dimpled. "My name is Sarah Mooreland. And this used to be my room. You're at my son's house, and you're safe."

Norie opened her mouth. Her throat convulsed. No words came out. She grasped the sides of her neck, though the gesture did nothing to jumpstart her speaking abilities. Panic edged through her. She was dreaming, right? She had to be. This was a nightmare. She looked at the . . . well, the ghost, and tried not to freak out.

"Can't talk, right?" Sarah gave her a sympathetic look. "Don't worry about that. It'll get fixed." She jumped off the dresser and float-walked to Norie. "You're very special. Goddess-blessed. She's calling you into Her service. That's why I'm here. To help you."

Norie stared at the spirit in shock. Goddess-blessed? Now, that was a laugh. She'd spent her childhood with a mother who was eight kinds of crazy. Norie's adult life had been given over to mundane, back-breaking jobs, and she had never, not once, been in love. She'd tried. Relationships were not her forte. If the Goddess had been blessing Norie, she sure had a funny way of showing it.

It wasn't even that Norie wanted big things. She wanted simple things. Love. Family. Home. She yearned for this dream so deeply, so often, that it was all she could think of . . . all she truly wanted. But she'd been denied the opportunity for love. Oh, her mother had loved her . . . as crazy as she was at the end. They'd moved so often, and Mom had been so paranoid, that Norie wasn't allowed friends. She never went to formal school. Her mother had homeschooled her and kept her protected from the world. And when Norie had gotten old enough to go out on her own, her mother had gotten ill. Doctors couldn't figure out what was killing her mother, or what was affecting her mental state.

At the end, when she was strapped into a hospital bed, her body nearly wasted away, her mind gone, she had grabbed Norie's hand and looked at her. "Star born," she whispered, her gaze flickering with insanity, "shine brightly."

Minutes later, she'd closed her eyes and breathed her last.

Norie felt her stomach clench. Mom may have been nuts, but she'd been the only person in the world who'd cared for her. And Norie had spent the next ten years figuring out a few things . . . such as being cursed. Attempting relationships . . . Well, it never ended well—especially for the man fool enough to like her. Something bad always happened to him.

So she'd accepted her loneliness. She'd tried to build a life. It may not have been glamorous, but she'd been okay. Sometimes, though, when she woke up in the middle of the night, her chest aching, her heart pounding, a nightmare crimping the edges of her memories, she wondered if she'd inherited her mother's insanity.

"Our lives are a series of choices," said Sarah kindly. "Not always our own. There's so much you don't know, sweetie. So much you must learn before your thirtieth birthday."

Norie stared at the ghost. "Why?" she mouthed.

"The spell that's bound your powers and your memories will disappear. You will know your destiny then. There are very difficult things ahead for everyone, especially for you. But you must have courage."

Sarah was echoing the speech of the raven in her dream, the one she'd had before she woke up chained to a stone. Black Robe had also talked about her destiny. She was tired of strangers telling her what her life should be like. She'd listened to her own mother map out Norie's life in a way that only a crazy person could. *You'll know, Norie. You'll know. And then he'll know. He will know. And you won't be safe. Have to keep you safe. Pack! Pack now!*

And off they'd go. To another city. To another ratty apartment. For a while, her mother's mind would settle enough to get a job, to build a home, and then a couple months would go by . . . and it would start all over again. Goddess or not, Norie would not be beholden to Her will. How could she serve a deity who hadn't helped at all, ever, during the constant hardships of her nearly thirty years?

"Sometimes, you choose," said Sarah. "And sometimes, you are chosen." She laid her fingers against Norie's brow; her forehead tingled. "In the morning, you will have some answers."

Norie didn't want to go back to sleep. She wanted to get out of this bed, out of this house, and out of whatever trouble she was in.

"It's not wise to leave," warned the ghost, as if she'd read Norie's mind. Huh. Maybe she had. "If you venture outside this house's protections, they'll find you. You're cloaked here. Safe. Understand?"

Fear skittered like snakes up her spine. She nodded, suddenly chilled.

"Good." Sarah smiled. Then she slowly faded into nothing.

Norie slowly sat up and stared at the space where Sarah Mooreland had stood looking all motherly and concerned. Something flickered in her mind, a memory she couldn't quite grab hold of. She chased it for a minute, but it eluded her too well. Was it weird that she found the sight of a ghost familiar? She had seen one before, but it was a feeling of surety, rather than actual memory.

She looked around the room, approving of its loveliness. She was glad to be here, safe and sound, rather than in the company of Black Robe and his asshole cohorts. She had no idea if she was embedded in a similar pit of vipers, but she doubted it.

Oh, how she wanted to go back to her old life, but she knew it was gone. It didn't matter now if she returned to California. Would she be on the run for the rest of her life? And for what? She didn't understand why Black Robe needed *her*. She was no one.

No one at all.

Norie figured the best thing to do was to rest. At least in her dreams, she was safe.

Taylor held her hand and led Norie through the garden. The trees were cut in whimsical shapes, the flowers as lush and beautiful as any she'd ever seen, and the path was lined with smooth, black rocks.

"Here," he said. The small clearing was surrounded by a wall of verdant trees, these with long thin leaf-covered limbs that drooped to the ground like a lady's wrinkled ball gown. "Weeping willows," said Taylor. "My favorite." He glanced at her, smiling. "Not that I walk around thinking about trees a lot."

Norie laughed.

He squeezed her hand and took her to the checkered blanket. She saw the wicker basket, and beside it, two wineglasses and a bottle of Chablis.

He waited for her to sit, and she realized she was in a long dress, the same white one she'd worn in the raven dream. Her heart tripped, and fear shot up her spine like cold lightning.

"You're all right," said Taylor. "It's okay."

The fear receded instantly. He poured the wine and handed her a glass. "To us," he said, tilting his glass in her direction.

"To forever," she said.

They clinked glasses.

Later, they lay on the blanket, hand in hand, and she listened to the low, comforting sound of Taylor's voice. She couldn't discern the words, but it didn't matter. Not really. She was where she belonged.

With him.

Above them, two stars glowed in the night sky. It was odd, thought Lenore, that only two stars should be visible. They looked like eyes gleaming in the dark, but she wasn't afraid.

Destiny, said a voice that sounded like the white raven's.

The garden faded.

Now they stood in the middle of the nemeton, the ancient stones buzzing with energy.

She was naked.

And so was he.

She turned in Taylor's arms and kissed him, mating her tongue with his, reveling in his gasp of breath, his tightened embrace.

"I want you," she whispered. Whoa. Was she really doing this? Love me, *she wanted to say.* Love me.

But the words wouldn't come out of her mouth. She couldn't bear to ask for love, only to receive judgment and rejection. Just like so many times before.

She couldn't say it. No. But she could show him. She kissed the strong column of his neck, the rough line of his jaw, the dent in his chin. "Taylor."

He took her hand and lowered it to his cock. Her heart pounded fiercely as she encircled the smooth, warm flesh, then trailed her fingers from the base to its tip.

Taylor tipped her chin so that she would look at him. "I want you so much."

"Then take me," she said. *"I'm yours."*

He lowered her to the ground then and used his hands, his mouth, to give her such pleasure. She gave the same to him. Touching his muscled flesh, stroking, kissing—it was beyond what she believed possible.

And when he finally rose above her and slid inside her, she thought, I belong to him.

"Lenore. Oh, Lenore." He clamped on to one of her tight-ened nipples and sucked. Bliss bubbled through her. She wrapped her arms around his hips and matched his strokes. She wanted to reach that promise of pleasure that felt so close. Her body trembled; her heart pounded.

"More, Taylor," she said. *"More!"*

Her breath caught in her throat when he abandoned her breasts and pounded into her, his head cradled in the crook of her neck. Sweat rolled down her breasts, but all she felt was the great need filling her belly, the spark he ignited.

"Lenore," he muttered. "Lenore!"

She shattered. Her hands grasped his shoulders, her nails piercing his flesh.

Then Taylor found his pleasure. He held on to her, shuddering. Only when he lifted his head and looked at her did she see the utter desolation in his gaze.

Norie woke up and shoved off the covers. Her body was suffering the aftereffects of such a vivid dream.

Wow. She had it bad for her rescuer.

But there something about . . . What did the stars mean? And why had Taylor looked so desperate?

She put her head into her hands. She knew the price of falling for someone. Every guy she'd ever dated, whoever had the misfortune of being with her for longer than three dates, ended up hurt—literally.

Her mother had told her, numerous times, that she had to wait for the key. *Only the key can be yours*, she'd muttered in some of her most insane moments. *Save yourself for him. He'll save you. He'll save the stars!*

Oh, Mom. Norie shook her head. Whatever voices had infiltrated her mother's thinking, whatever crazy thoughts spun in her head, she'd been right about Norie's luck in love. She wasn't allowed to have a relationship.

Well, she wasn't going back to sleep. Who knew what else her brain would come up with?

She eyed the opened door to the bedroom and then shoved off the covers.

It was creeping toward four a.m., well past the witching hour and edging into the territory of time owned by roosters and farmers. Trent Whitefeather, knee-deep in his uncle's office crap, kept glancing in Elizabeth's direction. It was almost as if he needed to make sure she was still there and that she was still his.

He stopped pretending to work and just watched her sort through the stack of paperwork that had never made it into Uncle Atwood's poor excuse of a filing system.

"Can you stare at me *and* work?" she asked, her tone teasing. "Not that I don't enjoy digging through garbage service receipts. I found one from 1952. How long has Atwood owned this place?"

"Family biz," said Trent, trying to sound nonchalant. He was embarrassed she'd caught him acting all moon-eyed. He needed to keep it cool. "The Stephens were one of the founding families in Nevermore. Started out as just the go-to people for the newspaper. When the Guardian decided to add in garbage services, the Stephens ended up with that duty, too." He snorted a laugh. "To hear my unc tell it, nobody wanted to be responsible for picking up the town's trash—even with extra incentive money for trucks and workers. He said all the business owners had to do a lottery. My great-great-grandfather ended up with the short stick."

"I suppose it's a better method than 'Eeny, meeny, miny, mo.'"

Trent looked up and grinned. "Yeah. But not by much."

She grinned back, her eyes going soft, and that look . . . *Oh shit.* That look was what set his heart to pounding and his dick to hardening. He wanted to bend her over the desk right now. Claim her in the space that was his legacy. Give himself, too. To her. Show her that he understood there was something special between them. She was Mordi to everyone else, but to him, she'd always be Elizabeth.

"What will you do with the businesses?" she asked.

"Carry on," he said absentmindedly. It seemed weird to be trying to organize Atwood's things. He kept thinking his uncle would barrel in, demanding in that hoarse huffing voice just what the hell Trent thought he was doing. He'd attempted to put some order to the madness before, and every time, he met with furious resistance from Atwood. Why the man liked living in such a horrific mess was beyond Trent's comprehension. His own room was neat as a pin, as organized and clean as Atwood's living and working spaces were disorganized and filthy.

Still, he'd happily live in this crap hole forever, just as it was, if it meant he'd get his uncle back. They'd never been too close, at least not before he'd moved to Nevermore. He always got the feeling that Atwood didn't necessarily approve of his sister hooking up with . . . Well, a nonwhite was probably the kindest way to think about it. Not that Atwood ever messed with him. He'd like to think his uncle actually loved him.

Trent's dad had been a Cherokee, and Trent preferred to follow the tenets of his father's people. There were magicals in the native peoples of this continent, just as there were magicals in any race. And Atwood didn't seem particularly fond of magicals, either, though he lived in a town with them. And yet, he hadn't hesitated when Trent's parents died, coming to Oklahoma to pick him up and give him a home, a purpose.

His uncle hadn't tried to interfere with his magical studies, either. Trent practiced his gifts with the same intensity and purpose he had when studying for school or for crushing on Elizabeth. He barely managed to stop the goofy grin that wanted to crease his face as his thoughts returned to her.

He couldn't believe that Elizabeth liked him the way he did her. Sure, they were young, but young didn't mean a person couldn't commit to another, or shout from the rooftops about falling head over heels for her. They could marry. Have children. Run the garbage service, and the newspaper, and the cemetery together.

He stared down into the dark drawer he'd opened. He'd been emptying it absentmindedly, and now that there was nothing in it, he used it almost as though it were a crystal ball. What was their future? Would it eventually end? Or would it go on, as he hoped, until their dying days? Maybe they'd share a nursing home room together. They'd be old and wrinkly and wouldn't care. Love didn't see with the eyes, only with the heart.

"What's so funny?" asked Elizabeth.

She was staring at him now, her expression etched with an emotion he couldn't quite discern. Shit. He'd been doing the goofy grin after all as he imagined their future together. But that expression of hers . . . He shivered. The way she was looking at him made him uncomfortable. That look so subtly carved on her face was somehow caught between love and regret. He felt his heart drop to his toes, and his throat closed. Was something wrong already? Was she going to let him go before they'd even had a chance to really explore what could be between them?

He couldn't breathe.

"Trent." She moved from the floor where she'd been sitting and crossed to the desk chair he occupied. She sat on his lap and kissed him gently. "I'm yours," she said simply.

His lungs filled with air, his heart with tenderness, and his mind with plans for a future with sweet, sweet Elizabeth.

"Lenore." Taylor lay on the grass, naked and aroused. Above them was the night sky, and all around them were the huge blue stones that guarded the nemeton.

Lenore's small, pale, perfect body lay next to him. She was trembling, her gaze luminous. What emotion glittered there?

Lenore offered him what he wanted—not just her body, but sharing a life together.

You can't save her.

The hell, *he said to the voice that echoed inside his skull.*

Her hands slid up his chest, making him writhe under her touch. He slid his hands over her breasts, those perfect, beautiful breasts, and nearly died from the sensation.

"It's been so long," *he said.* "It's almost like I was waiting for you."

"I know I was waiting for you," *she said.*

He brushed his fingertips across her trembling belly, dipping down into the soft curls at the apex of her thighs. He stroked her clit, watching her eyes go dark. Her breath hissed out of her mouth, and she bit her lower lip, moving closer to his touch.

Taylor cupped the most intimate part of her. She moaned and rubbed her slick flesh against his palm. She knew only pleasure—not his anguish. I can save her, *he thought desperately.*

But he couldn't think about that.

Only this.

He trailed soft, slow kisses down the curve of her stomach. He pressed his lips against her belly and prayed to the Goddess—and yes, he prayed—that Lenore would live.

Sweat dewed her skin. He licked the tiny droplets, drawing patterns in her flesh with his tongue before parting her trembling thighs.

Her swollen clit was as juicy, as sweet, as a ripe berry. He tugged the morsel between his lips and sucked. She arced against his mouth, her restless hands tugging on his hair.

"Please," *she begged.*

He slid his hands under her buttocks and pulled her close, breathing in her scent. It was earthy, intoxicating.

Mine.

He stroked her with his tongue, torturing her clit with tiny, brief suckles. She moved against his mouth, taking her pleasure with an innocent wonder that pierced the heart of him.

"Only you," *she murmured.* "Only you, Taylor."

She stilled, thighs quivering, and cried out as she came.

For a long moment, Taylor stared at her, watching as she recovered from her orgasm. She was luminous. That female satisfaction that curled in her smile made him want to do it all over again.

Taylor kissed his way up her belly. He paused at those gorgeous breasts and paid glorious attention to them. Her nipples were beaded, and he pulled one into his mouth, licking and sucking.

She moaned.

Everything inside him tightened in pleasure. Taylor positioned himself above her and slowly entered. She was wet and ready and tight. He closed his eyes and drew in a steadying breath.

Oh, sweet hell.

Another stroke sent more pleasure rippling through him. She pulled him close, grasping with hungry hands; her body moved against him, and he thrust harder and faster, her breathy moans battering away at his control.

"Taylor!" She moved her hips, her hands sliding to grasp his buttocks. "More," she whispered, her breath feathering his ear. "More."

He gave the lady what she wanted.

The pulsations of her orgasm tugged at his cock, and he tried to hold on, tried to give her the time to savor her pleasure again.

Then he was sailing over the edge with her, saying her name, desperation and love pounding in every beat of his heart.

Then the scene changed. . . . Darkness flowed over them.

"You can't help me," Lenore said. Her voice held placid acceptance. Goddess above! She made his heart ache. "Just go, Taylor."

"Not without you." He reached for her, but the darkness swirled, as heavy as iron, yet as intangible as smoke. He couldn't reach through that magical ether. He wasn't powerful enough. She needed him, and he was failing her all over again. "Don't do this."

"Save Nevermore," she said. "Save yourself." Then she was fading, fading into the raven blackness, into the night embrace of Ekros, who had once ruled the world of death. The smell of incense was thick, the chanting voices rising higher

and higher, and inside, Taylor felt something claw through him, something electric and cold and vengeful.

Claim what's yours.

Pain exploded in the middle of his forehead—a lightning strike that left him breathless, helpless.

"Lenore!" Taylor woke up with her name bursting from his lips. His head hurt, and he cradled it in his hands while he tried to catch his breath. Fuck all. What was going on?

The nightmare was already fading, and so was the pain that had taken root in his brain. And Holy Goddess! Making love to Lenore?

He needed to keep his brain—and his dick—in line. He shoved away the covers and stood up. In deference to their female guest, he'd pulled on a pair of sweats. Usually he just slept in his boxers.

Scrubbing his hands through his hair, he got out of bed and walked out of his bedroom. He needed to check on Lenore—just once—and make sure she was still resting well, still safe. That damned dream had tainted his sleep; he didn't think he could lie down again. He'd try, but he had no doubt he'd spend more time staring at the ceiling than getting any shut-eye. He wasn't functioning on all cylinders, so he decided to table the self-flagellation for later.

He yawned so hard that his jaw cracked. He stumbled down the hallway, scratching at his belly like a true Neanderthal, and paused by the open door of Lenore's room.

She was gone.

Taylor snapped fully awake. He hadn't even processed that he was moving before he found himself taking the stairs two at a time. *Where did she go?* Had she awakened and taken off? Had someone kidnapped her? With the protections that Gray had added around the house, there was no way anyone could've gotten in or out without setting off an alarm. Although Lenore *could* leave. . . . What if she'd woken up and gotten scared or upset? Was she wandering around outside?

His heart skipped a beat.

He skidded into the kitchen, only thinking about getting his boots on before he took off outside to find his lost Lenore.

She was standing in the kitchen, a glass of orange juice in her hand. She gave him a startled look, and then her gaze dropped appreciatively to his chest. Taylor resisted the urge to cross his arms over his pectorals, and then he had to kill the impulse to puff up like a rooster. He kept in shape, and he had the muscles to show for it.

Not that he had to prove anything.

"You okay?" he asked gruffly.

She nodded. Then she took a long drink of juice. She licked the residual liquid off her lips, and that small gesture of tongue against mouth had his cock jumping.

Shit. That was all he needed—a big ol' hard-on. That would inspire confidence in the woman, no doubt. She didn't seem to notice his discomfort, focusing instead on finishing off the OJ.

To forestall further potential embarrassment, he strode to the fridge and opened it wide enough to let the cold air flow over him. He leaned down and grabbed the milk, then poured himself a glass. He wasn't much of a milk drinker, but it was too early for coffee, and Lenore had effectively commandeered the orange juice.

"You hungry?"

She looked at him for a moment, and then her gaze skittered away. He knew pride when he saw it, and he was amazed she had any left after what she'd been through—whatever it might have been. He wondered exactly how she'd ended up bloodied and bruised and naked in his woods.

Her gaze meandered back to his, and she touched her throat, almost apologetically.

"Oh," he said, nodding. "You can't talk. Gray and Ember said they detected a spell on you."

One dark brow lifted, and he realized she had no idea who Gray and Ember were. "Gray Calhoun is the Guardian of Nevermore. That's where you are—Nevermore, Texas. Ember and her husband run the tea shop. She's . . . uh, a sorta prophet, I guess." He knocked back the milk, then put the glass in the sink. She followed suit with her own glass. Standing next to each other at the farmhouse sink created an awkward moment. She glanced up at him, her lips quirking; she reached up and used two fingers to wipe off his upper lip. The strangely intimate gesture stalled out his lungs. She seemed to realize how familiarly she was acting, as though they'd stood in this kitchen next to each other all their lives and had the right to touch each other in such familiar ways.

And he wanted to touch her.

A lot.

"Thank you," he said. He tore off a paper towel from the roll he kept on the counter and gave it to her so she could dry her fingers. Then he took one and scrubbed at his mouth. He saw the pink taint her cheeks and watched as she drifted away, obviously abashed, the paper towel crumpled in her fist.

"You . . . uh, going back to bed?"

She turned and glanced over her shoulder. For a moment, Taylor's brain short-circuited. Lenore was the kind of pretty that had no doubt driven better men than he to their knees. And who wouldn't worship such a delicate, ethereal beauty? He was tongue-tied, and he felt the heat of embarrassment crawl up his neck.

She studied him, as if she could see right through him, into the conflict that knotted his gut. He wanted to claim her, and . . . It was stupid to feel that way. He didn't know her. She was—hell, she didn't even know who she was.

"Your name. Is it Lenore?"

Her eyes widened. She made a gesture between a nod and a shrug. Then she lifted her hand in a pen motion as though writing. He grabbed the pen and notepad he kept by the kitchen phone. She scribbled on the pad, then handed the paper to him.

"Norie Whyte," he said. He looked up and offered a smile. "Hi, Norie. I'm Taylor Mooreland. I'm the sheriff of Nevermore."

She smiled back; then she wiggled her fingers in a shy hello.

He felt as if he'd been punched in the chest. How could just looking at someone make a person feel like an arrow was penetrating his belly? More like a dozen arrows. Taylor realized then that he hadn't followed up on the question of feeding her. She had to be starving. And though it seemed she had no problem getting herself a drink, it appeared she hadn't been bold enough to grab something to eat, too, or she hadn't had a chance. Maybe he'd made her self-conscious.

"You know, I'm feeling peckish. I make a mean sandwich. You want one, too? We got some ham, turkey, and roast beef, and all the fixings."

Norie's glance skittered toward the fridge. She visibly swallowed, and then, after hesitating a moment more, she gave a slight nod.

"Terrific. Go on and have a seat." He grabbed a chair and pulled it out, gesturing toward it for her to sit.

She stepped forward, then paused, her head tilting and her lips forming a *moue*.

He felt it then, the tingle in the air.

Magic.

Chapter 5

As he turned to locate the magical threat, Taylor saw
that Norie's eyes were as wide as saucers. She wrapped
her arms around herself and started trembling.

The air felt tainted—as if it were slowly turning metallic. The heat came next, waves and waves of it, and
then a smell so putrid, he gagged. Taylor knew evil had
somehow wiggled through the protections on his
home. How, damn it? Was Gray's power weak? Or
someone else's magic just a helluva lot stronger?

There was only one reason why: Norie.

He crossed the kitchen in three long strides, swept
Norie into his arms, and headed toward the stairs. The
only magical he knew was on the second floor, snoring
away in his bed, and he had to get Norie there, to safety.
And Gray had said he'd be alerted if the protections
were somehow broken, so his Dragon ass had better
show up soon, too.

Ant was already in the foyer, working his mojo.

Taylor had never been more relieved to be related to a magical than at that moment. Whatever had infiltrated his home was coming for Norie, and it was damned scary to know he had no way to combat it. But his baby brother did.

Holy Creator Goddess. He hadn't realized the extent of Ant's powers, but as the blue and green swirls of magic ribboned together from his brother's hands to create a globe of protection, Taylor could feel its depth; it was fulsome, mighty.

Norie clung to him, still shivering, while her cornflower blue gaze was pinned on Ant. His brother was muttering under his breath, doing long movements with his arms and little flicks and twists of his fingers. Taylor had seen Gray work magic plenty of times, but the Guardian didn't seem to require much in the way of gestures and such.

"What the hell is it?" asked Taylor.

Ant's eyes were closed, his face scrunched in concentration. He shook his head, obviously unable to concentrate on whatever spellwork he was enacting and have a conversation at the same time. That only confirmed Taylor's suspicion that whatever was trying to enter his home was big, nasty, and powerful. He clutched Norie and muttered a prayer to the Goddess.

Claim what's yours.

Taylor frowned. That phrase kept popping into his head, and he didn't know what to make of it. He didn't know what it meant. A pulse started to beat in the middle of his forehead. It felt as if light were gathering in the crevices of his brain, bringing heat and pain, and trying to shove something electric into his skull.

He groaned, trying to push out the agony and stay upright. Norie held on to his neck even tighter and balled up, as though she knew he might take a dive. She didn't seem inclined to actually let go, and he was glad. So as long the woman remained in his arms, he could protect her. She wouldn't be alone. She wouldn't be in danger.

He managed to stay upright, but he was swaying, his legs threatening to buckle; sweat beaded his brows and dripped down his temples.

"Can't," cried Ant. "Shit!"

He was driven to his knees, his arms dropping to his sides. He was breathing heavily, as if he couldn't get any oxygen into his lungs. His eyes rolled until the whites showed; then he threw back his head and screamed. His voice held such an awful sound of suffering that it rived the pain away from Taylor's own head. He staggered backward, his hold on Norie viselike, and tried to think about what to do.

How did he save them both?

"Ant!" he yelled.

The bubble around them burst, the colors slithering off like multicolored snakes into the awful darkness that filled the house with its vile thickness and stench. He watched helplessly as his little brother fell forward, his body seizing as though someone had touched him with a live wire. After an endless moment of quaking torments, his brother lay still. Horror filled Taylor as he realized his brother wasn't breathing.

"Release the sacrifice."

The sulfuric tones pullulated, filling the foyer with hissing demands.

Demons.

He didn't think it was possible for Norie to cling to him any tighter, but she managed to fasten to him like a barnacle on the underside of a boat. He didn't think he could shake her off if he tried. But if demons wanted her, they well could separate the sheriff from his charge.

"Release her."

The commands issued in a multitude of sibilant tones, and the darkness seemed to push in on them, as hard and unyielding as obsidian stone. Still, there were no attempts to take Norie from him. He wasn't even sure there was anything out there. . . . He could detect no real forms, clawing and writhing. It was the pervasive feeling of evil that made the hairs go up on the back of his neck. He edged closer to his brother, unsure about what rescue he could attempt. There was no way for him to carry both his brother and Norie, and certainly not through the oppressive blackness. He knew without a doubt that touching that darkness for even a second would mean getting sucked into it, getting lost in it, getting the forever kind of gone.

"You and your brother's freedom for hers," offered the voices.

"Fuck you."

The laughter echoed all around him, and the joyless sounds made his stomach knot in gelid fear. Something bad was gonna happen. He wouldn't be able to stop it.

"Your brother lives, but he's injured. Would you trade his life for hers?"

No, he wouldn't.

But he would trade his own.

Maybe if he blundered into whatever hell had snuck into his house, Norie and Ant would have enough time to escape. He gazed down at his brother, relieved to see him stirring. Ant groaned, obviously in pain, but at least his limbs were twitching and his lungs working. Then Ant rolled onto his back, took a huge breath, and opened his eyes.

His expression was seven kinds of pissed off.

Good. Ant would know to get Norie to safety. He wouldn't waste any moments gained from Taylor by leaping into the black madness twisting around them like a demented band of ghosts.

Taylor looked at Norie and offered her a reassuring smile. She studied his expression and frowned. He didn't know what she'd seen in his eyes, but she practically leapt out of his arms. He tried to hold on to her, but she was light as a bag of feathers and fluid as sunshine. She was on her feet, arms akimbo, staring at him. She pointed at his brother and shook her head. Then she pointed at him and shook her head again.

She blew him a kiss, then turned, fully intending to walk into the arms of demons.

"No." Taylor grabbed her shoulder and yanked her back. "I won't let you."

She whirled and gave him a look of disbelief. Then she waved her arms as if to say, "Hey, moron, what choice do we have?"

The voices started in again, demanding the sacrifice be given to them. Taylor realized they weren't taking her because they couldn't. He had to hand her over freely. That was why no one had tried to reach out and pull Norie into whatever wasteland lay in the darkness. He wondered why . . . and then he figured it didn't much matter.

These demons were almost wheedling now, and those awful voices took on the ferocity of a thousand toddlers whining.

He whirled Norie around and pulled her tightly against him. "I won't give her to you."

"Noooooooooo!" the voices protested. The noises of their dissent rose and fell like ocean waves crashing against the shore. "She belongs to the master. To him alone. Give us the sacrifice!"

"Go fuck yourselves."

Howls issued, and the atmosphere changed. It got darker, and the suffocating heat dissipated into a wretched chill. The stench became so foul, Taylor found himself breathing through his mouth to keep the stink out of his lungs. The howls faded into a silence that offered far more menace than the petulant yawps.

"Give me the woman," intoned a resonant male voice, "or perish."

Norie shrank against Taylor, her fear as palpable as the evil pulsing around them. He didn't know if she recognized the voice, or if she was reacting to the final-offer tone it emitted. Whoever this new asshole was, he meant business.

"We'll perish anyway," said Ant. "So, like my brother says . . ." He trailed off. Then he jumped to his feet and made a show of picking lint off his T-shirt. "Go fuck yourself."

Ant's moment of defiance ended quickly. He lost the color in his face, and his eyes bulged.

Taylor clutched Norie as he watched his brother once again go to his knees. His eyes rolled around like those of a wild animal trying to escape a snare. His entire body went still, and then it was almost as if he were being squeezed by an invisible python. He seemed to get smaller; then he lost his breath, and blood started to drip from his nose and his ears.

"No!" Taylor held firmly on to Norie as he reached

down and tried to pull Ant free of whatever tortured him.

He couldn't stop the attack. Hell, he couldn't get to Ant. His hand was bouncing away before he could grab his brother's shoulder and try to haul him to his feet.

Pain shot through Taylor and electrified him. He couldn't keep his arms around Norie. Instead, he felt as though a big metal hand were pressing against his skull, forcing him to his knees. The excruciating sensations attacked every nerve ending, invading his lungs and stealing his ability to breathe. He felt something in his brain snick, and then he felt the blood dribble from his nose.

Goddess almighty! He felt as though he'd been wrapped in a net of bee stings and set on fire. He couldn't move; he couldn't tell Norie to run, to just fucking run. He sought her out, and she was like a beacon of light in the terrible darkness of his nightmares.

"Come to me, Lenore," said the single voice again, as patient as a father trying to corral an errant child, "and I will stop their suffering."

Tears streaked Norie's face, and, from her expression, Taylor knew it was her compassion, not her fear, that drove her to turn around.

He wanted to cry out, to grab her, to protect her.

She was important. It shouldn't be true. Shouldn't mean so much for a woman he didn't know, for a woman who stirred in him emotions he had no right to feel. He'd made a promise, and he wanted to keep it. He wanted to keep her.

Over her shoulder, she cast him one last glance and wiggled her fingers in that childlike good-bye.

Then she marched toward the realm of demons and dark magic.

Chapter 6

"Gray!"

Gray Calhoun crawled through the foggy layers of sleep and found his fully dressed wife leaning over him and shaking him.

He sat up, exhaustion disappearing under the weight of his wife's panic. "Baby, what is it?"

"Ember and Rilton are downstairs. They said we have to get to Taylor's right now."

"What? Something wrong at Taylor's?" He frowned. "I should've gotten a warning if my protections were broken."

"I don't know," said Lucy, her gaze worried. "If whatever-it-is got to Taylor, it got through the town's spells, too."

"Shit." Lucy moved back as Gray threw off the covers. Then it hit him hard. The spells he'd created to protect his friend were being wormed through by a much more powerful, darker magic. He was connected to his

143

magic, to what he'd created. The spells that protected the town seemed intact. But how could something get to Taylor, all without setting off Nevermore's alarms?

"Gray?"

"It's okay." It took less than a minute for him to pull on jeans and a shirt, and slam his feet into a pair of Vans. Together, they hurried out of the bedroom. "Let's use the portal in the living room. It'll put us right in front of Taylor's house."

"What's going on?" demanded the scratchy voice of Orley Ryerson.

Gray didn't have time to explain the situation to the Raven, especially since he wasn't quite sure what was going on. Common courtesy, and the rules of Guardianship, had forced him to offer a room in his own house to the investigator; to his surprise and disgust, Ryerson had accepted.

"It's a local matter," he threw over his shoulder. "Sorry to wake you."

Ryerson followed. "Perhaps I can offer my assistance."

"No, thanks," gritted out Gray.

Taking the hint, the guy stopped at the top of the stairs, glaring at him and Lucy as they hurried down. Gray resisted the urge to flip him off—soul-sucking bastard.

Ember had already opened the portal. Her one dark eye was filled with worry and sorrow, and that look, that awful look, made his stomach sink. Then she and Rilton stepped through the black oval that looked like a giant's winking eye; Gray and Lucy followed.

There was a tingling rush of cold and color, and then they were stepping out into the front yard of Taylor's farmhouse.

"Sweet Creator Mother," murmured Ember.

Gray stared at the house in horrified awe. It looked as though the bottom half had been dipped in ink; it was thick with both substance and stench. He knew that feeling crawling like deadly spiders over him, and that terrible smell of dying and decay.

"What is it?" asked Lucy in a choked whisper.

"Demons," said Gray.

"Dey after dat girl," said Ember. "She important t' 'em. Gather your powers. We must use all dat we have t' disperse dis evil."

Rilton stood back. Not being a magical, Ember's husband could not help them conquer what was currently invading Taylor's house.

Gray shuddered, old fears rising up inside him like ghosts. Then his wife took his hand and clasped it tightly within hers; strength flowed through him. With Lucy, he would not fall into hell again.

He gathered up his powers and felt the vibration in the air as Lucy and Ember did the same with their own. Magic was strong in Nevermore, and with Ember's connection to the Goddess, the power of good and light streamed from all around them. They directed those sparkling beams of energy toward the swirling black morass.

The house shuddered.

The blackness yowled.

And a familiar male voice boomed, "No! She is mine!"

Kahl! Gray's focus wavered, but he managed to keep it together. Still, he couldn't completely shake off the shock of facing again the demon lord to whom he'd been sacrificed by his first wife. The very asshole who had tried to rend his soul from his corpse was after the woman named Lenore.

The sudden deluge of rage poured into his energy, throwing a red electric glow to the magic pouring out of the three of them.

Cries of fury echoed into the night, followed by a noisy array of hisses and screeches. It made Gray feel as though the gates of hell had opened up and let loose its minions. It made him cold with fear to think that might well be the case—as impossible as such a thing should be.

The darkness rolled off the house and boiled away, noxious streamers twisting into the sky like tossed ribbons.

Rilton was already running toward the porch. Gray, Lucy, and Ember had to take precious seconds to release their powers back to elements from which they'd been borrowed, and offer their prayers of thanks. It was necessary ritual for every wizard.

When Gray entered the house, followed closely by Lucy and Ember, Rilton was already kneeling among the three unconscious people lying on the floor.

"Holy fuck."

The muttered expletive came from behind Gray. He whirled around and had his hand on the male's throat before he'd even registered that it was Trent standing behind him.

"What are you doing here?" he snarled.

"Used the portal at my unc's. Jeez! Chillax, dude," the kid choked out. "I felt a disturbance in the force."

"Real funny," said Gray. He let go, trying to stamp out his anger, and within the red beat of that emotion, the bone-chilling fear that Kahl had somehow found a way into Nevermore. "There were demons here. How does that rank with your necro magic?"

"Not demons," said Trent, rubbing his throat and staring stonily at Gray. "Ghosts."

"Bullshit. We . . . *I* heard the voice of Kahl." Lucy gasped, and Gray turned to grab her hand. "It's okay, baby. He can't hurt us."

The worry didn't leave her gaze, and he lifted her palm and kissed the center of it. "Let's get our friends walking around again, okay? Then we'll discuss what to do."

She brushed her lips over his, which sent a frisson

right down his spine. If the demons got to Lucy, if anything happened . . . Fear invaded him. He couldn't lose her. He wouldn't. She was his heart.

He watched her walk to Taylor. She crouched down, and within moments, the gold glow of her healing magic emanated from her hands and swirled into the prone sheriff.

Gray turned back to Trent. "It felt demonic."

"I'm not saying they were good spirits," said Trent. "Maybe they were some evil motherfuckers. But the spirits of the dead aren't demons. Not that all demons have corporeal forms. They don't. But their energies are different, and I'm not in tune with that kind of juju. I'm a necromancer. Believe me when I say I know dead people."

"Okay. So a bunch of evil ghosts descended upon Taylor's house, probably to get at Lenore, and these spirits were somehow controlled by Kahl?"

"What does any of that have to do with Norie?" Taylor's voice sounded like a bucket of rusted hinges. He sat up, sending Lucy a grateful smile. She brushed his brow, then went to Ant and began healing him. Ember was hovering over the girl, concern marring her brow.

"Who's Norie?" asked Trent.

"Lenore," said Taylor. He got to his feet, not looking exactly spry. He rubbed a hand over his hair and shook his head. "Her name is Norie Whyte."

"She talkin'?" asked Ember.

"Nope. She wrote it down for me." He looked down at Lucy. "Ant gonna be okay?"

"Yes," she murmured.

Then Taylor turned and knelt next to the girl. Gray was surprised at the look of tenderness that crossed his friend's features. He knew the sheriff felt a sense of responsibility for her; after all, she'd been found naked and beaten in his own woods. But that look . . . Oh, he recognized it. He'd seen it on his own face often enough, mirrored in the reflection of his wife's love.

"Is she all right?" asked Taylor.

"She will be," soothed Ember. "Rilton, I tink da sheriff needs some water."

"Maybe some breakfast, too," he said. "I'll cook."

Taylor's lips thinned into a mulish line, but with just one look at Ember's quirked eyebrow, he sighed. Gray empathized with the man. No one won a battle with Ember, especially when she was in full mother hen mode. The sheriff got to his feet again and followed Rilton into the kitchen. Gray and Trent followed. When Rilton refused their help with fixing breakfast, the other men sat at the kitchen table.

"What happened?" asked Gray.

"I woke up and couldn't go back to sleep, so I went and checked on her. On Norie. She wasn't in her bed, and I just about broke my neck trying to get downstairs. She was in the kitchen drinking orange juice. I was gonna make her a sandwich and . . . shit. It was as though hell descended on my house. It blinded us, choked us with its stink. I was trying to get her away, up the stairs, to Ant, but he was already in the foyer working his magic." Taylor stopped, and Rilton put a glass of ice water before him. "Thanks." He drank it all, and then wiped off his mouth. "Whatever those things were, they just about killed Ant. They wanted Norie. Kept asking me to give her to 'em. That was when I realized they couldn't take her. Why do you think that is?"

Gray frowned. "I'm not entirely familiar with protocols for human sacrifice. Maybe Ant did something. Or maybe they could encroach on your territory but not take anything from it. It's possible there are different rules because we're dealing with spirits and not demons."

Then Gray and Taylor both looked at Trent, who offered a shrug. "Dudes. Never heard of anything like this. Ghosts working for a demon lord? It's possible, I guess, but that's a lot of spirits. Where did he get them? And how's he controlling them?"

They contemplated those questions in silence. Gray didn't have the answers. Between the suicides, his mother's impending arrival, trying to get Banton's gun secured in Dallas, and . . . hell, even the now almost-silly idea of hosting an All Hallows' Eve party weighed on his soul like a stack of anvils.

"Hey." Ant wandered in, waved hello to everyone, then headed to the stove to sniff at all the scrumptious food Rilton was whipping up.

"You okay?" Taylor asked gruffly.

"Got the Lucinda treatment," said Ant. "I'm great. You?"

"I'll live."

"She will, too," said Lucy.

Taylor almost tipped over his chair getting up. He grabbed onto it, then held it out so Norie could sit down.

Gray caught his wife's knowing look, and they shared a quick smile. Then Lucy crossed to him and slid onto his lap, right where she belonged.

"Well, den," said Ember as she entered the kitchen. "We all fine now."

"You mean all fine *for* now," said Ant. His gaze skittered toward Norie. Gray watched Taylor send his brother a dark look, and Ant returned to watching Rilton plate up eggs, bacon, and toast.

Norie held out her hands in a placating gesture, her eyes filled with regret and fear. Lucy reached across the table and took her hands. "Don't worry. You're safe here. We'll protect you."

Norie looked even more dismayed. A notepad and pen were on the table, and she quickly wrote a message.

"'I need to leave,'" read Lucy. "'Then no one else will get hurt.'"

"Do you remember where we found you?" asked Gray softly.

She scribbled again and handed the new note to Lucy.

"'I remember being on a big stone. And people in black robes trying to hurt me.'"

Lucy smiled kindly. "Do you know why they wanted to hurt you?"

She shook her head. Then she wrote, "'Sacrifice. Apparently, it's my destiny.'"

"Are you a Raven?" asked Gray.

She wrote, "'Not magical.'"

Trent whistled. "Is she serious?"

Norie's gaze whipped toward him, and she raised her eyebrows.

"Oh. Sorry. The not-talking thing is kinda weird." His cheeks flushed, and he cleared his throat. "You're a magical. You're like me. The power's all locked up, but nothing necro can be hidden from me."

Norie shook her head violently, her long black locks swishing. "Not magical," she mouthed.

"I'm not wrong," said Trent in a matter-of-fact voice. "Maybe that's why the Ravens want to sacrifice you. Although it's not as if they can siphon off her abilities . . . or can they?"

"Nope," said Ant. He stole a slice of bacon. "Kill the magical; kill the magic. That's the way it is."

"Well, maybe they don't want her to unleash her power," said Trent thoughtfully. "So they're offering her to . . . well, whomever. And getting rid of whatever threat she reps."

"Kahl wants her," said Gray quietly.

"Okay. That's not good," said Trent.

"Enough. We eat now." Ember helped her husband distribute the plates of food and cups of coffee. Ant dug up a couple more chairs, and everyone crammed in around the table and spent the next ten minutes filling up on calories and caffeine.

"Seems to me that Norie would be safer at my house," said Gray. "The farther she is from the *nemeton*, the better."

"There's a *nemeton* nearby?" asked Trent, wide-eyed. "Can I see it?"

"Shit," muttered Gray. "Don't tell anyone, okay? We're still figuring out its purpose."

"The Ravens know the purpose," put in Taylor. "Why not ask that Ryerson fellow?"

"Right," said Gray, a wry smile twisting his lips. "Because he'd love to help us. He's here to find evidence proving someone in Nevermore killed Franco. It's no coincidence he showed up around the same time Norie found herself strapped to an altar."

"You think he's a Raven spy?" asked Ant. He was eyeing the slice of bacon Norie had left on her plate. She noticed, and pushed the plate toward him. He grinned and swiped it.

"Of course he's a Raven spy," said Lucy. "I'm sure Franco's murder is part of the reason he's snooping around, but there's something else. Either he knows about Norie and the *nemeton*, or he wants to find something on Gray's mother. She's one of the most powerful Dragons in the Grand Court."

"And you said there are rumors about the Ravens seceding?" Taylor directed the question at Gray.

Gray nodded. "Rumors. If it happens . . . well, it won't be pretty."

"Maybe sacrificing Norie is part of that," mused Trent. "Maybe they're using her as a bargaining chip to get more power or demonic support."

The idea chilled Gray. Rogue wizards with demon backup? The world would be torn apart. He couldn't imagine the horrors that would be inflicted on magicals and mundanes if a war actually started. He hoped diplomacy would win out.

"So," said Lucy, "we're all exhausted. Maybe getting some sleep would be best now. We can reconvene at our house later and discuss strategies."

"We'll have to figure out a way to get rid of Ryerson," said Gray.

"Let's meet at da tea shop," said Ember. "Neutral ground will put him at a disadvantage, so he won't cross da threshold."

"Okay," said Gray. He was enervated; his mind felt

too full of cobwebs for him to think straight. "Norie? You ready?"

She shook her head. She reached over and placed her hand on Taylor's arm. "Stay," she mouthed.

Gray shifted his gaze to Taylor, and he saw the fight in his friend's eye. Well, hell. He knew better than to try to separate them. He knew exactly what that kind of possession, and protection, felt like. Lucy was his, and he'd die for her. He didn't know, not yet, if that was the case for Taylor and Norie, but it seemed strange that they had formed so strong a bond in mere days.

Then again, who was he to question it? It had taken him less than a week to fall in love with Lucy, even though he hadn't wanted to admit it. And he'd almost lost her. They'd nearly died trying to fight off evil, and he didn't want anyone else in Nevermore being killed because of some asshole's diabolical agenda.

He'd had enough of that crap.

"She stays with Taylor," said Gray. "Let's help clean up, and then get to our beds."

The Guardian had spoken.

And everyone complied.

In the early-morning light, Happy Ness's decision to follow Ant to the testing grounds seemed . . . well, stupid. Happy's heart pounded so hard, she could feel the erratic beats pulsing in her ears. She shouldn't have followed

Ant to the open field behind the Dragon temple. And she shouldn't be hiding in a copse of trees, spying on him.

Last night, Lucinda and Gray had gone off with Ember and Rilton—to where she didn't know. She hadn't been able to sleep, so she heard them return. It had been almost three a.m.

Ant dropped by the Guardian's house this morning to say hello, and to have a private conversation with Gray. The way he offered a quick hug and a quicker good-bye, she could tell he was eager to meet Elandra and start the magical testing. If he wanted to be part of the House of Wolves, well, then he totally should. But if he did well and he went away for a whole year . . . she'd *die*! So, instead of going to school—and not going to class would piss off Lucinda and Gray big-time— she'd watched Ant walk to downtown, and then she'd snuck along like a stupid, immature, jealous moron.

She'd seen Elandra in the tea shop and knew how pretty she was . . . and how *mature*. Of age, as Ant would say, especially when he was trying to resist the urge to kiss her.

Didn't he know she'd give him anything he wanted? She understood he was honorable, and she liked that about him. She did. But if they were gonna be together, then why wait? Why did their ages matter, when their hearts had already decided? Why all the freaking torture? She was starting to feel as if they were Romeo and Juliet, and the ending to that story sucked.

Not that she wouldn't die for Ant—or die for love. She would. But she thought it was kinda stupid Romeo and Juliet didn't have, you know, a conversation. She would've found a way to send a note, or something, saying, "Hey, I'm gonna fake my death. Just chill until they put me in the crypt; then we'll run away." Seriously. How difficult would that have been? It bothered the crap outta her that they didn't get to really be together. All that love and angst and drama.

Felt familiar.

Like her and Ant.

Only they weren't star-crossed lovers. They weren't even lovers. Not that she'd ever been with a guy, 'cause she hadn't. She was pretty sure Ant had been with girls, though. He was too confident and sexy to be a virgin. That didn't really bother her. She knew he wouldn't date someone else while he waiting for her an' all. Worry gnawed at her. At least she didn't think so. And was it really fair of her to expect that? Sure, she'd jump his bones in a heartbeat if he let her. But then . . . he wouldn't be Ant. He wouldn't be the guy worth waiting for. Honor was important. All the people she looked up to had loads of honor, and she could, too. She could be patient.

Though it hurt. A lot. Some days, it was as if a big stone were sitting on her chest, crushing her lungs, and she couldn't take a breath. Ant was always on her mind. Even if she was thinking about other stuff, thoughts of him hovered on the perimeter.

That was love, she thought. It wasn't all wonderful, all the time. Lucinda told her once that love left the heart open to be either embraced or wounded. Sometimes, the heart ended up embraced *and* wounded.

It seemed to Happy that love shouldn't hurt, and it kinda sucked when it did.

Like now.

She crouched down, peering around the trunk of a tree, and watched Elandra put Ant through the paces. He looked to be doing well, or maybe his tester was just doing warm-ups or something. Happy didn't see the House of Wolves mage as someone who'd mess around. She had a sorta serious vibe. Ant did, too, for that matter, and it seemed to Happy that it was just one more thing for them to have in common.

Damn it.

Happy wasn't sure what exactly Ant was proving by making the earth move, plants grow, and animals appear. Nor did she get why it was so important that he do those fancy swirls of magic. For a brief, awful second, she wanted him to fail. Then he'd stay in Nevermore, wait for her, and they'd be together.

And Ant would be miserable.

Shame filled her. Man, she was being so selfish. She couldn't think about anything beyond how *she* felt and what kind of pain *she'd* be in if Ant moved away. A year seemed a lifetime. And Canada? It might as well be the moon.

What would she do?

How would she cope?

"Miss Ness."

Happy nearly jumped out of her skin. She grasped the tree to steady herself and gulped in some oxygen. Good Goddess. The rasping voice of Orley Ryerson made her feel as if a viper were slithering near her ankles. She only recognized his voice because it was what creeped her out the most when Gray had reluctantly introduced them. She'd known right away that the Raven wizard was not a nice man.

When she felt as though she had some control back, she got to her feet. She pivoted, putting one hand on her hip and an annoyed expression on her face. She'd learned it was better to go on the offense than be on the defense. "Gah! What are you doing skulking around here?"

"Perhaps you're the one skulking." Orley offered a smile as sharp as a blade. He studied her for a long moment, so long, in fact, she wanted to squirm. He knew it, too. Hell, he was probably waiting for it. She barely resisted the urge to shiver. Blech. The dude gave her the mondo creeps.

Happy knew Orley was staying at the Guardian's house, but she hadn't actually run into him there yet. The house was big enough that she probably didn't have to see his stupid face if she didn't want to . . . and she didn't. And Gray and Lucinda had told her to steer clear of the mage and to not talk to him without one of them present. They would shit kittens if they found she'd skipped morning classes to spy on Ant and then had ended up alone with the Raven mage.

"You're Bernard Franco's daughter."

"Duh." Happy hated to be reminded that Bernard was her sperm donor. He'd killed her mother, and he had tried to kill Lucinda and Gray. Then he transferred his demonic curse to her, and she'd had to die just to get away from it. She hoped he was rotting in the deepest darkest pit in hell.

"When's the last time you saw your father?"

The question was asked tonelessly, but it was delivered as sharply as that knife-blade smile. Her stomach jumped as fear did the cha-cha up her spine. *Special investigator, my ass.* He had no right to be here poking around. She didn't like the Raven mages, and she especially didn't like Orley Ryerson. He was here to mess everything up; she knew it.

"Well?" prompted Orley.

"Last time I saw my father . . . *hmm.*" She put a finger to her chin and looked up, as though the sky held the answer. Then she shifted to face him and pinned him with all the hate she could muster. "Oh, yeah. That would be when he killed my mother."

Orley's eyes narrowed to slits. "Do you have proof of this supposed murder?"

"Sure. I'm the freaking CSI. Here, let me get the pictures we took of the crime scene and show you the knife he used to slit her throat." She tossed the sarcasm at him as if she were throwing acid. Goddess, he was such a prick. She couldn't stand being near him. He made her skin crawl and her gorge rise.

"Careful, girl. Making such an accusation against one of our own merits a serious response from the House of Ravens."

"Is that a threat?" she asked boldly, even though her heart was stuttering and her palms were clammy. "'Cause it sounds like one."

"I'm merely sharing a fact with you, Miss Ness. You would not want the full weight of the Raven's judgment aimed at you."

He was scaring her, and he knew it. She couldn't resist the impulse to swallow the knot clogging her throat. Nor could she stop herself from taking a step back. She could sense magicals, sense their magic—which was how she knew Orley had some serious juju—but she had no abilities of her own. His expression had shifted in a way that set off alarm bells. He looked as though he wanted to hurt her. The air went stagnant, and the little hairs on the back of her neck stood up. Orley didn't move, but he gave her the impression he could strike at her in the blink of an eye. He was capable of melting the skin right off her bones. She wanted to call out for Ant, but her throat closed up. Besides, if she screamed for him, then Ant would know that she followed him. He'd be furious, too.

No. She'd faced assholes like Orley before. She could handle him. Happy squared her shoulders and kept her gaze steady. Her knees wobbled, but she didn't move again. She wouldn't let him scare her.

"Bernard was murdered," said Orley in an oily voice. "Do you have the same hatred for the killer of your father?"

"Where's *your* proof of this supposed murder?"

"The truth spells were designed to enact only if he had an unnatural death, which is an indisputable fact. It's my job to find out what happened to him, and to bring his murderer to justice. You believe in justice?"

"Yeah," said Happy. "And if someone offed his sorry ass, then he got justice. And so did the rest of us."

"Did you kill him, Miss Ness?"

"He killed me first," she said, her voice breaking. Tears gathered hotly in her eyes. Happy couldn't stand another moment in this jerk-off's presence, and she didn't care anymore if he knew he was putting the fear of the Dark One in her. She ran, right past him, through the trees, and toward the temple. She just wanted to get away.

From him. From Ant. From everyone.

But that was the thing about running—eventually there was nowhere else to go.

Chapter 7

At the noon meeting that took place at Ember's tea shop, it was decided that Taylor would bring Banton's gun to Dallas as well as do the research on its history. Gray needed to stick around for his mother's impending arrival the next morning.

"I think Norie should go with you," said Gray. "I think she's the link to why the protections on the town are failing."

Taylor glared at his friend. "What is that supposed to mean?"

"She was at the *nemeton* and the house." Gray shook his head. "Ember and I did a quick check around the perimeter. The spells weren't broken."

Ember nodded. "Whatever came through was allowed inside Nevermore."

Norie pointed to herself and shook her head fiercely. Taylor took her hand under the table and lightly squeezed. She sent him a grateful look.

"She's not a resident," Taylor pointed out, "so she can't be used as an entry point."

"Now, now," said Ember soothingly. "Dis isn't about hurtin' her, Taylor. We just tryin' to find the source."

After a while, it was determined that Norie would go to Dallas with Taylor. Gray had theorized that removing her presence from Nevermore might confuse the Ravens who might be honing in on her, but doing so might also give Gray and Ember a chance to seal whatever portals had been opened and to reinforce protections. As an additional insurance, Ember put more protections on them, and Gray had handed over some kind of woo-woo crystal that would summon the Guardian if needed. Taylor felt all tingly from the magical "overcoat," as Ember had called it.

No one had anything new to offer about the situation regarding Norie. The debate about the *nemeton*, the Ravens' intentions, and Norie's role were hashed and rehashed until theories reached the ridiculous.

"My mother might be able to give us better insight," Gray said. "And I'll run it past Grit, too."

Grit was Gray's grandfather. He was actually deceased, but he had authorized his soul to be imprinted on a book. Along with his pal Dutch, another soul-imprinted book the old man had befriended in the Great Library, Grit resided in the Calhouns' private library. And he was still an ornery ol' cuss.

When the meeting adjourned, Taylor pulled Norie aside. "You okay with going to Dallas with me?"

Norie nodded, and he could see the wariness in her eyes. He didn't blame her for wanting to find some kind of safety. Still, he wasn't exactly comfortable leaving the town behind while it endured yet another crisis, and this one appeared to be even worse than what they'd gone through in March. But if Norie's presence really was the cause of the Ravens' being able to get through Nevermore's borders, then it was probably best that they get her out of town, at least until Gray could determine for sure what was allowing demonic ghosts and evil wizards into town. Still, it irked him to admit there wasn't a whole helluva a lot he could contribute. What needed to be done in Nevermore required magic. At least in Dallas, he could protect Norie and get Banton's gun secured right and proper. Gray had already called ahead to the Dragon embassy and made the arrangements.

"It takes about three hours or so to get to Dallas," said Taylor, "so we should probably get going."

Norie gave two thumbs-up.

She wore clothes borrowed from Lucinda, who was also a slim woman, but the T-shirt and jeans looked baggy on Norie's too-thin frame. Taylor decided they'd hit a mall, too, and get her some decent clothing. There was no reason she had to walk around looking like a little girl playing dress-up. Then again, the alternative was for her to go naked. For an uncomfortable moment, that image stuck inside his head, along with the number of things he could do to a naked Norie. . . . Then he felt like an asshole and tried to scrub the porn out of his mind.

Sweet Mother Goddess. He needed to knock that shit off. He was Norie's protector, not her lover, and she deserved a lot more respect.

He said their good-byes to the others and then guided Norie to the battered SUV. He opened the door and helped her inside. She squeezed his hand in thanks and then put on her seat belt.

In no time at all, they were headed out of town.

"Not much in the way of radio stations out this way," he said apologetically. "I've got some CDs in the glove box, if you want to pick something to listen to."

He kept his eyes on the road, but he heard her rummaging around. Finally, she picked one and slid the silver disc into the player.

Seconds later, he recognized the opening strains of Carlos Santana's "Black Magic Woman." He glanced at Norie. She looked back at him and grinned. He saw the sparkle in her eye and was glad she still had a sense of humor.

They arrived at the Dragon embassy a little after four p.m. They found a spot in front, fed the meter, and then walked up a hundred marble steps to get to the entrance. With his Dragon-issued ID and the paperwork from Gray, they were allowed inside. A woman with graying hair, thick glasses, and an unfortunate penchant for wearing plaid led them down a hallway and into a lushly appointed study. Or maybe it was just a fancy waiting room. Taylor couldn't really put a name to it. The lady gestured for them to enter and said nothing at all, barely offering them a glance as she left.

"Nice to meet you, too," muttered Taylor. He held the lockbox with the gun in his left hand. He couldn't wait to be rid of it. He didn't like that holding the damn thing made him nervous, but he couldn't shake the foreboding sitting in his stomach like a bad bowl of chili.

Norie sat down in a plush leather chair and picked up a magazine with the headline, "Martha Stewart's Magical Makeovers." Restlessness ate at Taylor, so he wandered around the room and looked at the paintings. Most were medieval landscapes, a few were scenes from magical history, and the biggest one, which hung above the massive stone fireplace, was a portrait of Jaed and her dragon. It was a monstrous red and gold beast, and it looked very much like the creature that Gray shifted into when he took on the form. Taylor hadn't paid much attention to magical history in high school, so he couldn't recall if Jaed could shift into a dragon herself. Even in a world filled with the unusual, the idea of people turning into mythical creatures was still astonishing.

Taylor was eyeing that portrait when a panel next to the fireplace slid open and a young man hurried in.

Startled by the mage's sudden appearance, Taylor put his hand on his gun holster. The kid didn't even notice. He had a distracted, harried look that didn't sit well on his youthful face. He wore the traditional red robes that indicated the House of Dragons; his Converse sneakers peeked out from beneath.

"Hey. Um, hi." He was pale-skinned, wore round glasses that made his brown eyes look owlish, and his blond hair looked as if it hadn't been brushed in a week. "You're the sheriff?"

Taylor held out his free hand. "Sheriff Taylor Mooreland."

The man shook hands heartily, with far more strength than Taylor would've given him credit for. The firm handshake made his estimation of the boy rise, well, a smidge at least.

"Emmett Lee," he said. "I'm your . . . er, mage, I guess. Did you bring the—" His gaze landed on Norie, and his mouth dropped open. "Wow! I mean, wow!" He hurried to the girl, his arms waving and his robes fluttering. "Awesome. So awesome. Never thought I'd ever meet one of you!"

Startled, Norie rose from the chair and found herself nearly shaken to death as Emmett grabbed both of her hands and juddered enthusiastically. Taylor crossed the room and extricated the stunned woman from the mage's grip.

"Sorry," said Emmett. He blushed. "I just didn't

think I'd ever get to meet a thanaturge. They're practically nonexistent, you know." He paused, his gaze zeroing in on Norie's neck. "Hey, that's weird. You get some kind of magical blowback or something?"

Both Taylor and Norie stared at Emmett.

"What does that mean?" asked Taylor.

"Yeah, that must've been some spell. I've never seen a thanaturge in action, but I've researched a lot about them. Ekros is so cool, you know? I'm a dragon. Totally a dragon, heart and soul, but being able to necro? And see ghosts? Man, that's awesome." He turned his gaze to Norie. "You see any ghosts here? I think this place is haunted. It's old and people have died here, and sometimes I get that funny feeling in my stomach, and my hair stands up on the back of my neck. So I was thinking we have spirits hanging around or something."

Taylor's head was starting to throb from Emmett's rapid-fire commentary, and when he opened his mouth to start another round, Taylor grabbed the kid's shoulder. "She can't talk," he said. "And she doesn't exactly remember what happened. We think she got bespelled."

"Oh." He gave them a strange look. "Well, sorta. I guess. Whatever went down was really badass. It happens sometimes when the magic is so strong, it kinda . . ." He flicked out his hands and wiggled his fingers while making sounds of an explosion. "Chances are whatever happened, the magic wasn't released properly and it, you know, got all globby. I mean, it'll go away on its own eventually, but why wouldn't she just remove it?" He cast an unsure glance at Taylor. "Don't you want her to talk?"

"Of course I do!" Taylor wondered why Gray and Ember, two of the most powerful magicals he knew, hadn't offered up the "globby" theory. "Is it demonic?"

Emmett blinked at him. "You know her better than I do. I've never heard of a thanaturge controlling demons, but anything's possible." He looked askance at Norie. "She seems really nice, though."

"I'm talking about the spell. The magic. Did demons do this to her?" Then Taylor thought: *What the hell is a thanaturge?*

"Er . . ." The mage looked at Norie, and then at Taylor. "Demons smell bad, and so does their magic. She smells really, really, *really* good. And she's pretty." He blushed again. "So I don't think she's possessed or anything. Um, not that pretty has anything to do with magic. Just with her."

Taylor wanted to shake Emmett until some sense fell into his cotton brain. "Norie isn't possessed, and she doesn't control demons. But we had a run-in with one earlier, and I just wondered if the magic clinging to her voice box has anything to do with the Dark One."

"Um. Well. Y'see, it's her magic," said Emmett slowly. He glanced at each of them, his expression confused. "Don't you get it? *She* cast the spell."

Chapter 8

Stunned silence followed Emmett's announcement.

"Um, yeah," said the mage, his befuddled expression bleeding into apprehension. "When magic gets, well, globby, it only does that with the person who accessed the power. You know, return to sender, that kind of thing." He readjusted his glasses. "How come you don't know this stuff?"

"I'm not a magical," said Taylor.

Emmett slanted him a look of disbelief. Taylor ignored the mage and met Norie's panicked gaze. He felt badly for her, but along with that empathy was a sliver of suspicion that curled up in his stomach. How could she not know she was a magical? Was she really a victim, or was she playing him?

Norie stroked her throat as though doing so might remove the clinging magic.

He took her shoulders and gently turned her to face him. "Do you remember casting a spell?" he asked.

She shook her head. Her eyes glistened with tears. Her lower lip quivered, but she caught it between her teeth. He believed her. He also realized that Emmett was the second young magical to see what the older, more experienced magicals had not. Trent had also mentioned Norie's necro powers. And Taylor couldn't help but wonder why no one in Nevermore had detected she'd been a victim of her own magic.

Taylor put his arm around Norie, and she accepted his comfort. She fit just right against him, as if she belonged there. He wished he didn't feel this way. She made it difficult to think straight. But she needed him, and he'd already committed himself to her safety. *I won't let anything happen to her.*

"Can you remove it?" asked Taylor.

"Me?" squeaked Emmett. "No way. It's Magic 101. Only the wizard who cast the spell can undo it, or you know, a convocation from his House, which is like, huge, and hardly ever done anyway. And magic globs aren't a big enough reason to get her House to work a removal spell."

"She doesn't have a House," said Taylor. "Because she says she's not magical."

"I thought she couldn't talk."

"She wrote it down."

"Oh." Emmett stared at Norie. "She's . . . That is, *you're* the only one who can remove it. I can tell you how, if that'll help."

Norie's gaze slid up to Taylor's. Fear flickered in her eyes, and he gave her a one-armed squeeze. "It wouldn't hurt to try, sweetheart."

She looked at him a moment longer. Then her gaze cleared, and she gave a firm, decisive nod. She moved away from Taylor and then stood before Emmett. She lifted a hand and made a "c'mon" gesture.

"Yeah. Um, okay. You're necro, so your power origi- nates from . . . well, spirits and residual death type stuff. The older the place, the better the necro vibes. Like here's good 'cause this place has been around awhile, and people have died here an' stuff. But, you know, cemeteries are like the ultimate mojo for you." Emmett cleared his throat. "Like everyone else, you borrow from the elements, from nature, but it's . . . not quite the same. And thanaturges are like . . . way, way out there. Like überness, you know?"

"I've heard of thaurmaturges," said Taylor. "But not thanaturges. How do you know that's what she is?"

" 'Cause that's her vibe," said Emmett. "Every mag- ical has a vibe. It's kinda how we know who's who. Anyway, she's a necro, for sure. But she's like *pulsing* with the death energy. I mean, honestly? I didn't know any existed. The last recorded thanaturge was . . . jeez. A hundred years ago, at least."

Taylor was reassessing his idea of Emmett helping Norie. The kid was a damned mess and appeared so scatterbrained that it seemed unlikely he could teach

Norie anything useful. And if Emmett was wrong, and his own magic somehow harmed her, then Taylor would have to kill him.

"Is there a master wizard around?" he asked. "Or maybe a Raven who could help us?"

"Ravens aren't altruistic," said Emmett. "And I'm good. Really good. If she can call up the magic, I can show her how to use it."

Taylor opened his mouth to protest again, but Norie punched him in the arm. He looked down at her. She made a slashing motion over her throat that he took to mean, "Shut up."

He took a few steps back, readjusting the lockbox in his left hand. He wasn't sure what to expect, and tension ribboned through him.

"Okay," said Emmett. "You know the first stance, right? The one you use to call the magic for the elements? In your case, that's the ghosts. Or decay. Something's always dead or dying somewhere. That's your conjure point. And you know it's one of the five points you use to call for the magic from the elements and commove into your spell."

Taylor bit back a grin at the look of astonishment on Norie's face. Emmett kept describing the process without taking notice that his student wasn't exactly keeping up. The fact that the kid was so excited about describing what to do without any regard for Norie's obvious cluelessness didn't exactly inspire confidence in the sheriff.

Taylor had never really paid attention to the ins and outs of magical instruction. When he went to the academy to get his police training, he had to take the required courses in uses of the law enforcement–approved magical objects, and, of course, the courses that taught him how to survive magical attack and take down magicals. Neither of those situations had occurred in his nearly six years as sheriff. Still, the information was useful to have. It wouldn't help him in a full-on magical onslaught, but mundanes rarely came out from those altercations smelling like roses—or alive, for that matter. So, he knew how to use the tools given to him, though he tried not to implement those things too often. He preferred the direct, mundane route, though he certainly didn't mind having magicals for friends. They sure did come in handy from time to time.

He stifled the urge to interfere. Norie had asked him, sorta, to stay out of it. The lockbox with Banton's gun felt heavier by the moment, and he was startled to feel itchy. Still, he knew it was important for Norie to get her voice back, and even though he had a bad feeling about what was going to unfold in the next few minutes, he decided there wasn't much he could do about it. Sometimes, you just had to go with the flow and assess the damage afterward. Yep, sometimes it was all about the cleanup.

Norie was trying to keep up with Emmett's instruction, even following some of the kid's moves. He didn't think for a minute that Norie would be able to conjure up anything viable, much less fix the whole "globby" issue. It made sense that the girl was a magical, maybe even this so-called *thanaturge*, and that would draw the attention of the Ravens. But Kahl? How did he come into things? And demons? Or ghosts, as Trent had insisted on. What was the end game? And why taint the portal to the Goddess fountain, which was, at this point, still just a working theory about Nevermore?

"Okay," said Emmett. He had a self-satisfied expression on his face. "I think she understands."

Taylor gave them both a thumbs-up and prepared to watch the show. Or rather, he prepared to watch nothing. Still, his mama didn't raise no fool, so he stepped back—*way* back.

"So, you start with feeling around for the dead stuff," said Emmett. "Start the first point of the five you need to create the energy."

Norie nodded, though she didn't seem too sure about "feeling around for dead stuff." Still, she made an effort, going so far as to close her eyes and scrunch up her face.

Goddess, she was cute.

"Got the first point?" asked Emmett. "Think of it like strings that you're gonna tie together. You draw out the first one, then the next, and the next . . . until you've kinda braided all five together. Then you have the convergence and the magic. Then you direct it what to do." He pointed to her neck and made wiggling motions.

Yeah, thought Taylor, *easy as pie*. If the pie were made of disconcertion and calculus.

Norie cracked open one eye and offered a half-moon glare. The boy offered a somewhat pompous smile, as though his quick and twisty instruction hadn't just confused the living hell out of his student.

"Ready?" asked Emmet.

Norie nodded, squeezed her eyes closed, and lifted her arms. She pointed her fingers, took a deep breath, and then went very still.

Seconds ticked by, and nothing happened. Emmett didn't seem entirely concerned that Norie wasn't calling forth any magic. Taylor wasn't too surprised, though. He wondered how long he should let this craziness continue.

The air went suddenly electric.

All the hair on Taylor's body rose, and then an ungodly wail shot through the room. The lamentation was filled with pain and terror and echoed off the walls, bouncing around until it split into several terror-filled exclamations. As the noise faded, the temperature dropped—one minute, Taylor was breathing normal, if not stale, air, and then the next, he was drawing in air so cold, it scraped his lungs.

"Uh-oh," said Emmett.

Taylor glanced at him sharply. "What?"

Emmett's teeth were chattering, and everyone's breath issued little puffs. It was as if the room had been turned into a walk-in freezer.

"Emmett," said Taylor, his voice low with warning.

"She's way powerful," offered the mage. "But she's blocked. It's like her power is bleeding around . . . oh." His eyes went wide. "Do you think her powers were bound, or something? I mean, that would make sense. Probably cursed as a kid, before she really knew what she could do, or whatever. The thing is, curses can't last forever. There's always a time limit, so maybe hers is almost over. That's why she can sorta access the magic, but it's all weird and stuff, 'cause she doesn't know what she's doing." He tapped his temple. "She's winging it. Instinctual, you know?"

"Maybe," managed Taylor through clenched teeth, "you should've figured that out before your damned magic lesson."

Emmett looked wounded. "It's not like curses are always obvious."

Taylor resisted the urge to unsnap the gun from his holster so he could shoot Emmett. The mage took one look at Taylor's face and scuttled away a few steps, his nervous gaze switching to Norie.

Norie hadn't moved at all. Her eyes were still closed, her breathing shallow, and she remained eerily still.

"What's going on?" demanded Taylor.

"Um." Emmett swallowed nervously. "I don't know."

"Terrific." Taylor tossed the lockbox to Emmett, who caught it out of reflex. At least the fool boy didn't drop it. Three strides toward Norie, he rammed into something flat, cold, and immovable. The shock of hitting something *not there* sent him reeling backward, cursing the whole way. "What the hell!"

"Weird," said Emmett.

Taylor retraced his steps more carefully, putting out his hands to feel for the obstruction. His palms slid across an icy surface, solid and real but invisible. He felt his way around, and ended up making a complete circuit. The blockade had Norie fenced in, and she wasn't moving at all. In fact, she didn't even seem to notice that she'd been cut off from them.

"Norie!" he yelled. "Can you hear me?"

She didn't even twitch. Maybe she couldn't hear him, or maybe she'd gone comatose. *Damn it*. He should've listened to his gut. His instincts had never done him wrong, but no, he had to go and trust some idiot kid. The air around Norie seemed to be going gray. He peered closer and saw swirls of silvery mist. Shock rendered him immobile. He saw faces, lots of faces, most of them with expressions of horror. They swirled around Norie like hateful children, their mouths wide as though they were screeching.

"Norie!" Taylor banged his fists against the barricade.

Frustration curled through him. How could he get to her?

Pain seared the middle of his forehead. *Claim what's yours. You are the key, Taylor Mooreland.*

The voice echoing inside his skull, the one he'd heard before but hadn't wanted to acknowledge, was feminine—as soft and comforting as a fleece blanket. *What do you want from me?* He thought. *I'm not the key to anything.*

You're the key to everything.

The pain ratcheted up. The excruciation drove him to his knees. He pressed his palms against the magical wall, his skull throbbing in agony.

Claim what's yours, urged the voice.

"No," he whispered. "I don't want this." Taylor gritted his teeth. Sweat beaded his brow as he tried to fight the pulsing torment.

"What's happening to her?" asked Emmett.

Taylor directed his gaze toward Norie. She, too, had been driven to her knees. Her body quaked, her eyes widened, and her mouth opened in a soundless scream. No! He wouldn't let her be harmed.

"I claim it," he uttered hoarsely. "Whatever the hell it is, I claim it as mine."

The pain flared, hot, acute, and damned near unbearable. Then he let go. He stopped struggling. And the agony receded. Silvery light filled him. Energy flowed. He felt the skin on his hands blaze with lines of heat, and, to his amazement, he saw swirls and lines appear—tattoos, and he could feel their ancient power.

His hands sank through the wall, and then the rest of him melted through it. The mist was as thick as cold soup. Voices murmured and sobbed. He realized the spirits were trying to tell their stories to Norie, and she couldn't handle the strain of so much emotion, so many voices pouring out despair. He stumbled toward the overwhelmed woman and grabbed her, lifting her into his arms. "Leave her alone!" he shouted.

A great, sorrowful howl issued from the entities. The temperature dropped, and it seemed as though all the air had been sucked out of the space.

Taylor's hands went blazing hot, and he found himself shouting, "Be gone!"

Silver, sparkling light emitted from the markings on his hands and seemed to somehow ignite Norie. He felt the power within her, the dark coldness of it, the heavy burden of communing with the dead, and then his luminosity joined with hers. Magic flared from them both, joining, twisting, and then exploded in a rush of brightness. The spirits yowled as they were dispersed.

Taylor slipped to his knees, still clutching Norie. She slumped in his embrace, her head lolling on his shoulder. He held her tightly, trying to shake off the power buzzing inside him. His skin prickled painfully.

"Are you guys okay?" asked Emmett. He hovered a couple feet away, hugging the lockbox.

"Help me get her to that sofa." The oversized red couch faced the massive fireplace, and it was the only place in the room where Norie could stretch out while she recovered. For a moment, Taylor wasn't sure he could get to his own damned feet, but he sucked in a huge breath, and, keeping hold of Norie, he stood up.

Emmett shuffled the lockbox into one hand and used his free arm to wrap around Norie. Together, they managed to get the prone woman to the couch. Taylor knelt down and examined her. He could see the steady rise and fall of her chest, so he knew she was breathing. But her eyes were closed, and her limbs seemed boneless. "You have a blanket around here?"

"Yeah," said Emmett. "Yeah, sure. Maybe some water, too. It's usually better to hydrate after using that much power."

Taylor looked up at Emmett, his temper simmering. "You got any idea what the hell just happened?"

Emmett blinked down at him, his eyes looking huge behind those ridiculous glasses. He swallowed visibly. "You . . . uh, said you weren't a magical. You have a kinda weird vibe. Some mundanes have enough magic to make them . . . er, have vibes, I guess. Not enough power to work with, but enough to sorta make stuff happen. Usually not good stuff. Anyway, I've never seen anything like what you did. It wasn't magic as much as . . . well, I don't know."

"You're mighty helpful," drawled Taylor.

The young man flushed. He pushed the glasses up onto his nose, more out of nervous habit than a real need to fix his eyewear.

Taylor sighed. "Just get the blanket, son. And some water. And maybe fetch someone who knows what he's doing."

Emmett opened his mouth to protest, assessed the look on Taylor's face, and snapped his mouth closed. "I'll put this up while I'm at it."

"Good idea," said Taylor. He watched Emmett scurry away, and then he turned his attention to Norie. He brushed back the dark strands of hair clinging to her face and resisted the urge to kiss her. She wasn't Sleeping Beauty, and he sure as hell wasn't a prince. Laying his lips on hers wouldn't wake her, and he might just get a slap for his trouble.

Although she was beautiful.

His heart skipped a beat.

He put his hand on her shoulder and grimaced as he noted the silvery marks on his hands. He had no idea what the gobbledygook meant, but he'd accepted it as a gift, or more likely, a curse. He got the feeling it wasn't something he could give back. And if being the so-called key, whatever *that* meant, allowed him to save Norie . . . then that was all right by him.

And he would save her.

Even if it was the last thing he ever did.

Chapter 9

"Where is she?"

Orley peered into the bowl of water. The face glimmering there was half concealed by the wizard's black cowl. It didn't matter. He knew the man's reputation well enough to be afraid. He tried to keep his expression passive, but it was difficult to deny the urge to shiver.

"Dallas. They went on some kind of mission for the Guardian."

"Mission?"

Orley swallowed nervously. "I couldn't glean the exact nature of their trip," he admitted. "Only that the sheriff and the girl went together."

"Do they know who she is?"

Orley shook his head.

"The spellbonds are already weakening," said the wizard. "If she gains her full powers before we can sacrifice her, we will not be able to use her. Only her pure blood can open the portal for Kahl."

"You're sure she's still . . . virginal?" He shouldn't doubt the master, but it seemed strange that a woman nearly thirty years old—especially one as beautiful as Lenore Whyte—hadn't had sexual relations with anyone.

"Yes. The protections that were used on Lenore to cloak her from us had a residual effect. She's poison to the opposite sex. The original spellwork has a thirty-year limit."

"Thirty years? How is that possible?"

"It's an ancient spell. One that's never used—hell, it's not even known to modern wizards. Its potency was ensured by human sacrifice."

"A blood spell, then."

"Yes. And it makes Norie nearly impossible to kill."

"That's what happened?" asked Orley. "At the ritual?"

"We moved too quickly," he admitted. "We assumed we could complete Kahl's sacrifice since her birthday was so close." The master sighed, an obvious sign of impatience. "Anything else you need to know, or are your fears allayed?"

"I don't have fears, Master. Nor do I have doubts about our success." Orley's tone was submissive and respectful. He knew how the chain of command worked. If he played compliant now, he would surely be rewarded later. Still, he wondered why the girl had been allowed outside of the Ravens' protections, especially if they'd known her importance. He didn't know much about her history—only that the girl had disappeared from Raven's Heart orphanage. The master had been searching for her for years, one of the star twins, the only one whose magic and blood could serve as the way for Kahl to enter the world. Magic was neutral. It was the intent of the user that mattered. If the prophecy was correct about the power of the star twins—then Lenore's virgin blood, her sacrifice, would be the key to unlocking the doorway between worlds. Lenore had only recently been discovered in Los Angeles laboring as a mere waitress. She wasn't hiding, and she didn't fight. She had no idea what kind of power she had.

"When will the girl return?" asked the master.

"Tomorrow evening," said Orley.

"That will be enough time to recapture her."

"Should we attempt to retrieve her in Dallas?

"Why expend the time and manpower when she's coming back to the location?"

"Yes. Of course." Orley cleared his throat. "Leticia Calhoun arrives tomorrow as well. Apparently, she's bringing a guest."

"I'm aware. That presents a problem. You'll have to deal with him."

Surprise jolted through Orley. "Deal with him? In what way?"

"In the way that I'm inferring, you idiot." He issued a long sigh. "To put it plainly, I want you to kill him. But not until Friday." Lenore Whyte's birthday. Why wait? Oh, but it wasn't wise to continue annoying the master. He'd pushed enough with his questions. Orley nodded as though eager to fulfill this request, but his stomach roiled. He'd never been much for murder. He didn't like getting his hands dirty. There were plenty of others who had a better taste for it. "What about Bernard's daughter?"

"She is of no consequence. Continue to use the pretense of the investigation to follow through with our plans. You will be ready when Lenore returns to Nevermore?"

"Nearly everything is in place," said Orley. He hesitated to question the master again, but he needed assurances. Though he was not yet high enough in rank to participate in the ritual, he knew that the first attempt to use the girl in the *nemeton* had resulted in five deaths. Only the master had somehow escaped the power of the girl's unfettered magic. "The others are ready, too?"

The resulting pause was long enough to cause anxiety. Sweat beaded Orley's temples.

"We will not make the same mistakes that cost us our brethren," said the master slowly. His gaze pierced Orley. "Perhaps I should send along Lyer to make sure all goes as planned."

Terror chilled Orley to the core. Lyer was one of the master's loyal minions—and a crazy, murderous bastard. "No need," he said hastily. "I have it under control."

"Good. I'll see you soon."

The face disappeared, and the water went blank. Orley moved away from the copper bowl and withdrew a handkerchief from the inner pocket of his robe. He blotted the moisture off his face. He'd been given this task because he'd proven his loyalty to the cause. He was organized, methodical, and without conscience. Indeed, he was the perfect man to carry out the master's orders. There would soon be a new world, one shaped by the Ravens and Kahl. It would be glorious.

And if the start of that reign meant killing Cullen Deshane . . . well, so be it. He wouldn't be the first human to die in the coming war. As far as Orley was concerned, the mundanes weren't equals and never would be. They were fit enough to be slaves, he supposed, but really they had no purpose. It didn't matter if they all perished in the flames of Kahl's insurrection.

"The bowl's ringing," said Lucinda.

Blearily, Gray looked up from his perusal of *Prophecies of the Magicals* and stared blankly at his wife. She leaned against the doorway of the library, looking as beautiful as ever. He grinned at her.

She offered a smile and then nodded at him. "Honey?"

"What?"

"The bowl. The one next to your elbow. It's still ringing."

The tinkling noise that indicated an incoming magical communication penetrated the fuzziness in his skull. He caught the magic, dispersed it, and leaned over the bowl. Taylor's pale, concerned face appeared in the water.

"About damned time," grumbled the sheriff. "Your magical rock isn't working, by the way."

"What?"

"Never mind. I got a situation."

"The gun?" asked Gray.

"No. The girl. And me. I'm a damned key, and she's comatose."

"None of that made sense," said Gray. "You're a key? What kind of key?"

"How the hell do I know? One minute, we're trying to get the magical globs off Norie's vocal cords, the next minute she's getting attacked by spirits, and now I have tattoos."

Gray looked up at his wife. She offered him an I-have-no-idea-what-he-means shrug. "And the gun?"

"It's taken care of," said Taylor. "Locked up in one of the most secure vaults they have here. Or so says Emmett, who's a taco short of a combination platter, if you ask me. Well? You coming, or what?"

"To Dallas?"

"Yes," said Taylor, his tone full of exasperation. "Get your scaly ass to the Dragon embassy in Dallas."

Taylor disappeared, and the water wavered until it

reflected nothing more than Gray's dazed expression. "You understand any of that?" he asked.

"Just that Taylor needs you."

Gray shut the book and leaned back in the chair. "Scaly ass, huh? He wants me to go dragon. Flying, I could probably get there in an hour."

"It's nearly seven o'clock now," said Lucinda. "By the time you get there and fix whatever it is . . ."

"We'll have to drive back tonight. I can't miss my mother's arrival. She'll kill me if I'm not here."

"I can handle her," said Lucinda.

"I know." He stood up, rounded the desk, and crossed to his wife. He pulled her into his arms and kissed her lightly.

Lucinda cupped his face. "Be safe, Gray."

"I will, babe." He went in for a longer kiss, the kind that made a man think about scooping up his wife and taking her to their bedroom. His arms tightened, but Lucinda knew him too well. She broke the contact and gazed up at him, her eyes shining.

"There'll be time for that when you get back," she said. "I have a thousand things to do before your mother gets here, so . . . go already."

Gray kissed the tip of her nose. "I'll be back before you know it."

Ant leaned against the old oak tree, the one that had been part of Nevermore since its founding. It stood, once proud, once protective, at the crossroads. The road to the left led to the lake, the one to the right went to the cemetery, and on past that was Daisy Estates. He often communed with Tree, sitting against its trunk and taking solace in its calm, steady presence. Tree had been through a lot, not only recently, but also throughout the history of Nevermore. It was a symbol of the town, of its continuity, its importance to stand strong against adversity.

Tree was dying.

Ant could feel the chill stealing into its limbs. It was weary. It knew it had a purpose, an important purpose, but it was old and had been too abused, too ignored. No one had known its worth until Ant.

Not a single one of Ant's spells or earth-healing gifts had given Tree what it needed for renewal. Sometimes, death could not be deterred.

All living things had essences, but only people had souls. Plants didn't have consciousness, not in the way a human being did. And when a plant, or a tree, died, it released that energy, that pure essence, back into the world, a gift for new life.

But Tree had been around for so long, it had developed a consciousness. Hell, Tree had a personality. And it knew it was dying. *Being sad serves no purpose, friend.*

That had been its message for the last week.

Ant put his hand onto the base of its trunk. Yes, death still whispered there. He was going to lose his friend. Not today. But soon.

Tree was practical. Its concern was not for its own life, but for abandoning its purpose. The founders had given it life, and put it in this location, for a vital reason. Ant did not know what, exactly, Tree was meant to do. It would not tell him.

"Ant."

Startled, Ant looked up and saw Mordi standing next to Tree. She wore a dress the color of sunrise, and her blond hair was pulled into a long, sleek ponytail. She offered him a lovely, distant smile as she placed a hand on the trunk and stroked. He swore Tree purred.

"Can you hear it?" he asked. "I mean, does Tree talk to you, too?"

"That's your gift," she said. "But I know death. And I feel it here."

"Do you know you how long before . . . ?"

She shook her head. "How can anyone know when his time is over?"

"Now, there's a question." Ant glanced up, staring at Tree's foliage. Sunlight played peekaboo between the broad, leafy limbs.

"When do you leave for your training?" asked Mordi.

"I'm still testing," said Ant. "Elandra's pretty hard-core."

"You'll pass," said Mordi. "You're going to the House of Wolves. You'll be a great wizard, Ant. One of the greatest, I think."

"Thanks." He peered up at her. "You seem kinda sure about all that."

She offered another smile, this one much warmer. "I am. And you shouldn't worry so much about Happy."

"You're not gonna give me the time-apart-will-do-you-good speech, are you? 'Cause I've heard that one about a hundred times from Taylor."

"Time apart will be excruciating," she said. "You two are bonded. But there are things you both must do. And some of it you cannot do together."

"You sound a lot like Ember." He chuckled. "You turning into a prophet, too?"

"Not so much." She laughed, but the sounds tinkled into silence. She was considering Tree in a peculiar way. "Can trees have souls?"

Ant looked at her, startled. It was almost as if she'd tapped into his thoughts. Or maybe being a death keeper just made her think more about dying, death, and souls than anybody else.

"This one probably does," he said. He thought about the ancient stones in the *nemeton* and thought they had something close to souls, too. He'd never run across any living thing that emitted such power and such terrible sorrow.

Mordi was staring at Tree now, her expression one of incredulity. "I understand now," she said. She patted the trunk. "Ant, there may be a way to save Tree."

"How?"

She turned her gaze to him, and in that moment, she reminded him of the stoic blue stones coated by blood and magic. It was as if Mordi were as ancient, as knowing as those magical monoliths. "I have to tell you something, and I must ask you to keep it secret."

"And whatever this is can save Tree?"

"I believe so."

"All right," he said slowly. "But I think I should hear this secret before I agree to keep it."

"I'm sorry," she said, her voice soft with regret. "I know you'll hold to your word, Ant, and that's why I must ask for it now."

He stared at her, trying to get a hint about this particular mystery. But Mordi had always been enigmatic, even in school. It was her nature to keep secrets, especially those of others. It was part of being a grief counselor, and being in charge of a cemetery. Still, he felt wary about her request. He had a strong feeling he wouldn't like what she had to say . . . and promises were important to him. She knew that, too; yet Mordi wasn't a manipulative kind of girl.

"All right," he said. "Tell me how to save Tree. And whatever you need to say will stay with the three of us."

Mordi nodded. "Good."

Then she sat next to him, tucking her dress primly under her legs, and began to talk.

Chapter 10

Cullen Deshane entered the tiny, dark confines of the Mystique Salon and followed the smell of clove cigarettes to the back booth.

The man lounging there blew out a thin stream of smoke and peered up at him. He grinned. *"Mon frère.* How ever did you escape prison?"

"That metal file you sent in the last shipment of beignets finally did the trick, Laurent."

The grin widened. He put out the cigarette in the already-full ashtray, and then slid out from the booth. He grabbed Cullen in a crushing bear hug, then stood back. "You are a sight for sore eyes, Cullen."

"What you're wearing is making *my* eyes sore," said Cullen. "Did you decide to go into privateering? Or modeling for romance covers?"

Laurent swept a hand down his outfit. He really did look like a pirate, especially with the billowy white shirt, tight black pants tucked into calf boots, and the gold hoop earrings. His long brown hair was swept into a queue at the back of his neck. He looked outrageous and dashing—and pure Laurent Chevalier. "You do not like?"

"It fits you." Cullen slid into the booth, and Laurent resumed his previous seat. "I can't stay long. Tomorrow morning, I'm going to Bumfuck, Texas."

"Interesting name." Laurent raised his head and waved at the waitress lounging against the bar. "The usual, darling. Two."

"Oui, Laurent."

"Leave it to you to find a place like this in Washington," said Cullen.

"They cannot offer the same as what we find in New Orleans," said Laurent, "but it is adequate. What is it that you will do in this . . . Bumfuck?"

The waitress arrived with two tumblers, an amber bottle, a bowl of sugar cubes, and two flat slotted spoons. She also put two carafes of chilled water on the table.

"Thank you," said Laurent. He winked at the waitress, and she offered a flirtatious grin before flouncing away.

"You're incorrigible." Cullen eyed the tumblers. "Not Pontarlier, I see."

"Don't be such a snob. Not everyone is as sophisticated as we are." Laurent chuckled. He opened the amber bottle carefully. "This is a verte absinthe."

He poured the green liquid into the tumblers, a

quarter of the way. Then the men put the slotted spoons across the rims, added one sugar cube to the middles, and each took a carafe. It took a careful, slow pour—a fast drip was preferred—over the sugar cube to get the desired louche. He and Laurent had spent years practicing such a pour. Still, fountains were more convenient, especially because they allowed the proper louching of the absinthe and people could converse. Self-pours required concentration and patience.

And Cullen had both.

Eventually the sugar cubes melted, the louching completed. Cullen removed his spoon and picked up the tumbler. He inhaled the licorice scent of his favorite drink and smiled. It had been too long since he'd been able to indulge.

"*La fée verte*," said Laurent, holding up his glass.

Cullen held his up, too. "To the Green Fairy . . . and to dreams reborn."

Laurent smiled.

And they drank.

"What are your plans, *mon frère*?"

"Indulge in some family nostalgia. Then, you know, get my revenge on all those magical bastards."

Laurent made a *tsk*ing sound. "Revenge is so passé. Perhaps we could do something else . . . like go to Europe and bed pretty French ladies."

Cullen stared down into his absinthe. "Do you know how long I spent in prison? My own father testified against me. The magicals, with all their powers, all their truth spells and sorcery bullshit, didn't see the truth. They wanted someone to pay for killing those children. I was the goat."

Laurent said nothing. Well, what the hell was there to say? Cullen had gotten screwed. And he'd spent a lot of time in his cell thinking about all the ways those bastards in the Courts should pay. He hadn't been guilty. He'd been railroaded.

And that resentment boiled in his guts like acid.

"What do you hope to find in your past, Cullen?" Laurent asked. His gaze had a laser focus.

"Nothing," said Cullen. "Or maybe everything. I don't know. But I have to look. It's my mother's life, her family there. She deserves that much from me, don't you think?"

"I think a man who lives in his past has no future."

"And the man who lives in the moment like nothing else matters?" asked Cullen, taking a dig at his friend.

Laurent smiled, but there was a sorrowful glint in his eye. "That is a man who knows well the price of revenge."

"You honored Katherine. You took the sword up in her name and—"

"And nothing." Laurent's carefree expression hardened. "Did my actions bring her back? Did she live again? No. She is still ashes scattered on the sea, and I still live with her ghost."

"I'm sorry, Laurent."

"I know. And if you follow this dangerous path you are on . . . you will be sorrier still."

"Maybe." He sipped his absinthe. "But I'm determined."

"So, how long do I wait for you? We have plans, Cullen. Plans already put on hold by your unfortunate incarceration."

"I'm not giving up on the absinthe lounge," said Cullen. "As soon as I take care of business, I'll meet you in New Orleans. Is the location still available?"

"*Oui*. Especially since I bought it." He sighed dramatically. "But it is empty and needs work. A lot of work."

"We'll roll up our sleeves, then," said Cullen.

Laurent offered another long sigh. "My sleeves are Armani. I think not."

"Armani makes pirate wear?"

Laurent chuckled. "I have missed you." He eyed Cullen. "Are you sure about chasing these ghosts?"

"Yes."

"Then all I can say is"—he held up his glass—"*bonne chance.*"

Norie awoke on an uncomfortable couch with three male faces hovering above hers. She yelped, and Emmett, Taylor, and Gray nearly collided heads as they hastily backed away.

"What are you doing?" She grabbed the blanket, and, in a completely idiotic move, pulled it up to her chin. Because a fuzzy cloth would so protect her. *Sheesh*.

"You have a lovely voice," said Emmett. "It's like music."

"Shut your noise hole," grumbled Taylor. He nodded toward Norie. "You all right?"

"I'm thirsty," she said. She placed a hand against her throat, her gaze on Taylor. She couldn't look away from the man. He was good-looking in a solid, serious kind of way. He was the kind of man you could rely on . . . the kind that would stay no matter what. *What was she thinking?* She'd been cursed. Love would never be hers, and the men who'd had the misfortune to date her— even for a short time—ended up injured. She was lucky she hadn't managed to kill any of her would-be boyfriends. The last guy spent weeks in the hospital recovering from falling out of her second-story apartment window. They couldn't explain how he fell out. And those sorts of accidents happened all the time to men she showed the slightest interest in. Still. Taylor was the sheriff. It was his job to serve and protect. The interest he showed in her didn't necessarily mean anything. She wasn't particularly special; she was just the local damsel in distress. The thought was depressing. All the same, she could keep her attraction to herself, right? Right. He wanted to protect her . . . and she would protect him.

Emmett brought her a glass of chilled water, and she downed it greedily.

"Thank you," she managed. "It's nice to be able to speak again." She eyed the young wizard and then tilted her head up. "Are the globs all gone?"

"Y-yes," said Emmett. "Wow. You have a nice neck."

Taylor made a noise between a growl and grunt, and the boy took the glass from Norie, then scurried away. When she looked at the sheriff, she saw him scowling in Emmett's direction.

"He doesn't mean any harm," she said.

"That's worse," said Taylor. "He's like an overgrown puppy, all legs and enthusiasm and no damned sense."

Norie bit back a grin and looked down at the floor until she could school her features. She didn't think the sheriff would be too thrilled to know that she found his ire cute rather than fearsome. Wait. No. Not cute.

"Can you remember what happened?" asked Gray. He knelt down, his expression creased with concern. Nevertheless, she saw the shadow of suspicion lurking in his gaze. Well, why should he trust her? She wasn't exactly a reliable witness, not even to her own trauma.

"I called up some ghosts," she said. "I tried to do what Emmett told me, but honestly, his instructions were . . ." She trailed off, trying to think of a kind way to describe his harried teaching style.

"Stupid," offered Taylor.

Gray slanted a look up at the sheriff. Norie saw the

man's lips quirk, and then watched as he swallowed the laugh that had certainly threatened. He returned his attention to Norie.

"So, yeah, I tried to follow his instructions, but it wasn't like he said at all. The magical strands and tying them all together? It was more like . . . seeing this ocean of cold and dark. I could touch it. I was afraid of falling into it, drowning." She shivered. "Death really is all around us. I can see it. Well, I could."

"And the ghosts just came to you?"

"All at once. Dozens of them, and they were all talking and trying to tell me so much." She blew out a breath. "The worst part? All those emotions. Sad and scared and angry and desperate. They were like coiling snakes, squeezing me."

Gray nodded. "Emmett said you were a thanaturge."

"Yes," she said. "But I don't understand. I've lived my whole life without magic. I was raised mundane. If I really do have powers, I don't know how to control them. Or what my purpose is." She glanced at Taylor. He was frowning down at her, his arms crossed. "Taylor saved me. Again." Her gaze dropped to his hands. "What happened?"

"You're not the only one with powers," said Taylor. "Apparently I'm some kind of key." He tapped his temple. "Goddess wormed right into my brain and made me an offer I couldn't refuse. Still don't know what it all means, though."

"We'll figure it out," said Gray. "I'll do some research here before we go back to Nevermore."

"You up for traveling later, Norie?" asked Taylor.

"Yes." Norie had an urge to go to back to Nevermore, even though it seemed a moronic move. How could she feel any kind of safety there? She'd nearly been sacrificed there without anyone in the town having a clue. But she felt strongly she needed to return. She wanted to figure out what was going on and take on the bastard in the black robe. And she had to admit that being in that house with Taylor felt nice. If there weren't demons and Ravens trying to sacrifice her, then being there would feel close to her old dreams of love and family. Taylor was the kind of man she'd dreamed about.

She chose her life, damn it. She would not be ruled by some kind of uncontrollable destiny.

Once again, she found herself studying the sheriff. He really was handsome. It had been a long time since she'd been interested in anyone. Given her problems with intimacy—and that wasn't some kind of emotional metaphor—she'd never had any long-lasting or fulfilling relationships. She would be thirty in two days, and she'd never had sex. It was a fact that embarrassed her, but not as much as the inexplicable reasons she couldn't be with someone.

No, Sheriff Mooreland was not for her. No one was. She sighed, and that drew the gazes of Taylor and Gray.

"You all right?" Concern lit Taylor's kind green eyes. "Need more water? Something to eat?"

"Seems like you're always trying to feed me," she said with a slight grin. "But no, I'm fine. When are we leaving?"

"I need to go into the Great Library," said Gray. "I found a reference to an ancient prophecy that might indicate what the Ravens are trying to accomplish in Nevermore." He looked away, and she wondered if that prophecy had something to do with her, too. All this talk of destiny from friends and from enemies—well, why wouldn't there be some kind of prophecy motivating everyone?

"You think it has something to do with me?" she asked, just to confirm her suspicions.

"Maybe," said Gray. "I'm not sure yet. That's the shitty thing about prophecies, especially the older ones. They never spell out what's going to happen exactly, mostly because the future is malleable. Things can unfold in ways that change the course of whatever was foretold. It might not happen in exactly the same way. Or at all."

Norie studied his expression and realized Gray was holding something back. She tried to discern what it could be and made an intuitive leap. "I'm betting there are some hard-core predications, aren't there? Stuff that will occur no matter what else happens over time."

Gray nodded, shifting his gaze. "That's true." He offered her a smile, though it didn't convey a lot of comfort. "But I don't know if that's the case here. I need to check out a few references and put my thoughts together. Maybe then we can figure out what the Ravens really want and why."

"They want war," said Taylor.

"No," said Gray. "They want to win a war. They want to change the entire landscape of the world and create one that has demons living among us." He looked at her. "Are you familiar with Kahl?"

Norie shook her head.

"He's a very powerful demon lord," said Gray. "I've had run-ins with him before. Trust me when I say that his stepping just a hoof onto the earthly plane is a bad thing."

"Well, we can't allow that to happen," said Norie. She sat up and pushed off the blanket. "I might not buy into all this destiny crap, but I'll tell you this: I won't let the Ravens use me to bring Kahl and his minions onto the earth."

"Good," said Gray. "Neither will we." He paused. "Do you remember anything about the night Taylor found you in the *nemeton*?"

Norie couldn't stop the flinch. She had been hoping no one would ask her that question. It seemed with the restoration of her voice, she'd also been given the gift of remembering the horrible events that had unfolded the night the Ravens tried to sacrifice her. She owed

Taylor and Gray no less than the truth—especially after everything they'd done for her. No, she wouldn't lie or avoid. It wasn't her style anyway.

Norie took a deep breath. "Yes," she said quietly. "I remember."

Both men seemed taken aback, and then their gazes were riveted to her. There was no reason to explain about the dream with the raven familiar; she hadn't quite figured out what that all meant anyway. It wasn't as if the damned bird had shown up again. She knew that the white raven had drawn Taylor to her, not because he'd said anything. She just knew. And if that so-called familiar appeared in dreams and in—well, reality—she didn't know what to make of it.

So she plunged in. "I woke up on the altar. Um, naked. I remember that the stone felt cold. Really cold. Six, maybe seven black-robed people were around me. They all had blades." She stopped and drew in a shuddering breath. She hated being a wuss, but visualizing what had happened made her feel the terror all over again. "Anyway, the biggest asshole was at the top, I guess. Right by my head. He was the one directing the incantations and the . . . the other stuff. I don't remember exactly what they said. It was a different language."

"Most spells are in Latin," said Gray. "The Romans translated many of the ancient texts and spells. They work the same because it's the wizard's intention—and the ability to access his powers—that make magic work."

"Not Latin," said Norie. "I don't know what it was. I'd never heard it before—and I don't have any real comparisons about what it sounded like, either. I'm sorry."

"That's okay," said Taylor. "Doesn't sound like the important part. Tell us the rest, Norie."

She nodded, drew in another long, deep breath, and kept her gaze on Taylor. He made her feel steady. She knew in her core she could rely on him—and it was more than just the knowledge he continued to save her, and for whatever reason seemed to care about what happened to her. No, it was an innate quality. His sense of duty, reliability—that was Taylor's true magic.

"They cut me," she said. "It hurt. I screamed. Then I felt this pressure on my chest. No, in it. Then it was as if my insides had been set on fire. I heard other voices. Cold ones—like the ghosts here. There was a burst of light. . . . I could see it pouring off me. Then *they* were screaming. Pushed away from the altar as if they'd been swatted away by a giant's hand. I—I saw one hit the blue stone and just explode into ash. I closed my eyes after that. I was tired and scared and . . ." She shuddered. It was showing weakness, she knew, but she couldn't help it. This kind of abject fear wasn't easily controlled. She'd fight. She would. But she hated the idea that Black Robe would find her again and use her to bring evil into the world. Dying didn't scare her. The suffering did—all that pain, all that fear . . . so unbearable.

A memory flickered, and she tried to snag it. A room in pink. An older woman screeching at her. The urgent whispers of children all around her.

What the hell?

Norie tried to hang on to the image, to the odd feeling of being someone different. No, of being a child. Maybe she'd once had a destiny—that felt right, true. But her life had shifted. It had somehow turned a corner and been shoved into a space not truly hers. The truth was that Norie had never felt like she belonged anywhere. How could she when she'd never lived anywhere long enough to feel she'd found home? Taylor's house was the closest she'd ever felt to . . . She sighed. It was useless to think about Taylor and that house, and their so-called relationship. Her curse had made it impossible to find someone who could love her, who could make her feel whole, normal.

Taylor had thus far been immune to her bad luck. Maybe he was different.

Her gaze flicked to Taylor. He was looking at her, his expression inscrutable. Why did she feel as though he could be the one? It was almost as if she'd been waiting for him. What a ridiculous thought. She should know better. But it didn't change the feeling.

Maybe she was suffering from some kind of magical hangover. She didn't quite feel herself, but she really hadn't been herself for the last few months, not since the night she'd been kidnapped.

"I'm going to do some research in the Great Library," said Gray. "I'll be back as soon as I can. Then we'll head back to Nevermore." He patted Norie on the shoulder. "Glad you're feeling better."

She offered him a smile. She wasn't exactly feeling better. She actually felt raw, exposed, and scared. What would happen to her? What if the Ravens found her again? Could Taylor and Gray really protect her?

Norie wished she knew more about her abilities. Surely having access to the magic would offer her a way to protect herself. If magicals were after her, then she needed to know how to harness her own magic. She needed to learn some defensive moves, but she couldn't trust Emmett to teach her. He was too excitable. And Taylor didn't know enough about his own magical changes to give her any advice. That left Gray, and he was gone.

"Are you really all right?" asked Taylor. "You still look peaked to me."

"Peaked?"

He smiled. "It's the Texas way of saying you look on the pale side is all. Maybe you should try to nap while Gray's in the library."

"I don't really feel like sleeping," she said. His smile

was gorgeous. It made him even more handsome. Her stomach fluttered. Whew. She had it bad for the man.

"I could show you around," said Emmett. He'd somehow popped back into the room but had enough self-preservation that he stayed clear of Taylor.

To Taylor's credit, he didn't draw his weapon, though Norie saw his hand twitch toward his weapons belt. Instead, he looked at the young man and asked, "Y'all got a cafeteria?"

Emmett nodded. "Well, we don't call it that. It's more along the lines of a five-star restaurant. It's really good. We have this chef from—"

"If the place serves iced tea and steaks, then it's good enough. Norie, you up for eating something?"

"Yeah," said Norie. Suddenly, she was starving, and a steak sounded like carnivore nirvana.

"I don't know much about the steaks," said Emmett in a superior tone. "I'm a vegan."

"Of course you are," muttered Taylor.

"Do you eat meat, Norie?" asked Emmett.

Her gaze collided with Taylor's, and she had to choke back a laugh. Taylor lifted one brow, his eyes sparkling with the same naughty thought she'd had.

"I do love meat," she said with a straight face. "Sorry, Emmett."

His face fell. "Oh. That's okay, I guess. Lots of my friends eat animals, even though it's really, really wrong."

"No lectures," said Taylor as he eyed the young wizard, "or I will shoot you."

Emmett turned his wide-eyed gaze to Norie, obviously looking for either support or reassurance.

Norie smiled. "Don't worry," she said. "I'm pretty sure it won't be a kill shot."

Emmett's eyes went even wider, and Taylor laughed.

And for a moment, everything was right with the world.

Chapter 11

Orley Ryerson stood in the middle of the dilapidated barn, staring up at the huge hole in the roof. The edges were blackened, as though there had been a fire. Indeed, there was plenty of broken and burned debris on the hay-strewn floor that supported this theory; yet the building had somehow escaped damage. He studied the area some more. Obviously, the barn had fallen into disrepair long ago. It smelled awful, not only because of the manure and moldy hay, but because of the magic undertones. Whatever had happened here left a taint that seemed to film the air. That slightly greasy resonance had penetrated his lungs, and that undetermined stench coated his nostrils.

Yes, there was an oddness in the atmosphere. And it was exactly that kind of peculiarity he looked for during investigations. Magic had been dispersed here—lots of it. Raven and Dragon and . . . something else. There was a tinge of gold, too. Ah, yes. Lucinda Calhoun was a thaumaturge. So, she had been here during the event that caused the issues.

Of course, it was all theory now.

Orley finished making his notes and then began to prepare for the complicated spell that would reveal what had happened. He'd followed Bernard's magical energies, as faded as they were, to this location. Bernard hadn't been in Nevermore for too long; at least that was Orley's assumption, given how little of Bernard's essence he'd been able to track. It was a testament to his own skill that he'd managed to find what he suspected was the point of origin for Bernard's truth spell. It was likely that Bernard Franco, treacherous bastard that he was, had been murdered here. It seemed as if he'd chosen this abominable place to die. Not that Orley believed that Bernard intended to die. He wasn't the type to circumvent his own agenda just to promote the Ravens' righteous objectives. The only reason Bernard proved useful at all was because his own goals coincided with those of his House. Or maybe, as Orley had suspected, it was really Bernard who had set all that was unfolding into motion right now. With his death, yes, but that had probably not been his intention. No doubt he had plotted the course with the master, with the council, with those who would lead the rebellion. He aspired to be part of the coming new world order.

In the meantime, Orley had his own role to play, and

if he did it well and pleased the master, he would be rewarded. He liked being on the winning team. The perks were so much better. He started humming as he set up the magical instruments he would need to enact the complicated spell. It wasn't often that he had to use this kind of hard-core magic. But he needed results—something he could show the smug Calhouns and get their attention. And if the situation somehow personally tainted Leticia Calhoun, too, then so much the better. That was the goal at any rate—she was too potent a force in her House, indeed in the whole of the Court, to be discounted. No, she was a powerful enemy—one they needed to either control or destroy.

He wondered who would get that honor.

It took more than half an hour to complete the setup. He stepped back and looked at the cauldron with its special ingredients, the candles placed at its four corners, and the large white crystal hanging on the bar above the black pot. It would be the anchor point for the magic.

Enacting this particular spell could be draining, so he took a moment to drink water and to eat a magically enhanced power bar.

Orley began the incantations that would engage the revelation magic.

The magic spread out like an unfurling blanket, covering the entire area. Orley felt sweat bead his temple as he directed the magic. He'd done this spell often enough to understand how it worked, and what to expect, but for some reason this particular rendition required more concentration and more power than any other.

But he couldn't worry about the discrepancies. Instead, he focused on the unfolding scene, gritting his teeth as he tried to hold on to the spellwork.

Everything became transparent—ghost images of what had come before.

He saw a young man with dark hair and a tan uniform. He was carrying an unconscious blond-haired girl—Happy. Behind them marched a rather irritated Bernard Franco. Actually, Bernard's usual state of being was irritated. He directed the other man to lay Happy on a board that had been placed across two sawhorses.

The problem with this kind of reenactment spell was that while the images tended to remain consistent, getting audio was challenging. Sometimes, conversations, or more likely in these scenarios, arguments, would come in clearly; sometimes, they would fade in and out, and sometimes they would fail completely.

Even with all the magic he was exuding, and the power he was consuming to keep the spell on track, he couldn't hear what Bernard and the boy—ah, Ren Banton, no doubt—were discussing. He'd known about the deputy's death. His research had discovered that the deputy had died accidentally in a farming accident the same month that Bernard disappeared. Hmm. Given their expressions and the fury-filled gesticulation, arguing was a more accurate term.

It ended abruptly when Bernard made a sweeping gesture with one arm and expelled a wave of glittering black magic. Ren flew into the air as though he'd been swatted by a giant hand. He disappeared into the darkness. Had there been sound, Orley knew he would've heard a crash, perhaps Ren's screams of pain, perhaps even the grotesque sounds made by someone dying a violent death.

So, Bernard had killed Banton.

His stomach curdled.

The revulsion tingeing his insides caused his focus to waver. The spell loosened. For a terrifying second, he thought he might lose the hold on the magic. Even though the scene continued, he wasn't able to watch what Bernard was doing to Happy. It seemed to be some kind of energy or magical exchange. He didn't understand it because Happy was a mundane, and most mundanes couldn't handle magic even in its lowest form. It took him a couple of minutes to regain control of the spell, and by the time he did, he was sweating bullets. Salty moisture dribbled into his eyes.

When Orley was able to refocus on the scene, Gray Calhoun had arrived and gotten into a fierce battle with Bernard Franco. Fascinated, Orley watched as Gray gathered his magic.

A huge red fireball appeared between the Guardian's outstretched hands. Then he lobbed it—right at Franco. The Raven rolled away from the flames and popped to his feet. Gray made some other gestures aimed toward Happy, then appeared to yell at someone Orley couldn't see.

Then the sheriff appeared, running to the prone Happy, and sweeping her into his arms. He ran at full tilt away from the wizards' battle, and was gone.

Gray fully engaged Franco in a war of magic. Fire and lightning roared between them. Gray struck at Franco with the grace and power he was known for. But Franco retaliated quickly and forced Gray to move farther away from the woman he was protecting—the thaumaturge he'd married. She was the younger sister of Kerren Rackmore.

Orley smiled in thin satisfaction as it became apparent that Gray was losing to Franco. Every time Gray struck at him with fire or electricity or wind, the Raven handed it back twofold.

Franco yelled something, his expression filled with hatred. Then he created a huge ball of black-edged flames. Orley noted that Gray seemed to prepare his own magic to meet the new challenge, but he shouldn't have bothered. Franco was seconds away from defeating him.

Orley waited for the blow that would hurt Gray. Obviously, Franco had not come out the ultimate winner in this battle. But Orley had yet to see how the man could've died here. He certainly seemed to have the upper hand now.

But Franco didn't aim for the Dragon. The ball of flames went left of the Guardian—straight onto the injured witch. Franco had wanted Lucinda Rackmore to suffer.

Orley watched Gray turn around and run toward her, but he was too late. His wife was consumed by the dark magic.

Gray tried to grab her, but his magic failed him. To Orley's astonishment, Gray jumped into the pulsing, dark mess of magic that Franco had unleashed.

Together, they burned.

The entire scene froze.

Orley cursed. It didn't seem as though the spell had stuttered; no, the power was still flowing. That meant that everything had actually stopped.

He'd never seen anything like it.

What was going on? And why had the world literally stopped?

Was Gray Calhoun truly that powerful?

Fear snaked up Orley's spine. He hadn't counted on Gray being too much of a problem. The man was the Guardian of a backwater town in Texas. There was no way anyone here understood the magnitude of what Nevermore was supposed to protect. Oh, they had a hint or two. Maybe Gray and his idiot friends believed they knew more . . . but he doubted it. They still seemed to be bumbling around most of the time, especially that rude sheriff. He certainly wasn't very bright.

Orley watched as the flames returned, but they instantly turned to smoke. Lucinda had passed out, and Gray laid her down.

Franco stomped toward Gray, murder in his eyes.

Gray's scar pulsed with light, with purpose. His skin flaked away to reveal the shiny red of his scales. Then the magic burst forth, red fire and gold sparks, and the human receded, giving way to the dragon.

Horror chased the chill of fear right up Orley's spine. What he was seeing was impossible! Impossible!

The creature expanded, growing wider and taller, filling up the space in the barn. The red and gold dragon's massive head brushed the wooden ceiling beams. He lifted a wing to cover Lucinda, then aimed his snout at the ceiling and issued a fireball. The roof became instant ash, its crumbling edges falling to the ground below.

Franco, his mouth open in a scream, scrambled backward and stalled, cowering in the darkness beyond. His face was bloated with shock, his eyes bulging and his lips flopping open.

Orley could see that the dragon was speaking, and Franco looked like a man protesting. Once again, he wished the damned magic had some audio.

Franco turned and ran, but he tripped over debris and sprawled on the floor. Then the dragon spit fire—

just a little. Flames licked across the man's feet, melting his shoes and toasting his pants.

The magic wavered; Orley barely held on to it. He couldn't believe what he was seeing. Franco was rolling around, trying to douse the flames. The dragon leaned down, though it took some maneuvering. With one claw, he rolled the man onto his back.

Then the dragon rose to his full height, his massive head poking out of the ceiling's hole, and he stepped on Franco. Then the beast shook his foot to get off the bits before wiping his claws on a pile of hay.

Then the monster closed his eyes, and magic shimmered. In moments, all that remained was Gray Calhoun, naked and dirty. He collapsed next to Lucinda, and they both lay there, as still as death.

Orley immediately let go of the spell, and the release of the energy back to the elements made him shake. The entire scene faded away. The crystal above the kettle went dark and so did all the lit candles. With the magic gone, the barn seemed darker and more desolate.

He withdrew his cell phone just on the off chance he might have service. He should've known better. He needed a water source to enact a communication spell. He had to tell the master right away about Gray's ability to take dragon form. No one had counted on that complication. He wondered what other secrets this town held. Could anyone else turn into a dragon, or another type of creature? He couldn't quite accept that such a thing could happen. Even in the world of magic, being able to assume an animal form was fantastical.

"Well, *that* didn't go exactly as planned, did it?" said a sultry female voice.

Startled, Orley whirled around and found himself face-to-face with Kerren Rackmore, the most feared witch on earth and the bride of the demon lord Kahl. She was as beautiful as everyone said, and her eyes were soulless, too.

"W-what are you doing here?" He swallowed nervously. He hated that he'd stammered, showing her his fear. He straightened and tried to switch tactics. "You're not needed."

Her slow grin held no humor at all.

Sweat dribbled down his temples, and he resisted the urge to step back as she sauntered toward him.

"Now, Orley, is that any way to talk to your future queen?" Her grin widened into pure maliciousness. She reached out and, with one fingertip, followed the trail of sweat down his cheek.

"Queen?"

"Kahl is my husband, and when he takes form on this earth, I will accompany him. He and I have big plans for this world."

Orley frowned. No one had mentioned what Kerren's role would be in the new order. He hadn't even considered the possibility that Kahl would give her any power at all. It had already been decided: Kahl and the Ravens would rule together.

Kerren had no place in the new order. Everyone knew she was just a . . . a minion. She was Kahl's whore—certainly not a queen.

It was Orley's turn to smile. He understood now why she had shown up. She was hoping to secure her position, perhaps by stealing his information. Wouldn't she look useful and important if she were to tell Kahl about Gray's transformative ability before he could inform the master?

"I see your little thought hamster spinning in its wheel," she said. "You think you have it all figured out, do you?" She laughed. "You really think you or any of the Ravens will have a place of equality once my husband enters this plane? You're all suckers. You crack open that door and let him and his demon horde through. Whew. It's all over. Demons don't need humans. Trust me, cupcake."

Orley let his smile turn into a smirk. The Ravens weren't stupid. A plan had already been put into place to ensure that Kahl kept his word and to keep the demon horde under control. The demon lord had no doubt underestimated his human cohorts. The Ravens would be the ones in control.

Kerren backed away and put her hands on her hips. She wore a red dress that swirled at the knee, and a pair of red high heels. And the outfit matched the bloodred lipstick on her mouth. With her black hair and ice-blue eyes, she looked every inch the devil's bride.

Orley readied himself to access a defensive spell. Foreboding crawled around in his stomach like a nest of spiders. He couldn't hope to defeat the half-demon witch, but all he had to do was stall her long enough to escape.

"Don't worry, Orley," she purred. "You are serving a greater purpose—just as you wanted."

He drew in the magic and started weaving a protection spell while he waited for her strike.

He expected magic.

He expected demon trickery.

But he did not anticipate the dagger.

The simple, gleaming blade appeared in her upraised hand. She tossed it almost casually at him, and it embedded easily into his chest cavity, into his heart.

The magic he'd called died instantly. He sank to his knees, his gaze on the cold bitch who'd killed him.

Orley fell to his side, sucking in liquid breaths as blood filled his lungs.

"Don't worry. I'll see you soon. We have in a special request for all Raven souls. You'll make a spectacular addition to our ghosties." She chuckled. "You know what? It's so nice when you can kill two Ravens with one stone."

Before he could make sense of her declaration, the darkness caved in on him, and he took one last, shuddering breath.

Chapter 12

Emmett told them where the restaurant was located, and Norie felt so sorry for him that she invited him to come down later for dessert. Taylor nodded, but she knew it was a sacrifice for him to tolerate the boy's presence. Emmett perked up and then headed off, waving as he hurried away.

They were seated quickly, and it didn't take long for them to order steaks, salads, and iced tea.

"This is nice," said Norie.

"Yeah," said Taylor. He cleared his throat. "You feeling okay?"

"I am, thank you. How about you?"

"Well, I got new tattoos, so there's that." He looked at his hands.

"Everything that's happened is so strange," said Norie.

"That's just the way it is for folks in Nevermore. Used to be a lot more boring. Which I liked."

Norie laughed. "I can imagine that boring is better for sheriffs than . . . well, not boring."

"Damn straight."

It didn't take long for the food to arrive, and they settled into a comfortable rhythm of conversation in between eating. It was a wonderful moment, one that Norie hadn't experienced in forever. Taylor relaxed, and his smiles came more easily.

"So, you live on a farm? But it's not one anymore?" asked Norie.

"Used to, sure. It's just me and Ant now. I worked the land when I was younger, but when I got the chance to go to the police academy, I took it. Eventually, all my siblings moved away, and it just got to be too much. I had to choose between farming and law enforcement."

"So, how many Moorelands are there?"

"Seven."

Norie goggled. "Seven?"

Taylor laughed. "Yes. We grew up in what my mother called 'happy chaos.'" His smiled faded a little. "She's been gone awhile now. You want to hear something crazy? The other night I smelled sugar cookies. She used to make 'em all the time." He shook his head. "The mind's a funny thing."

Norie looked down at her plate. Sarah had made it quite clear that Taylor shouldn't know she was hanging around as a spirit. Norie didn't like keeping secrets from him, but neither did she want to admit she'd had a conversation or two with Sarah. She had a feeling that little bit of info wouldn't go over too well with Taylor.

"My mother died, too," she offered. "It leaves a hole inside you. Nothing can quite fill it." She reached across the table and took his tattooed hand. She felt a sudden, tingling rush of electricity, and she gasped. She and Taylor stared at each other.

"What was that?" he asked.

"I . . . don't know," she said. She withdrew her hand, and the energy surge faded into vague tingles. "Maybe your magic affects mine." She shook her head. "I can't believe I have powers. I don't even know how to make them work. And I don't really feel different, either." She looked at him. "When something changes you so significantly, shouldn't you feel different?"

"Seems like," said Taylor. His gaze flicked over her shoulder, and he took on a pained expression.

Norie looked behind her and saw Emmett eagerly making his way toward them. She hid her smile. Then she glanced at Taylor through her lashes. She wondered what it would be like to have dinner with Taylor every night—to be there when he got home from work, to talk about their days over meat loaf and mashed potatoes and apple pie.

Oh, how she wanted that.

And she thought, maybe, maybe she could have it. With Taylor.

*   *   *

It took nearly three hours for Gray to follow the sketchy trail started with one vague prophetic reference. He'd gained some assistance from the soul books in the Great Library, although not all of the tomes were helpful, especially as he got into the older sections. Some of the books hadn't had a real human to speak to in years and simply wanted to converse—without sharing any useful information. At the end of his search, though, he'd found exactly what he needed. And it wasn't all good news, either. Actually, he wasn't sure any of it could be called good news.

He found Taylor, Norie, and Emmett in the embassy's twenty-four-hour restaurant. The embassy worked like its own city, and it never ceased operations. It was almost like Las Vegas except without the gambling and desperation.

"Hey, Emmett," he said as he sat down. "Can you give us a minute?"

Emmett nodded, his adoring gaze sliding toward Norie. Norie was peeking at the sheriff through her lashes while sipping a cup of coffee. The discarded plates with smears of devoured food—and was that cheesecake?—made Gray realize he hadn't eaten in a while.

The young wizard said his good-byes, then left.

Gray made a space for the book he'd checked out from the Great Library. Luckily, it wasn't a soul-imprinted book, just a very, very old one. He had almost had to promise his life's blood in exchange for taking the dusty little guide. He opened it to the appropriate page and then looked up.

"Good news first," said Taylor, eyeing the book with distaste. "I'm kinda tired of bad news."

"Sorry," said Gray. "I'm afraid it's almost all bad."

"What's the almost good news, then?" asked Norie.

"Oh." Gray sucked in a breath. "You know how we discussed the flexibility of prophecies?"

She nodded. "And the written-in-stone kind." She frowned. "I take it whatever you found isn't one of the flexible ones."

"It's been around for centuries. I don't know where the Ravens found a version, but I have no doubt they did. It's not as though there's only one source. Usually prognostications are referenced in multiple resources, mostly to ensure their longevity. The prophet was Nelos—an ancient Greek thanaturge."

"Like me?" asked Norie. She shook her head. "Wow. Still can't wrap my brain around that."

"You'll probably need to absorb it all as quickly as you can. My guess is that the Ravens might've known about you for a while."

"So, they bound her powers?" asked Taylor. "How come you and Ember and the others didn't realize Norie was a magical?"

Gray shook his head. "I don't know. She seems to attract the attention of necros."

"Emmett isn't a necro," said Taylor sourly.

"But he's studied it," said Norie. "He knows a lot about it."

"It doesn't make sense," admitted Gray. "I don't think the Ravens bound her powers. And my guess is that they only recently discovered she was an asset, and was protected and controlled accordingly." He sent Norie an apologetic glance. "I'm sorry. I don't mean to talk about you in the third person."

"I almost prefer it," said Norie. "Then it doesn't sound like this person is really me."

"I'm afraid it is you," said Gray. He tapped the book. "I don't understand the whole thing. . . . Hell, I don't understand most of it. But here's part of it:

Goddess renewed
Through two born
Under the stars of Raven sky

Dark One revealed
Through virgin's blood
Under the stones of ancient earth

Magic reborn
Through the key's touch
Under the skin of one burns truth

"I think we'll need Ember to help with the translations. Anyway, it seems pretty clear that it's you." He cleared his throat. "Another part of the prophecy mentions . . . er, virginal blood. Again."

"Oh," said Norie. "Oh."

She ducked her head, and Gray could tell she was blushing. Shit. He hadn't meant to embarrass her, though there was hardly a polite way to ask about a potential sacrifice's sexual status. He glanced at Taylor and grimaced. Had his friend been capable of magic, Gray would be a pile of cinders right now. "Look, we don't have time to play getting-to-know-you in a classy way. I'm sorry. I really am."

Gray felt he was apologizing too much for crap that wasn't his fault. Still, it wasn't Norie's fault she was the gateway to Kahl's permanent entrance onto the earthly plane. It was damned difficult to be circumspect about this situation, though. They had, maybe, a couple of days to figure out everything, save Norie, save Nevermore, and oh yeah, save the world. And if it could all be done without telling his mother, that would be a bonus.

"I'm a virgin," said Norie. She faced Gray, her face still tinged red. "Not on purpose." She swallowed heavily and slanted a look toward Taylor. "It's . . . complicated. The short version is that I've been unable to . . . um, complete that act. I can't explain why, just that . . . anyone who's ever tried ended up hurt. Needless to say, my dating life has been nonexistent."

Gray thought Taylor looked a little too pleased about

that last statement, but he ignored the sheriff's foolish-
ness. He knew too well what it was like to fall in love
and to have it fuck with your brain. In fact, love still
fucked with his brain—but he wouldn't give up Lucy
for the world. So, yeah, he understood where Taylor
was coming from. They had to keep their heads in the
game, though, or their world would have a lot more
demons in it. And demons didn't give a shit about love,
or about anything, really.

"Maybe you should read us the prophecy, or at least
sum it up," drawled Taylor. "That way we can at least
start formulating a plan."

"I think it's better if we get everyone together," said
Gray. "Preferably without my mother's knowledge."

"Why not include her?" asked Taylor. "She might
know a lot more about Nevermore's past than she's revealed. You ever ask her about the Goddess fountain?"

Surprise bolted through Gray. "No. You know my
mother, Taylor. She's . . . overwhelming."

"She's powerful, and she's smart. I know you're
dreading what she'll do when she meets Lucy, but she's
a class act. We need all the help we can get." Taylor
blew out a breath. "Besides, there's no way in hell
you'll be able to keep this from her. She'll sense the
change in Nevermore's magic in one second flat. She
might even sniff out the *nemeton* all on her own."

Gray put up his hands in a gesture of surrender.
"Okay, okay. You're right. I'll introduce her to Lucy and

then say, 'Hey, Mom, you wanna help us stop Kahl from taking over the world?'"

Taylor chuckled. "That ought to do."

"Then I guess it's back to Nevermore, and a morning meeting at Ember's," said Gray. "It's after midnight now." He looked at Taylor. "You afraid of flying?"

"You're shitting me." Taylor looked aghast at Gray's suggestion.

"It's three hours in the car or an hour on 'Dragon Airlines.'"

"What are you guys talking about?" asked Norie. "I've never heard of Dragon Airlines. Is it local?"

"Yeah," said Taylor on a groan. "Real local." He pushed back from the table. "We'll need to bundle up and maybe find some pillows. It's gonna be cold . . . and scaly."

Norie turned a quizzical look to Gray. "He didn't drink a drop of alcohol with dinner, I swear."

"You're gonna wish you did," muttered Taylor. He gave Gray the stink-eye. "Me, too. Well, the SUV isn't gonna fit no matter how big your ass is, and I need it for work."

"Oh, don't worry," said Gray. "I'll make sure it's returned to you tomorrow." He closed the book and handed it to Taylor. "Hold on to that. If we can figure out what it all means, it might offer the answers we need."

"Why does this magical crap always have to be so complicated?" asked Taylor.

Gray knew his friend was just showing his nerves about the upcoming trip. He grinned. "Because it's the best way to annoy the mundanes, of course."

In the dark vault hidden beneath the Dragon embassy, the magically locked case housing the Colt .45 snapped open. The gun was removed, and the one holding it leaned close to the gleaming metal and whispered, "Our task is not done. To Nevermore, my old friend. To the next one who deserves punishment for breaking vows. For breaking hearts."

Together, the gun and its keeper faded until nothing remained but darkness and grief.

"Hello?" Happy's voice echoed into the dingy recesses of the barn. The early-morning light barely penetrated the dark interior. Like knives of burnished gold slashing leathery flesh, the slashes of light added to the weirdtastic vibe of the place.

She'd entered through a hole created by missing boards and had walked only a few feet. Now she stood ankle-deep in moldy hay, wondering if she should venture any farther. This place was where her own father had cursed her. She hated it there. Why would Ant ask her to meet in the one place he knew she couldn't stand?

It wasn't like him.

On the way there, it had occurred to Happy that

maybe she had somehow become part of his testing. She didn't want him to fail, not really, so she figured she'd show up and be the good girlfriend. Well, almost girlfriend. As she turned in a slow circle and listened to her own labored breathing, she got a bad feeling in her gut.

She felt the tingles that indicated recent magic. It was a real bummer that she could sense magic but not use it. It wasn't exactly an awesome gift. At least, she hadn't found much use for it. But she could definitely feel that something magical had gone down recently.

Maybe the testing for Ant had already happened? Sure. Elandra could've dragged him there and made him do some more stupid tricks. He could already be waiting for her. But why wasn't he calling out to her? Or at least doing some kind of magical woo-woo so she'd know he was around?

Her heart started to pound. She could be naive, and she knew it. She'd experienced enough ugly in the world to understand its follies, even though her youth kept her from getting too jaded. She had hope, and faith. At least that was what Ant and everyone else were always telling her. Sometimes, she didn't know if it was her own thoughts in her head, or the voices of all the people trying so hard to guide her.

That really bad feeling pulsed in her gut like an ancient drumbeat.

"Ant?" she called out.

Her voice echoed across the barn, boomeranging back to her in a lower, softer tone. Goose bumps pimpled her arms. Okay, that was creepy times twelve. She scuttled forward, peering into the interior of the barn. If she went forward, then she'd be close to the spot where her father had given her his curse. He hadn't cared if she lived or died.

In the end, he'd been the one to die. And she wasn't sorry. Not after what he'd done to her mother and to Lucy. He could burn in hell as far as she was concerned. She hoped his soul was being flambéed daily by the Dark One.

Happy sucked in a breath and marched forward. She wasn't a coward. And she wouldn't let herself be terrified. She'd survived death, after all. Not many people could claim that they'd died and returned. She didn't actually remember very much about dying, or where she was while Lucy was saving her. She'd had a vague feeling of floating, of feeling light and at peace. Then again, she'd thought about it so much, she was probably just adding touches to the experience, in case anyone asked. It seemed to her that no one wanted to know—not even Trent, and he was a necromancer. She supposed it was because everyone was there and had witnessed her death. Ant had described seeing her soul "bobbing in the air like a cork floating in a creek."

What the—

Happy stumbled to a stop and gawked at the strange

scene. A crystal hung over a still-boiling kettle, which was surrounded by candles that had obviously been blown out. Whatever the magical setup had intended to create, she didn't know.

Had Ant and Elandra made this mess? If so, why? And where had they gone?

Then she saw the crumpled figure at the edge of the circle that had been drawn in the dirt. Her mind went blank, and bile rose in her throat. "Ant!" she screamed. She skidded to a halt and dropped to her knees. Something had gone wrong. A spell had hurt him—or Elandra had. Her thoughts whirled and collided, until she couldn't grab on to even one that made sense.

She grabbed at the robe, the black, silver-edged robe—and her mind tugged at that detail, but she couldn't stop and unravel the knot. She pulled hard. The man rolled onto his back, his sightless eyes gazing at the singed hole in the barn roof.

"Shit," whispered Happy. Her gaze went to the gold handle of the dagger embedded in the man's bony chest. Her entire body went cold. It couldn't be. . . . It *couldn't* be!

Orley Ryerson was dead.

She had the urge to yank the dagger from his chest, to hide it, to run and run and run . . . but logic asserted itself. No. She had to deal with this the way Lucy and Gray would expect her to. She touched the small red orb that hung from a gold chain around her neck and said, "Help."

The magic crystal glowed, its magic released, and her message traveled instantly to Lucy and to Gray.

Happy moved away from the man who'd scared her when he was alive. He wasn't exactly friendly looking now. But dead was dead, she knew. So she crawled to the opposite side of the circle, sat down, wrapped her arms around her knees, kept her gaze on the corpse, and waited.

Chapter 13

"Not much to look at," said Cullen as the limousine trundled down Main Street.

"It's not a thriving metropolis," agreed Leticia. "But Nevermore has its perks."

"If you say so." He returned to gazing out the tinted window. The Consul had insisted on showing him the town, as though doing so were some sort of grand favor for him. But Cullen suspected the woman just wasn't ready to meet her new daughter-in-law.

He almost felt sorry for Lucinda Calhoun. He'd heard she'd once been a Rackmore, and the rumor mill had churned out plenty of scenarios about Gray marrying the younger sister of his first wife—the one who'd sold his soul to save her money. What a bitch. Either Lucinda was the most awesome woman on the planet—and hell, that kind of woman plain didn't exist—or Gray was Grade A Fool. Cullen was betting on the latter. The dude obviously fell for the wrong kind of girl.

The private airplane ride from Washington to Dallas had been pleasant, if a little boring. Leticia spent a great deal of time signing paperwork and reading things her assistants kept putting in front of her. The two comely women had not accompanied them, however. Only the lictors—all freaking twelve of them. He'd spent most of the flight pretending to sleep, not that he believed the Consul would've insisted on a conversation. She'd been keeping a distance between them, and he wasn't sure if the switch had been flipped because she'd gotten him to Nevermore, which had been her goal, or because she now had bigger fish to fry—or rather, witches to burn.

They made a slow circle in a roundabout.

"The temple is open," said Leticia.

Cullen couldn't tell if the Consul was pleased or pissed about that development. He gave a cursory glance at the Temple of Light. It was nice enough, he supposed, like most magical churches. In fact, the place seemed almost welcoming. Still, he wasn't exactly a venerating-deities kind of guy. He left the worshipping to the suckers.

He noted the large brass dragon in the center of the circular drive and gave a low whistle. "Well, I guess there's no mistaking this is a Dragon town."

"No," said Leticia in a voice that held both warning and pride, "there's no doubt at all."

Okay then. He said nothing, turning his gaze once again to his window. As they finished the circuit, the limo slowed to a stop, right around the middle of Main Street.

"That's the old Sew 'n' Sew," said Leticia. Her voice had softened. "Your grandmother's place. It's been in your family since the founding of Nevermore." She offered him a slight smile, even though her eyes remained guarded. "You have a history here, Cullen. Roots. Family."

"No offense, Consul, but why do you care so much?"

"It's not me so much as the Goddess," said Leticia. "You are important to Nevermore."

"The Goddess told you that?"

"Her prophet, Ember, told me. She's the reason I pushed the committee to make a ruling on your case and release you. And, Cullen, you cannot underestimate the value of family."

"Except that I don't have one anymore." Cullen studied the faded gold lettering, the dingy picture window, the weather-worn door that may have been dark green once. He felt something long dormant shake off the grave dirt and try to push through the debris of his apathy. Wanting something or someone only brought misery. And he'd had enough pain for a while . . . hell, for a lifetime. No. He wouldn't look at this place and consider the possibilities. He wouldn't go in there and try to get to know a grandmother long dead, a family that had never been his except by blood. It was pointless. And he didn't do pointless.

"I appreciate what you're trying to give me," he said, even though he knew her motives were less than altruistic. "But all I see here are ghosts."

Just as the words left his mouth, Cullen saw movement inside the shop. He jolted. "Did you see that?"

Lucinda leaned forward and peered out his window. "What?"

"Someone's in there."

He saw a flash of white, something pale and fluttering. "Definitely someone messing around in there." Cullen grabbed the handle to the car door, but it was locked. He looked down at the black handle in disbelief. "Damn it."

"Roan! Unlock the doors," demanded Leticia. She glanced at Cullen. "I don't see anything in there. Are you sure?"

"I'm looking right at whoever it is," said Cullen. He pulled at the handle again, and this time, the door swung open. He was out of the limo and onto the sidewalk before he realized he didn't know how he was going to get inside the building.

Leticia followed him out, her gaze still on the plate-glass window as though trying to discern what he was seeing. He couldn't believe she couldn't glimpse the fluttering white. It was right there. Too far back, maybe, for him to determine what it was—or who it was—but there all the same. And it was as obvious as the two of them standing on the sidewalk in the early-morning light.

"Here." Leticia reached into her robes and pulled out a brass key. "I procured this for you."

Cullen took the key, not particularly caring how the Consul had managed to get it, or why she had it on her at this moment. He went to the door and unlocked it.

Leticia followed him, peering over his shoulder.

"Consul." The smooth, deep voice of Lictor Roan had them both turning around. "Allow me to check for intruders."

Cullen eyed the big man, and shook his head. "No offense, but this is my property. And if you go in to look for intruders, I'll feel like a pussy."

Roan's flash of a grin was so quick, Cullen wasn't sure he saw it. Then he glanced at Leticia. "I apologize for my language."

She rolled her eyes. Then she stepped back, closer to Roan. "Go check out your inheritance," she said. "I'll stay here and be protected, apparently."

The lictors who had been following the limo in a big black SUV were now exiting the vehicle and lining up on the sidewalk. Five men had accompanied them on the "tour"—well, six counting Roan. The remaining six were securing perimeters, or whatever.

Cullen turned back toward the door, opened it, and entered. The daylight barely penetrated the darkness. It smelled musty, and the air was stale. He shut the door, and the loud bang echoed. The hair on the nape of his neck rose.

"This is my place," he said. Man. Saying those words felt good. He'd never really owned anything. He'd always been a Deshane, which meant having access to his father's money and possessions, but really, nothing he could call his. And even though he wasn't sure he wanted it, this building was his.

It felt good.

The white fluttered again.

Okay. Now he was just getting annoyed. He felt along the wall for a light switch, but found only smooth, dusty surfaces. *Shit.* Since this was a business, it was likely that the lights were in the back, where it was more convenient for the owner to control them.

He walked farther into the darkness. He maneuvered between bins of fabric and shelves filled with thread and needles and other sewing-related things. If he were to stay—and that possibility ranged between nil and none—he'd have to redo everything. He wasn't going to be a purveyor of girly things. And yes, he knew that made him a chauvinist, but he never claimed to be a sensitive kind of guy.

He walked slowly, carefully, keeping his eyes and ears open. He couldn't see the white anymore—and what had that been? The swirl of a skirt? A handkerchief clutched in a fist? His fucking imagination gone stupid?

He reached the checkout counter. It was really dark back here, but his eyes had adjusted to the interior. He followed the rectangular glass case until he reached a gap. He went through and stopped. He heard only the rasp of his own breathing, but he could feel someone here. Someone was watching him. His body electrified, and goose bumps popped out on his skin.

"Who the hell is there?"

"I am."

One minute, the darkness hid nothing but unfamiliar shapes, and the next, an older woman stood before him. She wore a pink dress with matching pink flat-soled shoes. She wore her graying brown hair in a knot, and her face held the wrinkles of age, which had been tempered by beauty and kindness.

"Hello, Cullen," she said. "I'm Sarah. Welcome to Nevermore."

"Mom?"

Leticia Calhoun turned at the sound of her son's voice. All six lictors closed around her before she even had a chance to see his face. "Oh, for Goddess' sake! It's Gray!"

Roan stepped back and created a narrow gap so she could get through her human shield. Gray stood on the sidewalk staring at her with a decidedly unthrilled expression. It hurt her feelings to know he wasn't happy she was visiting, even though she'd spent a great deal of time avoiding Nevermore. Obviously she had some motherly repairs to do.

"Darling!" She opened up her arms and forced him into a hug. He caved quickly and squeezed her hard before pulling back a little. He looked less tense, although still far too wary. "It's good to see you, Mom."

"I've missed you." She straightened up. "Where's your . . . um, Lucinda?"

"My Lucinda is at Ember's tea shop, along with a few other folks. I think you may want to join us."

"Oh?"

He nodded. Then he glanced at the Sew 'n' Sew. "What are you doing here?"

"I told you about Cullen Deshane, dear," she said. Then she proffered a small lie. "He wanted to see his grandmother's property before we headed to the house. So! How's my father?"

"Cranky. And he makes too many Wild West references. I think we should've imprinted his soul in a different book."

"That wouldn't change his demeanor," she said. "Why the meeting at Ember's?"

"It's a long story. Actually, it's a couple of long stories." He sighed. "Maybe Mr. Deshane should make himself comfortable at my home before we—"

Cullen chose that moment to exit the shop. He looked shaken, his face pale. His gaze locked with Leticia's.

"Cullen? Are you all right?" Leticia moved toward him, worried about his terrible pallor.

"Holy shit."

Gray's hoarse, shocked declaration made everyone turn to look at him.

"Gray?" Leticia reached out and grabbed his forearm. "What's wrong?"

"Everything," said Gray. "I think Cullen needs to go to Ember's, too."

Cullen seemed to shake off his stupor, and as he stared at Gray, his eyes narrowed. "What the hell is going on?"

"Good question," said Gray. "Let's find out."

"They're coming for you," Sarah said to Norie. "Tomorrow is your birthday, honey. They can't risk that you'll regain your powers before they can complete the ritual. Once you tap into your true affinity, you'll be able to protect yourself. They can't have that."

"I know." Norie had figured that out during the prophecy discussion at the Dragon embassy. "I rode on a dragon's back last night. I loved it." She thought about her shock when Gray took the dragon form, and then how it felt to climb up his scales and sit behind Taylor, her arms wrapped around his waist. She loved how it felt to soar above the cities. Gray had used magic to ensure they stayed seated. Taylor had been less than thrilled with the entire situation. She'd gotten the feeling he wasn't fond of heights, though he was too much of a man to admit any weakness. "It was wonderful. I felt a kind of freedom up there. As if I belonged to the sky, too, somehow."

Sarah chuckled. "That's a good thing, sure enough."

Norie stopped detangling her freshly showered hair to stare at the ghost. "What does that mean?"

"All will be revealed in time." Her kindly gaze assessed Norie. "You like him, don't you?"

Norie didn't play coy. She put the comb on the dresser and sighed. "Yes. Taylor is amazing. He makes me feel safe."

"That's nice, dear." She reached out and patted Norie's hand. "But you'll have to save yourself. He won't like it, mind you, but that's the way of it. But maybe there's a little bit of saving each other later."

"Sounds ominous."

"Norie?" Taylor's voice echoed down the hallway, followed by the staccato rhythm of his cowboy boots.

Sarah put her finger to her lips—a reminder to keep her presence a secret—and faded away. It wasn't as if Norie wanted to discuss that she'd been talking to Taylor's dead mother. She wasn't sure why Sarah wanted her presence to remain hidden, but Norie would honor the woman's desire.

In the next moment, Taylor stood in the doorway, looking fit and handsome in a T-shirt and jeans. He wore a black felt cowboy hat, and man-oh-man he looked yummy.

"You look real nice," he said. Something sparked in

his eyes, something hot and needy, and . . . primal. It just lit her up inside the way he looked at her—as if she were the only girl for him.

"Thanks," she said. "You look very handsome."

He grinned and tugged on the brim of his hat. "Thank you, miss."

Norie didn't know why she did it. Maybe it was being tired of getting told how she had a destiny. Or maybe it was just that Taylor had been kind to her, and he was cute. And something about him touched her soul-deep. There was a rightness to being with him, a rhythm between them that indicated they'd been together before and were meant to be again.

Or maybe she was scared. Terrified of what would happen today—or tonight. The Ravens would have to try for her again. And she knew they'd get her. Sarah had as much as told her so when she said Norie would have to save herself. What else could that mean, anyway?

No, in the end, Norie didn't have one explanation for why she crossed the room, wound her arms around Taylor's neck, and drew him down. They stood there like that for a long moment, hearts thumping as they stared at each other and breathed each other's air.

He closed the distance.

Her whole body went electric, especially as he wrapped her tightly in his arms. He was so warm, so safe. She wanted this; she wanted him. And for a moment, she'd pretend that she was normal, and that this man could be with her—that he could be hers.

It was a lovely fiction.

Taylor was patient. He brought his lips over hers in a slow, gentle sweep that had tingles racing down her spine. He did it again . . . and again . . . and *ooooooh* . . . again . . . making each contact longer, building the tension so sweetly between them.

Her fingers dropped to the collar of his shirt and twisted in the fabric. Her heart pounded so hard, so fast, as if it were trying to burst out of her chest. She couldn't stop gasping. It was his air she sucked into her lungs, his scent that she breathed in, his essence that infiltrated her skin.

And still . . . oh my Goddess . . . *still* . . . he kissed her in that patient, drawn-out way. She was dying. Just dying. And he was holding her and torturing her and kissing her. It was wonderful.

Beautiful. She had never known anything like this.

"Taylor," she whispered. Her lips were swollen from his kisses, but he wasn't finished. And she was so glad when he went for another taste.

This time, his tongue parted the crease of her mouth, and she welcomed the sensations he invoked. She met each of his slow thrusts with her own. She felt tentative, but he held her tighter, and as she matched the pace of his sweet invasion, he groaned.

The sound vibrated right through her.

He pulled away just a little, tipping up his hat. "I want you, Norie," he said. His eyes were glazed with his passion, with his sincerity. "No matter what it takes. No matter how long I have to wait, babe. I can be patient until we've sorted out whoever is after you and you're feeling stronger. The important thing is . . . I want you."

"I want you, too," she said. She felt luminous. She felt . . . as terrific as she had during the "Dragon Airlines" flight, when she was soaring close to him through clouds and wind. Taylor gave her that same feeling with his kiss, with his words.

"All right then." He leaned in for one last honeyed kiss, then let her go.

She felt bereft, while at the same time her body buzzed with need, with desire. Oh, if only she could have Taylor. Damn the cursed luck in love. Then he took her hand and raised it, turning it over so he could plant a soft kiss on the pulse of her wrist. He looked at her, with that promise, that adoration glittering in his dark eyes, and she was lost. No, she was found.

She had finally found a place where she belonged.

"Well, den," said Ember as she stood in the small entryway of her tea shop, eyeing Gray, Cullen, and Leticia as well as the six really big men. "You all here."

"You know my mother," said Gray.

"Yes. Nice t' see you, Consul." She turned toward

Cullen and waggled a finger at him. " 'Bout time you got here. What took you so long?"

"Um . . . prison?"

Ember rolled her eyes. "Dat no excuse. C'mon, den. We got work to do."

She turned and walked past the empty bar, leaving them no choice but to follow her. Cullen thought the whole thing was fucking weird, but since he'd just had a conversation with a ghost . . . well, the meter for weird was a lot higher than it used to be.

"Gray!" The slim brunette had been standing near a table conversing with a tall, thin blond man. She hurried to the Guardian and wrapped her arms around him. An eternity seemed to pass as they held each other—and as though no one else existed in the room—or hell, the world.

Cullen felt something clench in his gut. It felt a helluva lot like envy. He'd never known love like that. He'd never had a relationship that lasted longer than breakfast.

Finally, the lovebirds broke apart. Gray turned toward Leticia. "Mother, this is my wife, Lucinda."

"It's so nice to meet you," said Lucinda. She offered her hand, and Cullen could tell she was trying to hide her nervousness. Leticia had no doubt noted the girl was anxious. He wondered if she would try to exploit that. Or maybe she'd also noticed that her son was completely in love with his wife—and she had better tread carefully.

"It's nice to meet you," said Leticia with a polite smile. She shook the girl's hand perfunctorily. "Welcome to the Calhoun family."

"Thank you." Lucinda moved closer to Gray's embrace, and Cullen saw the man flash his mother an irritated look.

Family drama. Sheesh. This kind of crap made him glad he didn't have a family.

"Oh my Goddess." The exclamation came from Lucinda as she noticed him standing slightly behind Gray. "He looks just like—"

"I know," said Gray.

"This is Cullen Deshane," said Leticia. "Mary Clark's son."

Gray looked startled. He shared a look with Lucy. Then turned to Ember. "Is Taylor here?"

"On der way," said Ember. "Bot' of dem. Everyting's comin' together as it should."

"You knew about him?" asked Gray.

"Well, I did when I laid eyes on him," said Ember with a harrumph. She turned toward Leticia and Cullen. "You come, and I make tea for you." She made shooing motions at the lictors. "Go find somewhere to sit. I bring you someting, too."

"Thank you," said Leticia. "Earl Grey, please."

Ember snorted. "You don't know what you need." She glared at Cullen. "Do you?"

Cullen grinned. He really liked this woman. "I don't know a damned thing."

"First step to knowing anything is admitting you know nothing," she said approvingly. She waved at them. "Sit, sit." She walked away, her purple dress swishing around black boots.

"Does she have an accent?" he asked Gray. "Because I swear she did a minute ago."

"Think of it like a radio that tunes in and out," said the Guardian. "The stronger her accent, the more trouble you're in."

"Ah. Got it."

"Gray."

Cullen looked at Lucinda. She'd gone pale. The red jewel that hung from her necklace glowed red. Gray cursed and grabbed the gem. Then he closed his eyes. A few seconds later, his eyes popped open. "She's at the Banton farm."

"Why would she go there?" asked Lucinda. Her voice was tinged with panic. Cullen felt the tension in the air. Something was definitely up.

"We'll find out." To his mother he said, "You'll have to make do without us." Gray took Lucinda's hand, and they hurried away.

"Where are you going?" asked Leticia as she followed them.

"To get Happy," said Gray.

Cullen wondered if that was a drug reference. He wheeled around and followed the line of lictors that trailed after Leticia like a drunken snake.

"Happy? That girl you took charge of?" asked Leticia. "Is she in trouble?"

"Yes." Gray and Lucinda turned at the door. "Let us handle it, Mother."

"Of course," said Leticia. "But I'm coming with you. And Roan, too. He's very handy when it comes to trouble."

"I'll go," said Cullen, surprising himself with the offer. He wasn't much of a team player. But he was still shaken up by his conversation with Sarah—the dead woman. She'd said to stick close to Gray, so that was what he was going to do.

"Thanks. We have to go the sheriff's office," said Gray. "There's a portal there. It'll take us close to the barn where Happy is."

Cullen had heard of portals, but he didn't really know of any still in use. It was an old-school magic, and since most cities ran on technology, it was difficult to use complex magic without affecting the electricity on which everything ran. But in a small town like Nevermore, magic was far more prevalent than tech. He kinda liked it.

"Consul," said Roan in a smooth, respectful voice, "it may not be wise to accompany your son on this venture."

"Wise or not, I'm going. And don't argue with me about taking the other lictors. This is Nevermore, Roan. I'm safer here than anywhere else."

Roan looked as though he wanted to argue, but he made a formal half bow instead. "As you wish, Consul." He turned toward the lictors that had piled up behind them. "Stay here. I'll call you if necessary."

Silently, the other lictors turned away and strode toward the back of the tea shop. Cullen wondered if Ember would make them drink tea.

"Let's go," said Gray.

Leticia, Roan, and Cullen followed Gray and Lucinda down the street and into the sheriff's office. A robust brunette sat at a desk in the lobby, typing efficiently on a typewriter. She looked up at the new arrivals and quirked an eyebrow. "Help you?"

"Just need the portal, Arlene," said Gray. "Happy's at the Banton farm."

Arlene's friendly expression hardened. "Well, don't just stand there," she snapped. "Get going. I'll send Taylor to you as soon as he gets here."

"Thanks."

Gray led them to the back of the building and made a right turn into what was obviously a break room. He went to the back wall, put up his hands, whispered a spell, and a big black oval opened like a giant's sleepy eye.

Gray went through first, then Lucinda. Roan made a

sweeping gesture at Cullen, indicating that he should go next. He didn't argue. He stepped into the portal. *Whoa.* His body went hot, cold, and then electric. He felt as though he'd imploded. There were lights and colors and faint music, and then he was spit out into the cold air. His feet hit the soil, and he surged forward, barely managing to stay upright.

Lucinda grabbed his arm to steady him. "The first time's always the hardest," she said.

"Yeah," he managed. He still tingled, and for some reason his mouth tasted metallic. In the next instant, the Consul popped through, and then Roan.

A couple yards away he saw a dilapidated barn.

Gray was already moving toward it. Lucinda followed, and Cullen went next. The Consul and Roan came after. Gray found a section of wall that had rotted away. He went through it. When they were all in the barn, they waited for the Guardian to decide what to do next.

It smelled like manure, and the dust tickled Cullen's nose.

"Happy!" yelled Gray.

"Here," came a quivering female voice. "Over here, Gray!"

Everyone ran toward the sound of the girl's cries.

"Shit," muttered Cullen as he took in the scene. It was a spellcasting gone wrong, or might have been if it hadn't been for the blade planted in the chest of an old man. He was a Raven by the style of his robes. The girl was planted a few feet from the body, and she was being consoled by Lucinda and Gray. Cullen moved forward to get a closer look at the dead guy. Leticia and Roan followed him.

"Good Goddess!" exclaimed Leticia. "That's Orley Ryerson. He's a special investigator with the House of Ravens. What's he doing here?"

"Investigating Bernard Franco's murder," said Gray. He joined them, his expression seven kinds of pissed off.

"I didn't realize he'd traced back Bernard to Nevermore." She turned toward her son. "He was here?"

"I told you we had some long stories to tell you," he said. "It's not protected here. The telling will have to be saved for Ember's. Her place is neutral ground."

"Very well," said Leticia. "But I'd better hear the whole story." She glanced over her shoulder. "Did the girl kill him?"

"No," said Gray. "Happy said she found him like this. She touched the body, though."

"Unfortunate," said Leticia.

"What are you saying, Mom?"

"Gray, I'm an officer of the Courts. I have to process this scene. I have to call in proper authorities. The situation with the Ravens is tense enough—to see yet another of their elite murdered . . . with a connection to Nevermore. It's problematic."

Cullen thought that might be the understatement of the year.

"That's a bad idea," said Gray. "You don't know what else is going on, Mom. Inviting in outsiders— proper authorities, or not—could really fuck things up."

"Perhaps we can . . . delay notifications," said Leticia. "But action will still have to be taken. I'm sorry, Gray." She looked at Roan. "Arrest the girl."

Chapter 14

"I'll do the arresting around here," said Taylor as he sauntered into the unfolding drama. He held on tightly to Norie's slim hand, liking the feel of her skin against his. She'd insisted on going with him, and he hadn't put up much of a fight, considering the bad feeling roaming around his gut. He wasn't a fool. He knew the Ravens would have to try for Norie again—to fulfill the prophecy.

He leaned back on his boot heels, tipped his hat backward, and gave his best country-boy-aw-shucks grin. "Consul Calhoun. Nice to see you around these parts again."

"Don't pull that dumb-hick act on me," said Leticia. "I know you don't have biscuits for brains." She seemed to realize her country upbringing was showing, so she smoothed away her irritated expression. "The girl was found in the same place as a murdered Raven," she said in a more cultured tone. "She has to be taken into custody." Her gaze moved from Taylor to the girl standing beside him. Her mouth dropped open. "Holy shit."

"What?" asked Norie, looking down at her ill-fitting jeans and oversized T-shirt. "It's the best I could do on short notice."

"It's not your clothes, girl," said Leticia in a choked voice. "It's your likeness."

At that moment, a black-haired, blue-eyed man strode in from the opposite side of the barn. "Perimeter check done. No other dead guys. Just a bunch of moldy hay and really disturbing sharp objects hanging on the walls."

The entire barn went quiet.

Taylor couldn't believe it. The man who'd casually entered their presence was a mirror image of Norie— same nose, same chin, same blue eyes. The man was much bigger, of course, broader in the shoulders and narrow in the hips. He looked tough, as though maybe life had been hard, but surely no harder than it had been on Norie. She didn't have the same kind of wear and tear, though, and certainly not the kind of jaded, wary vibe that this man exuded.

Norie stepped forward, her hand loosening from Taylor's. "Who are you?"

"My name is Cullen Deshane," he said. He looked just as flabbergasted as everyone else. "And you are?"

"Lenore Whyte, but everyone calls me Norie."

They walked to each other, seemingly drawn like magnets. Taylor felt the tattoos on his hands tingle, and the center of his forehead felt hot. He reached out, thinking maybe he should catch hold of her, stop her from . . . well, whatever. But Gray grabbed his shoulder. "There's magic here," he said. "We must let it play out."

"The hell we do," said Taylor under his breath, but he left it alone. If one thing went wrong, he was going for Norie, damn the consequences.

Norie and Cullen seemed mesmerized. Together they lifted their palms, and, when they reached each other, they matched palms and threaded their fingers together. After thirty years, the spell that kept them blind and deaf to their pasts, to their powers, began to fray. Today, the star twins reached their thirtieth birthdays . . . and their destinies.

Light burst from their clasped hands and twisted upward, snaking out in thousands of glittering ribbons until white magic filled the entire barn. Taylor felt himself driven to his knees, and then he pitched forward into the abyss of unconsciousness.

It was Christmas Eve.

"Careful, Norie," whispered Cullen as they went down the winding staircase.

Lenore nodded, and she was glad that Cullen held her hand so tightly. He was her older brother by only four min-

utes, but he took his job seriously. Women deserved protection. He said this often, but she wasn't sure why. He was smart, though, and she trusted him.

Their bedrooms were upstairs at the very end of the wide hallway. Usually, they weren't allowed to venture downstairs without their nanny, but Mother had promised that they could each open a present. "Just one," she had said with a smile, "and only after your father goes out for the evening."

Lenore and Cullen rarely saw Father, and that was just fine by her. He never seemed to be a happy man. In fact, he frightened Lenore. She didn't like to endure the rare dinners they had with him. He seemed very interested in what they couldn't do. Magic. He really wanted them to do magic, but they couldn't, no matter how hard they tried. And Mother always seemed so sad after the dinners. Sometimes, she and Father argued, and it ended with the terrible sound of a slap and then Mother crying.

No, Norie didn't like her father very much at all.

"Sshh," said Cullen, even though Norie hadn't said anything. They stopped at the end of the stairwell. Voices filtered from the great room down the marble hallway.

"I won't let him!"

"Mother," said Lenore in a worried voice.

"C'mon." He gripped her hand tightly. "Be very quiet, Norie."

"Okay," she said. Cullen often said she was brave, and even if she was trembling on the inside, she would pretend *she wasn't. Mother said sometimes you could pretend your way to feeling better in no time.*

They crept down the hallway and peered around the doorway that led to the great room. It was very large and filled with big dark furniture, and big pretty paintings. But the best thing about it during Christmastime was the large pine tree by the hearth.

She loved how it smelled, and how pretty it looked with the colorful decorations. And she especially adored all the lovely wrapped gifts that spilled from underneath its wide branches.

"The prophecy is true," said a gray-haired woman Norie had never seen before. "We've hidden their gifts for as long as we can. Once your husband discovers they are the star twins, who Nelos predicted would end the world or save it, their fates are sealed."

"How can that be? End it . . . Save it. I don't understand."

"It would take only one to create a magical cataclysm, Mary. Leo can use them to do very bad things to this world. Your children are powerful, and they will only grow more so. We must hide their magic. Their gifts. Their true identities."

"What will it take?" asked Mother.

The woman shook her head. "The kind of magic you're asking for is . . . complex. It requires special energies."

"Sacrifice," said Mother.

The woman looked uncomfortable. "If the world's fate did not rest on the shoulders of your children, I would never consider it. To take the life of another is a sin against magic too strong to be forgiven. So that will be my sacrifice."

"He thinks I'm a mundane," Mother said softly. "But my father was a Raven."

"I know." The woman leaned forward and placed a hand on Mary Deshane's thin shoulder. "We must complete the spell."

"When?" asked Mary.

"The longer we wait, the more we risk that your husband will discover the secret you've been keeping."

"Tonight, then." Mary sighed. "Very well."

The woman nodded, then hugged Mother tightly. She moved back, her simple white robes glittering like snowfall in the firelight. She withdrew a dagger from her robe and then lifted her arms.

She started chanting. The fire grew brighter, hotter. Mary stood next to the hearth, looking the saddest Norie had ever seen her. Norie's stomach squeezed. Something bad was happening—something very bad.

"Cullen," she said, "is this because we can see dead people?"

"Maybe," he said. He leaned forward, his gaze anxious. "I don't like this."

The chanting got louder, faster. Wind came out of nowhere and rattled the furniture, the Christmas tree, the paintings. The floor underneath their feet rumbled. Cullen grabbed Norie and held tight. Their gazes were locked onto the gray-haired woman. She was screaming now, her eyes rolled back to their whites, and then she whipped forward with the blade and drew it across Mother's throat.

Blood sprayed everywhere. Black glittery light rose like wisps of smoke from the wound, and the caterwauling witch gathered those wisps and tied them into the white strands of magic that wiggled around the hearth like terrified worms.

"I want Mommy!" Norie struggled against Cullen's embrace. "Mommy!"

She got free of her brother and ran toward Mommy. She was hurt. She needed help. Tears streamed down her cheeks because she knew, she knew, she knew that her mother couldn't be helped. Cullen dashed past her, heading like a charging bull toward the woman who was in the throes of casting her spell.

Then the magic—black and white, shining like diamonds, like death—braided together and arrowed toward the children like striking cobras.

Norie screamed as the burning magic enveloped her. She heard Cullen's cries, too, and then there was nothing.

Cullen was five years old, his head throbbing because he'd been shoved into a table with the spell that stole his magic, his memories. He saw his mother lying on the hearth, and he crawled to her, crying. He knew he shouldn't cry because men weren't supposed to do that. But Mommy was dead. Mommy was dead, and he couldn't stop crying.

The pool of blood gleamed wetly in the flickering firelight. His father rushed in, his Italian leather shoes slapping *against the marble floor, his breath harsh and uneven, his face contorted with rage.*

Stumbling past the huge Christmas tree with its bounty of gaily wrapped gifts, he crouched next to him. He grabbed Cullen's face, his fingers digging cruelly into his son's cheeks. "What the fuck happened?" he screamed.

"I don't know," said Cullen, weeping.

His father hit him, hard. He was small, just a boy, so the blow shoved him away from his mother and into the wall. His head struck the marble fireplace.

Later, much later, he found himself in a room, his head throbbing. His father leaned over him. Beside him was another man, this one in a black robe.

"The spell is strong. Complicated. Whoever cast it was powerful."

"But why? Why cast spells on them?"

"Perhaps this is an enemy's attack on you. Kill your wife. Ensure your children never reach full powers."

Leo snorted. "They're both weak. They have so little magic." He rubbed a hand through his graying hair. "Mary's blood, no doubt."

"We don't know the full extent of this situation. The children should be separated."

"He should be dead," muttered Leo. "This feels like a nex spell. No one can do those."

"A few can."

"What happens if they stay together?"

"Who knows? Where's the girl?"

"She was unconscious on the floor." He frowned. "They don't remember each other."

"The spell, no doubt. Aftershocks, maybe. Who knows? Who cares? It'll make things easier."

Norie rode in the black limo. She was five years old. She wore her favorite pink dress and shoes, and Nanny had brushed her hair until it shone.

The man sitting across from her was elegantly dressed—as he always was. His brown eyes glittered with disgust, but Norie didn't shy away from it. Her father's anger no longer frightened her.

"Where are we going, Father?"

"To see a friend of mine. Her name is Millicent. She wants to have tea with you." He flashed a grin that gleamed like a sharp blade. "You like tea, don't you?"

"Yes."

The scene faded . . . faded.

Norie stood outside the orphanage, alone, uncertain about where to go, what to do. Then she appeared. Catalina, she said as she put her pale hand on the girl's forehead. "Your mother, baby. Remember?"

And suddenly, Norie did remember that Catalina was her mother. So she took her hand, and they walked together down the street.

*   *   *

Norie knew now that Catalina was the magical who'd worked the spell against her mother. And Catalina's powers had been warped by performing blood magic. That was why she'd gone slowly insane, her body paying the price for blood magic. But Catalina had taken Norie and protected her and kept her away from the Ravens. Until she'd died, without telling Norie anything about her past—or what her future might hold. No, she must have tried. It had to be hard to know she was losing her mind, suffering the consequences of what she'd done . . . and hanging on long enough for the girl to make it to womanhood.

Catalina had tried.

And Norie would, too.

Then Norie was sprawled in the back of another limousine, a blanket tossed over her naked form. Drugs and magic fuzzed her mind, but she saw him. Black Robe. The kidnapper. The asshole. Now she knew—it was Leopold Deshane.

Her father.

"We have to go," said Elizabeth.

"Go where?" asked Trent. They had just finished a late breakfast. He'd been thinking of taking her back to bed. He never tired of touching her, of finding the places that made her squirm and moan and sigh. She was playful, and he liked that. But she could also be serious. She made him feel as though he'd been missing a part of himself . . . a part he hadn't even known about until that night, that night she had changed his whole world.

He still grieved for his uncle. He still wondered what the hell was going on with the streak of suicides in town, and that damned Colt that connected those deaths. Maybe his uncle had been murdered. Screw the evidence. But who would do it? And why such random victims?

"Trent." Elizabeth reached across the table that was tucked into the small kitchen. "I think it's time."

"Time for what?"

She smiled—that wonderful, achingly beautiful smile—and once again, he pushed aside his sorrow and decided to live for the moment.

When Norie woke up from the dream that had restored her memories, she was being manacled. They were still in the barn, but now there were other people there—Ravens.

"What's going on?" she asked. Her voice sounded tinny. "What are you doing?"

"We're arresting you and your coconspirators for the deaths of Ravens Orley Ryerson and Bernard Franco and for colluding to cover up their murders."

The voice was familiar. Norie leaned back and stared up into the now-familiar face. "Hello, Father."

"That's Raven Deshane to you," he said in a haughty voice. "I have no daughter."

"Whatever."

Norie's mouth felt dry, and her head like cotton. She felt different somehow, more alive, as if something electric and foreign lived inside her now. But that power was somehow trapped. No, that was the wrong word. Inaccessible. As if she needed a key to unlock it.

Her father leaned close and whispered, "Don't bother trying to get to that precious magic of yours. The chains will dampen the powers of even the greatest mage. By tonight, you'll be bleeding out on the altar."

She saw Cullen lying next to her, unconscious, and he'd been manacled, too.

"Happy birthday to me," she muttered. Then she passed out again.

Chapter 15

Cullen came awake tied to a chair. Though his first instinct was to expend energy trying to free himself, he squelched the urge. Instead, he inhaled, waited for his vision to quit being so damned fuzzy, and looked around.

Lenore Deshane, his sister, was tied to a chair next to him.

"Hey," he managed in a low voice.

"Hey." It was obvious that she'd been awake longer. Given the sweat on her brow, she'd struggled to get out of the bonds. Her wrists were manacled.

"Where's dear old dad?" he asked.

She shook her head. She was scared, he could see that, but she was holding it together.

"I don't know about you," he said, "but he's off my Christmas card list."

She barked a laugh. "Mine, too."

"Now, children, is that any way to speak about your

271

father?" Leopold Deshane sauntered forward. Cullen got the impression that others hovered behind the perimeter of their little circle. They'd been placed in a shaft of light beaming down from a hole in the barn roof. But the rest of the place was in darkness.

"The star twins," said Leopold. "My very own children." His face went hard. "And your mother hid you from me."

"She sacrificed herself for us," said Norie.

"Mary was always prettier than she was smart," he said. "I tracked you down, Norie, didn't I?"

"How?" asked Norie.

"It took years to unravel the spellwork—starting with your brother. It took our best wizards to figure out what had been cast, and then we came across the prophecy. I knew then what Mary had done. And then I found out that Millicent hadn't done her job. You were alive. Turns out that was good news after all."

"You're a bastard," said Cullen conversationally. "And this isn't going to end well for you."

Leo shrugged, obviously unconcerned about his son's threats. "I almost had you killed, too," he said. "But getting rid of one child was enough of a risk. And a son . . . well, a son who could carry on the Deshane legacy was better than a girl." He eyed Cullen with disgust. "What a disappointment you are."

"Back atcha, Dad."

Leo's lips thinned. "You'll understand why you're not invited to the sacrifice," he said. "I just need the pure blood of the female star twin to open the portal to Kahl. And we really can't have you two together, can we?"

"Together, they can save the world or destroy it," said Cullen bitterly.

His father laughed. "As soon as your sister is dead, I'll come for you."

"Leave her alone," he said. Man, it hadn't taken long for him to fall back into the big-brother role. They may have been separated for twenty-five years, but he damned well remembered how he'd felt about his little sister. His mother had always told him to protect her, and he would. "I'll go with you. Willingly."

"No," said Leo. "You're not the sacrifice."

"Dad!" Cullen swallowed the pride, the fury that threatened to clog up his throat. "Don't hurt her. I'll go. I'll do whatever you want."

"Yes," said Leo. "You will." He rubbed his hands together and offered them an awful smile. "Well, there are preparations to make. And I've had enough of family time." He held up his hands, palms out, and two streams of black issued forth, hitting first Norie and then Cullen in the chest.

Cullen felt as if someone had punched him with a giant iron fist.

Then everything went dark once more.

* * *

Norie awoke in a jail cell that held Leticia, Lucinda, and Happy. They were awake, standing near the jail door and conversing with Taylor, who'd been imprisoned in the cell across the way. He was alone. He pressed fully against the bars, his gaze full of worry and anger.

"Norie!"

"I'm fine," she croaked as she rolled to her knees and sat up. "Where's Cullen?"

"Here." In the next cell were Cullen, Gray, and Roan. "The Ravens got us all. There were too many, and they were casting spells before we realized what was going on. We don't know what happened to the other townspeople."

"Bespelled is my guess," said Leticia. "Bastards! Holding us on such outrageous charges. And Deshane! What nerve!"

"It appears that the House of Ravens absolved Deshane of all wrongdoing," said Gray to Norie.

"Which they cannot do! When it comes to crimes of magic, the entire Court decides the punishment, not just one House, and certainly not the House from which the perpetrator belongs!" Leticia's anger vibrated in every word. "I bet the entire Grand Court is in an uproar. Washington must be in chaos right now."

"We have to focus on what's going on here," said Gray. "The prophecy said that the star twins accessed the key to the world. I think that's why they need the *nemeton*—it's where the Goddess fountain must be accessed. It's the only place with enough power to open a portal for Kahl. And Norie's blood has to be spilled on the altar to make that happen."

"Why my blood? Why not Cullen's?" She sent an apologetic glance to her brother, which he acknowledged with a quick grin.

"A woman's virgin blood," said Gray.

Norie felt her cheeks go hot. "Oh."

"At least we know how the Ravens got into Nevermore," said Gray. "The town's magical protections recognized your blood connection to Mary Clark."

"So I let them in?"

"Not on purpose," said Cullen. "This isn't your fault."

"If we can stop Deshane from completing the ritual," said Gray, "then the Ravens might rethink the whole idea of war. They can't win without the demons."

Norie stood up and made her way to the front of the cell. "Are you okay?" she asked Taylor quietly.

"Just pissed off," he said. His gaze softened. "You?"

"Bruised ego," she said. "Not much else." She looked at him, really looked at him, and saw that he truly was okay. She felt like her time was coming to an end, and she didn't want it to. For so long she'd felt she had nothing to live for. And now she'd found something meaningful in her life. She didn't want to give up Taylor. Goddess, what she'd do for that man. "Does anyone know what time it is?"

Everyone was suddenly quiet, and she knew then that the entire day had been wasted. Whatever plans they might've made, whatever preparations might've been made—it was all for naught. It was done.

The Ravens appeared to have won.

She would fight, though. She would fight until the bitter end.

It was as if her thoughts had drawn them into the jail. Four black robes entered the narrow hallway, gliding silently as though they were grim reapers.

Norie readied herself. If she was going down, she would go down hard.

The first black robe pulled down the cowl.

"Mordi!" said Taylor, a rush of relief in his voice.

The other three pulled down their cowls, too, revealing Trent, Ember, and Rilton.

"Well, now," said Ember. "Let's get you outta dere."

"Where are the guards?" asked Gray.

"Taken care of," said Ember. "How you tink we got dese fancy robes?"

It took precious minutes to unwind the magic used to reinforce the protections on the cells. Norie's heart pounded so hard, she could hear it thudding in her ears. She gripped the bars tightly, watching the wizards and witches do their mojo.

Finally, all the cells were opened. Ember passed out extra black robes. The idea was to get to the portal in the break room upstairs. It seemed that the Ravens hadn't figured out that aspect of Nevermore.

They all donned the robes. Taylor swooped in for a quick kiss and then pulled up Norie's cowl to conceal her face. It was stupid to feel so happy about that little show of affection, but she was. It made her feel loved.

Oh, wow.

Everything about her life had been crazy. . . . At least loving Taylor was the kind of insanity that was good. No, fantastic.

She got into the line of escapees heading up the narrow stairwell. All they had to do was get to the portal and go to the Guardian's house. Gray was sure that none of the Ravens would be able to penetrate his magical protections, especially since it had been reinforced by Lucinda's thanaturgical gifts. Norie had gathered that Lucinda was quite powerful, but the Ravens had no idea how much. *Good.* Because those bastards deserved to burn.

They filtered into the break room, only to find three Ravens taking advantage of the espresso machine.

"Son of a bitch," muttered Taylor. "How'd they figure out how to use it so fast?"

While they chatted as though they hadn't just overrun a town and planned to kill people and colluded with demons . . . Cullen, Gray, and Taylor walked toward them. As they all turned, the men punched each of them hard in the face.

All three went down, coffee flying and cups smashing. "Damn it," said Gray. "Get to the portal."

Taylor grabbed Norie's arm and dragged her to the portal. Ember opened it, and Taylor shoved her through, into the cold, dark magic of endless night.

Cullen watched his sister jump into the portal; then he watched as the sheriff went in after her. He'd seen the way they'd been looking at each other, and he had even spotted that kiss Taylor had planted on Norie. Since he'd only recently discovered he had a sibling, he couldn't exactly play the big-brother card.

He shouldn't, maybe. But he damned well would.

"You go next," Ember said to Cullen. "Go on, now."

He ran across the room. Just as he got to the magical entryway, other Ravens burst into the break room, magic already sizzling around their fingertips. Ember didn't give him time to make a decision about going or staying. She planted a hand on his back and shoved.

Ember closed the portal and turned her efforts to fending off the Ravens. More and more arrived, filling up the room with their black robes and foul magic. She'd had enough of this evil, and she called upon the Goddess for help.

White light flashed in the room, followed by a tremendous boom. When the light and sound relented, all the Ravens were sprawled on the floor.

"Go!" yelled Gray. Mordi and Trent went first, then Gray and Lucinda, then Happy. Leticia and Roan went next, and finally Ember and Rilton. As they rushed down the hall and out of the lobby, Ember stole another glance at poor Arlene. She was like a statue—one of the victims of the freezing spell that the Ravens had put onto the townsfolk. Everyone who'd had the misfortune of being within a mile of the town had been affected. Ember could only assume the farmers who remained outside of the spell were smart enough to go into hiding. Or maybe the Ravens were in the outer limits causing havoc with the mundanes. She didn't know. As soon as they rid Nevermore of these pests, the spell would be lifted.

But she couldn't be worried about that now.

They hurried onto the street, everyone who had magic calling it forth. Rilton stayed well behind the mages, knowing it was the only way to protect himself. She wanted him to go to the café, to stay safe in the confines of neutral ground, but he wouldn't do it. That was the beauty of having a life partner, a lover, a best friend.

Ravens converged behind them.

And Ember turned her attention to defending herself, her husband, and her home.

Ant didn't like this shit at all. He and Elandra had hidden out at Mordi's request. They made the necessary preparations, and while Elandra stayed behind to put on the finishing touches, Ant used the closest portal to get to town.

He came through in Atwood's office. The damned place was a mess. He stalked through the office and down the hallway. He peered out the window framed in the door. The battle raged fiercely, and he itched to be part of it. But he couldn't expend his magic. He needed it all to do what Mordi had asked.

Damn it all.

Mordi wasn't a full-on magical. She had a communion with the dead because that was her job, her calling. But the Goddess fountain affected everyone, or so it seemed. Or maybe it was just the Goddess sending on a message. Who knew? All the same, Mordi had a vivid dream one night and when she awoke, she knew what was to come, and what she was meant to do.

Trent must survive. He has a great task ahead of him. I know what I know so that I can help him achieve that. I don't mind, Ant. I'm glad for it. I love him. And I do this for love, and with love.

Mordi's words echoed in his head like a eulogy.

He stared out the window.

And like a fool, he waited.

Trent tried to protect Elizabeth as much as possible. She stayed behind him for the most part, but he was terrified for her. Still, he stayed focused, using his necromancy to strike at the Ravens who were flinging their magic at them as hard and fast as they could.

They got separated from the others, but it was obvious that the Ravens were weakening. Nevermore's witches and wizards were too powerful for the bad guys, and that was the truth of it. But he knew more would come, and more would try.

"Get to the office," said Trent. "Go!"

"No," said Elizabeth, somehow managing to stay calm among the sizzling magic battle. Then she yelled, "Trent!" And she shoved him out of the way.

He stumbled hard, falling to his knees as a black lightning bolt slammed into Elizabeth.

"No!" he screamed. "No!"

She fell backward, sprawling in the brick street like a broken doll. Trent slid toward her, throwing out magic at any Raven stupid enough to get close.

He put a protection bubble around them both, a bubble he knew would last only seconds in the magical onslaught. He slid his arms under her. "Elizabeth," he whispered. "Sweetheart."

Tears fell down his cheeks at the sight of her. He was a necro. He knew death, just as she did. She was fading fast, her soul clinging like so much smoke.

The bubble popped, and he didn't care. He didn't fucking care. Let the Ravens take them both.

"Trent." Somehow, some way, Ant was there, beside

him, trying to take Elizabeth. "C'mon, man. We have to go."

"Doesn't matter," said Trent dully. "Nothing matters without her."

"You may be right about that," said Ant. "But let's go anyway."

With Gray and Ember keeping the other Ravens at bay, a pathway was made to get Mordi, Ant, and Trent off Main Street.

Trent insisted on carrying her, and when they got to the portal, he stepped through with her dying in his arms.

Norie and Taylor found themselves stumbling onto a narrow dirt path. Taylor didn't know where the hell the portal had tossed them, until he saw the trees.

Shit.

They were in his forest, close to the *nemeton*.

He grabbed Norie's arm and started hauling ass away from the—

"Thank you, Sheriff," said Leopold Deshane as he stepped onto the path in front of them. More Ravens glided onto the path, effectively surrounding them.

"We won't need the sheriff," said Leopold as he yanked his daughter out of Taylor's embrace. "Come along, Norie. Your destiny awaits."

Taylor punched the first Raven so hard, the man crumpled. These mages were made of glass, too reliant on their magic to build up some muscles. Then three Ravens grabbed at him, and the fourth came at him with a surge of black oily energy.

All Taylor felt was sudden, searing pain.

Then nothing.

"What the hell is going on?" asked Trent, his voice dull with grief. "What does Tree have to do with saving Elizabeth?"

"She can't be saved," said Ant kindly, "and you know it."

"I'll put her soul back in," he said, "like I did for Happy."

"That won't work," said Elandra. "Necromancy cannot undo when a person's time is come. You know that."

"I don't care!"

"We have to do what she wanted," said Ant. "She wanted to save you, and she wanted to save Tree. With her life force—her soul—she'll be here forever, Trent. She'll always be a part of Nevermore."

Trent sobbed, but he let Ant extract Elizabeth from his arms. He sank to his knees, grief a vise around his heart. Elandra helped him lay her down on a blanket. She put Elizabeth's hand against Tree's trunk, and then Ant did the same with her other hand.

Together, they spoke the words, words so ancient, so magical, they permeated the air with life, with all that could be.

Trent watched as Elizabeth's soul loosened from her body, and with what he could only describe as love, sank into the stalwart trunk of Nevermore's true guardian.

The Ravens who had not been injured or dispatched fell back from the onslaught rendered by Ember, Gray, Lucinda, Leticia, and Roan. Rilton had relented in his insistence to stay with Ember only because Happy needed to be escorted to the café. "We must get to the café!" yelled Ember.

As the Ravens fell back and stopped trying to annihilate them, they all ran toward the café.

"Why did they stop?" asked Lucy as they all stood in the lobby, catching their breath.

"Why dey need to worry 'bout us?" asked Ember sadly. "Dey got da girl."

Cullen fell onto the dirt path, landing knees first. The jolt of the impact shimmed up his spine. Damn it. He just couldn't get the hang of traveling through the portals. He stood up and looked around. It took a moment to adjust his vision to the dark. And that was when he noticed the crumpled form just ahead.

Not. Good.

He hurried to the prone figure and realized right away it was Taylor. He smelled weird, as though he'd been barbecued. "Don't be dead," he whispered. Then he put his fingers against Taylor's neck. There was still a faint beat there, a pulse. Relief flooded him.

Then the world tilted.

The magic that had felt so locked within him, like a monster that slithered inside, waiting, burst forth.

It flooded over Taylor in sparkling white effervescence.

The sheriff sat straight up, sucked in a huge breath, looked at Cullen, and said, "Norie."

It killed Cullen to move slowly and be quiet as they trod through the forest. He wanted to rush in, to save the day—to save his sister. He remembered now what it had felt like to take care of her, to feel protective of her. Though born only minutes before her, he was still the older one. He couldn't believe that Norie was supposed to be a virgin sacrifice to the demon lord Kahl. Ravens and demons working together—that was fucked up. He wanted to hurry to his sister's rescue. She was the only family he had left, especially given that their biological father was a royal asshole.

He sensed the *nemeton* before he laid eyes on it. It was magnificent. Huge and ancient and . . . sorrowful. Magic was imbued in those stones, and the Ravens were trying to taint what the Goddess had wrought. Taylor signaled him to stop and stay low. They scurried toward the stone entrance and peered around its edges.

"What are these?" Cullen pointed down to a couple of misshapen clay bodies.

"Those are vigils," said Taylor. "I guess the Ravens destroyed them before they could send out warnings."

"And they didn't post any guards?" Cullen looked around.

"Arrogant bastards," said Taylor. "Or maybe there're not as many of them as we think."

They returned their gazes to the *nemeton*.

Seven black-robed figures surrounded the stone altar.

Norie was chained to it, naked, and she struggled against her bonds as they cut into her.

Beyond the altar, a portal—a huge dark oval—had opened, and the face peering out of it so eagerly was monstrous.

"Kahl," said Taylor, horrified.

"I say we go in and fuck up their shit," said Cullen.

"Sounds like a plan."

They charged forward.

Chapter 16

Cullen went around one side of the altar and just plowed into the Ravens. Taylor did the same to the ones on the other side.

They went down like bowling pins.

And then one popped up, tossed off the cowl of her black robe, and gazed at them with red eyes.

"Kerren," said Taylor. The horror in the sheriff's voice didn't bode well. Cullen eyed the half-demon magical. So this was the woman who'd sold her husband's soul for money and immortality.

What a bitch.

"So rude!" She aimed a hand at Cullen and issued a fireball.

Cullen dodged it, though how he didn't know. He drew her off, and she followed him, marching toward him and tossing all kinds of magic crap.

Taylor headed to the altar and grabbed at the chains that bound Norie. *Shit*. His hands tingled, but he couldn't get the magic to work. He didn't know how to be a magical. He just wanted to save Norie.

He looked at Cullen and watched in amazement as he got close enough to Kerren to coldcock her. Whether the recipient was immortal or not, a hard punch to the jaw had the same effect: She went down like a sack of rocks, sprawling onto the grass.

Cullen grinned, dusting off his hands. Then he was running toward the altar.

Taylor turned and saw Leopold, his lip bloody from his fall to the ground, his eyes insane. Leopold screamed in frustration. "No! Kahl must be brought forward. The Ravens must take their rightful place in this world!" He raised a gleaming silver dagger and plunged it downward, toward Norie's heart.

Taylor knocked his hand away, but the Raven was strong, and he came back, trying again. He nicked the side of Norie's throat, and blood flowed onto the stone.

"No!" Taylor punched Leopold, and the man fell back, stumbling while trying to catch his balance.

The portal was already opening. Darkness leaked out, snaking toward Norie.

Taylor felt his heart claw up into his throat. *No, damn it. No!*

Cullen reached them, and he and Taylor both grabbed at Norie.

The moment they touched, the magic within all of

them unlocked. It flowed like a river, and then the Goddess spoke:

Raven born, you are my Chosen. Brother and sister and key, work together to unlock that which belongs to Nevermore. Drive back the evil. And prepare for what must come next.

Cullen aimed his palm at his father, and white magic shot out, knocking the man backward. The dagger flew out of his grip, and he was sent crashing against the large blue stone.

They heard the crack of his skull as he collapsed onto the ground, staring at the night sky with sightless eyes.

"Damn it!" Kerren stalked toward them, murder in her eyes. "Don't bother, you irritating little humans!" She raised her hands, magic licking at her palms.

Kahl entered the doorway. He was big, powerful, built like a minotaur. He even had hooves, and his legs were as thick and strong as a bull's. He had to be nearly nine feet tall. His demon form was fearsome to behold.

One thick, black leathery leg slipped onto the earthly plane.

The *nemeton* shuddered.

Cullen aimed their power at Kerren.

Her eyes narrowed and then went wide. Her body stilled. Flames exploded around her feet, then wound around her legs like hungry snakes.

Her unearthly screeches echoed around the *nemeton* . . . and still the fire consumed her.

Then she exploded.

Ash that was once Kerren floated onto the ground like sullen snowflakes.

Kahl was nearly through the doorway, though it was obvious he was struggling. Something was keeping him from completely crossing into the human world.

Cullen directed their magic, the gift of the Goddess, into the portal.

It covered Kahl with gold light, and he screamed in agony.

Just as his wife had been annihilated by the magic created by love, by goodness, he was consumed by flames.

He fell back, his furious screams swallowed by the sound of flames, of vengeance.

Then his massive body imploded.

Hell's doorway disappeared.

The other Ravens had risen from being knocked down, and now they were scrambling to get away, but Cullen trapped them easily with the magic that still pulsed from his palms. They went catatonic in the grass.

Well done, Chosen.

Cullen looked at Taylor and nodded. They released Norie, and the magic receded, but it was no longer locked inside the star twins. It was there, an ocean of power, of Light, and of good.

* * *

"You okay?"

Norie looked up from the bed, finding herself once again tucked in between its cozy covers. The magic had overwhelmed her, but not Cullen. He'd always been the stronger one, and she didn't mind. But she would learn to use her new powers, and they would make sure that nothing else threatened Nevermore.

"C'mere," she said, and patted the edge of the bed.

Taylor crossed the room. He was wearing a T-shirt and jeans, but no socks. He looked vulnerable without his uniform on—like a different person, and maybe one not so weighed down by duty.

"What can I get for you?" he asked.

"I want just one thing," she said.

"Whatever you want."

"You."

His eyes widened. "I dreamed about you." He leaned over and stroked a finger down the side of her cheek. "I didn't think you . . . that we'd be here right now. I want this. I want you." He looked down at his tattooed hands. He sighed. "I'm a damned key."

Norie covered his hands. "You amplify the magic of others," she said. "That's a rare gift."

"Maybe," he said. He looked at her and offered a smile. "If it protects you, and Nevermore, then that's all right by me."

They looked at each other, their hearts open, their

future still yet to be written. Taylor pulled back. "Guess I'd better let you rest," he said. "We'll talk more in the morning."

"Stay with me," said Norie. "Please."

"There's a time and place for us to be together," said Taylor. "Mostly I'm thinking after vows have been spoken."

Norie grinned. Oh, this man. This wonderful, honorable man.

"Just hold me, Taylor. Tonight, that's enough."

"Oh." He offered a sheepish grin. Then crawling in next to her, he lay against her, wrapped his arms around her, and snuggled close.

Perfect, thought Norie.

She was finally home.

The funeral for Elizabeth Jones was held two days later. Cleanup still remained to be done, along with Ravens to arrest, suicides to investigate, and new residents to welcome to Nevermore.

But now it was time to say good-bye to the mortal remains of a beloved friend. Trent saw to the arrangements himself, refusing help from any of his friends. The funeral was short, and good-byes were spoken.

Then the coffin was lowered into the grave, and everyone helped to cover it with earth.

Mordi wasn't in the ground—no soul went to the grave with its body—but she lived on in Tree. This had been confirmed by Ant and Elandra, but Trent had known the moment he put his hand on the trunk that his love lived on within its essence.

It was small comfort.

Elizabeth had given Trent charge of Elysian Fields, and it seemed a more fitting vocation for a necromancer than garbage collector or paperboy.

But those concerns were for other days.

Taylor refused to let Norie out of bed. She was feeling better, but she liked all his fussing, so she let him feed her chicken soup and bring her cold washcloths for her forehead. Her brother knew her game and gave her some grief for it, but with a grin that warmed her heart.

They had decided to stay in Nevermore. She wanted a life with Taylor. And she and Cullen wanted to find their roots, their real family. Their mother had sacrificed her life for theirs, and they would find some way to honor that.

"No leads about Betty Mae?" asked Gray.

They stood in the break room of the sheriff's office while Taylor tried to get the infernal espresso machine to work. "None. My brother's outta his mind with grief. He's moving back in with me. He can't stand to step a foot into that place right now."

"At least the gun is secure." Gray paused. "You need any help with that?"

"No," said Taylor. "I'll figure out this thing if it's the last damned thing I do." He turned a knob, and the machine hissed. "I hear tell your mother's staying on."

Gray groaned. "Don't remind me. She wants to help protect the Goddess fountain and figure out what's going on around here."

"Well, I want to know that, too. Leticia's smart, Gray. And she's no slouch in the magic department, either."

"I know. But she's not exactly making things easy on Lucy."

"Lucinda can hold her own. Just give it some time. It'll work out." He cursed as the machine groaned but produced no coffee.

"And what about the suicides? About Betty Mae?"

"I'll keep digging," said Taylor. "I won't let it loose until I know what happened."

"And how do you feel about Cullen's staying around?"

"He's good for Norie. Though I heard him talking about some absinthe lounge, whatever the hell that is. I don't guess he plans on reopening the sewing shop."

"He's asked for a visitor's pass for a friend of his— name of Laurent. Looks as though we'll have some new faces around here."

"Just as long as they don't cause trouble. The Ravens are doing plenty of that for us."

"Well, they're not seceding from the Grand Court." Gray frowned. "At least . . . not yet."

"That whole mess! At least your mom came in handy for that."

"Thanks to the memory wipes she did on the Ravens, nobody will know what happened in the *nemeton*," said Gray. "And no one will miss Leopold Deshane."

"As long as we get some normal around here for a while, I'm okay with it."

"Good." Gray walked around, twisted a knob, pushed a button, and flicked a switch. Pure black nirvana poured into the coffee mug.

Taylor looked at his friend. "You're a bastard."

Chapter 17

It was midnight. Leticia Calhoun lay in bed, unable to sleep. Something tickled the back of her consciousness like a spider web caught in her hair. She couldn't relax; she couldn't sleep.

Cheater.

Leticia sat up. "Who's there?"

Liar.

Her heart began to pound, and she clenched the covers. She looked around, damned if she would show the fear that was crawling around her belly.

You killed him, you know. With what you did.

She looked at the nightstand, at the Colt .45 gleaming like vengeance in the moonlight.

Broke your vows.

Broke his heart.

Pay the price.

Suddenly, Leticia understood. Guilt wormed through her, acid in her veins. *I hurt him. He found out. Then he died.*

Yes. She should pay the price.

So she picked up the gun.

Read on for a sneak peek at the next book
in Michele Bardsley's Broken Heart series,

ONLY LYCANS NEED APPLY

Available September 2012
from Signet Eclipse

Ax was the best campfire cook, and he was punished for it nightly by having to make us all delicious meals (even with the sand that got into them—sand got into everything). I enjoyed tormenting my grad students, so I made them clean up. Again. *Mu-ha-ha-ha-ha-ha.*

"You turning in early?" asked Ax as he eased himself onto the ground next to me. I was sitting on a canvas chair, staring at the fire. Already the heat of the day was giving way to the chill of the night. I glanced at my companion. He was a big man, well aware of his height and girth, and generally a gentle soul. But I'd seen him riled a time or two, and he definitely had the kind of mean a female archaeologist needed in the south Sudan.

"Yeah. Dawn to dusk, that's the glamorous life of an archaeologist," I said.

"Quit being so bitter about Indiana Jones."

"It's directed more at Lara Croft."

He laughed.

"Permit will be up in three days." I sighed. "It's not enough time."

"You're lucky you got any sand time at all in these parts," said Ax. He chewed on a toothpick the size of a twig. "It's not safe, you know."

"It's not safe anywhere," I responded automatically. Granted, trying to extract ancient history from the desert while war raged around our perimeter was certainly more dangerous than trying to cross the street in Manhattan.

But not by much.

"I'm going to bed," I said, getting up. "See you in the a.m."

"I'll make the coffee."

I grimaced. Ax could cook like Martha Stewart, but his coffee had driven otherwise hardened souls to attempt suicide. "Dove will make the coffee. Your sludge is like drinking ass-flavored gelatin."

He grinned. "G'night, Doc."

"Yeah, yeah." I waved at him.

Dove was already tucked into her cot, snoring away. Ah, the sweet sleep of ornery bitches. I crawled onto my own cot and pulled up the scratchy blanket. Exhaustion weighed on me like the Great Pyramid.

I fell asleep before the discomfort of my crappy sleeping arrangements had the chance to annoy me.

* * *

"Moira!"

"Earthquake," I mumbled as my entire body was flung back and forth. I opened my eyes. A distraught Dove was inches from my face, shaking me by the shoulders. "If you keep doing that, I'm gonna need a Dramamine."

She let go of me, then dropped to her knees next to my cot. "Something just whooshed by our tent."

I leaned up on one elbow and stared at her sleepily. "Like 'death on swift wings'? Ugh. You're not gonna throw quotes from *The Mummy* at me, are you? I told you to knock that shit off."

"You are the worst waker-upper ever," she whispered harshly. "I'm telling you, someone is out there."

"Okay, okay." The real fear in her tone was almost like a cold dash of water to the face. Almost. I really was a bad waker-upper. I rolled off the cot on the other side, then reached under my pillow and took out my subcompact Beretta. It was loaded with thirteen 9 mm rounds.

"Sleeping with a loaded gun under your pillow?" she asked. "Really?"

"Relax. It has a manual safety and a decocker."

She snorted. "A what?"

"Decocker," I repeated. "It's a lever that lets the hammer—"

"I don't care." She smirked. "I just wanted to see if you'd say it again."

"I hate you," I said, feeling surly. "Go get Tikka."

"Or not." Dove imperiously pointed a finger at me. "You shouldn't name weaponry, you know that?"

"She already had the name."

"Nor should guns have gender. Personalizing the—"

"Look, kid," I interrupted. "Giving someone a dirty look doesn't exactly have stopping power—not even one of your patented I-wish-you-were-dead specialties. Get the fucking rifle."

"Whatever," she hissed at me. Then she flopped to her belly and crawled toward the footlocker that housed the rifle and other, more precious gear. As she pulled out the weapon and the box of bullets, I glanced around. A single lantern cast a muted glow in our tent. Dove wouldn't admit it, but she was scared of the dark. Why she was studying to be an archaeologist, a profession where exploring dark, cramped, and airless spaces was the norm, was beyond me.

As Miss Quiet as a Raging Storm rattled around trying to get the rifle loaded, I crept to the tent flap and peeked outside.

It only took a few seconds for my eyesight to adjust. The campfire had been doused, and the supplies put away. No one was prowling around. Still, it was ungodly quiet. The hair rose on the nape of my neck.

"Dove," I whispered as I turned around.   ·

I gasped.

A tall, lean man held Dove by the neck in one hand,

and the rifle in his other. How the hell had he gotten into the tent? He could've easily passed for one of my grad students, except he was dressed like fucking Indiana Jones, right down to the fedora and a faded leather duster. Seriously? We were getting jacked by a Harrison Ford wannabe?

He was too lithe to have the strength to hold my terrified assistant a foot off the ground, but he was doing it. He wasn't even breaking a sweat. *What the*— I nearly pissed myself. He wasn't even *breathing*. He was unnaturally pale, his eyes as dark as midnight. His black hair shone like a raven's wing. When he smiled, he revealed a set of sharp, ugly fangs.

Okay. I probably should've considered Dove's position on vampires with a little less skepticism. From my crouched position, I pointed the Beretta at his face.

"Vampire," said Dove, her voice choked and her eyes wide. Fear emanated from her in waves. Or maybe that was me, because I was more terrified than I'd ever been in my life. And I'd once thrown down with a Kardashian for a Bottega Veneta leather handbag (in butterscotch cream, if you were wondering), and won.

"Put her down!"

"Or what?" he asked, his voice thick with an accent I couldn't place. "She's merely the appetizer. You, my fine Amazon, are the meal."

"That's the worse pick-up line I've ever heard."

He grinned, and then he opened his mouth, showing off those awful, sharp fangs, and jerked Dove downward, aiming for her neck. She tried to struggle, but it was like watching a ribbon wrestle with the wind.

Shit! I lowered the gun and shot out his knees. The sharp crack of the pistol firing echoed in the tent even after the bullets thudded into his patellas.

He screamed in pain and outrage as he buckled, dropping Dove and the rifle. She grabbed Tikka, and hauled ass toward me.

"You have to remove his head," she cried. "Sever it! Sever it!"

"These are bullets, not hacksaws," I said as she scrambled behind me. "He's down, all right?"

"Not for long. He's the undead!" She wrestled with Tikka, then cursed. "It's not even loaded. I couldn't get the stupid bullets in before that asshole grabbed me."

"I will rend your muscles from your bones," said the dude, his gaze vitriolic. "You will die slowly as I feast upon you."

"And you thought me quoting *The Mummy* was bad?" murmured Dove.

"Go get Ax," I told Dove.

"The hell," she said. "We have to find something that will cut through a big, fat, stupid, undead neck."

"I'm not saying he's *not* a vampire," I said. Sweat dripped down my temple, but the gun I'd trained on No Knees didn't waver. "But is decapitation really the way to go here?"

"The only way to kill a vampire is to take off his head or expose him to intense light. It says so in *Vampires Are Real!*"

"Oh, my God. That Theodora Monroe book? Really? That's like taking advice from the Winchester brothers."

"And you know exactly *what* about supernatural creatures?"

"Silence!" bellowed the vampire as he wobbled to his feet. His pants were shredded and bloody, but his knees were nearly knitted back together. "You are both imbeciles. And you talk too much."

"Holy shit!" screamed Dove. "Holy fucking shit!"

I shot at him again, but he moved in a blur of motion. He was coming for us, so I shoved Dove to the side, and started shooting randomly. Yeah. That worked out well.

Then *I* was shoved to the side, and I flew backward, landing next to an outraged Dove. We watched, open-mouthed, as a huge black wolf leapt into the air, howling in triumph.

We both scrambled toward my cot and stayed at the edge of it. We couldn't see the vampire, but it was obvious the wolf could. He landed on the bastard's chest and knocked him to the ground. It was a short, brutal fight that ended when the animal tore out the vampire's throat.

The undead version of Indiana Jones went limp. Blood pooled in the sand around the ravaged neck.

Dove and I looked at each other, then back at the scene that seemed right out of a horror movie.

As if a vampire and a supersized undead-killing wolf showing up in my tent wasn't fantastical enough—and weren't vampires supposed to take wolf form, or something? I was rusty on preternatural mythology—our black-furred rescuer then padded to a nearby space and morphed into a man.

It wasn't like a transformation you might see on a late-night werewolf flick. It was sorta . . . magical, I suppose. His fur rippled into skin; his limbs stretched and plumped into human arms and legs. And long, silky black hair fell over his shoulders.

Also, he was naked.

Very, very naked.

He claimed one of my discarded T-shirts that was lying near the foot locker, and rubbed his face. I realized he was wiping off the vampire's blood. Then he returned to the dead guy, and wrenched off the head. The fedora fell off and rolled toward Dove's cot. The wolf tossed down the head next to its body.

Within seconds, the vampire parts turned to ash.

Dove and I shared a holy-shit-did-that-just-really-happen look.

"I call the duster," said Dove in a strangled voice.

"That baby's mine," I said.

"Fine. I get the hat."

"Whatever, Indiana."

"Are you all right?" The man walked toward us, and stopped on the other side of the cot, his expression a mask of concern as he studied our faces. He had the most amazing jade green eyes. I didn't even know eyes could be that color. He was gorgeous. Huge, muscled, beautiful. Well, except for the blood that streaked him from neck to . . .

"Is that real?" asked Dove in a reverent voice. "Because that's the biggest dick I've ever seen."

"He can hear you," I said. Then in a low voice, I added, "Don't you even think about taking dibs, you bitch."

"Then you are okay," he said drily. He grabbed the blanket from my cot and wrapped it around his waist. "My name is Drake."

"Moira Jameson," I said. "This is Dove."

"*Just* Dove," she said severely, as though to forestall any questions about a last name.

He inclined his head. "I must say, you handle yourselves very well. Not many humans are so . . . well, accepting of parakind."

"Parakind?"

"A general term. But in this case, I speak of the *droch fola*," he said, pointing at the pile of ash that was currently messing up my new duster. "And me, of course. The werewolf."

"Just another day in the desert," I said. I was starting to get the shakes. See, I was great at crisis-in-the-moment. But the aftershocks got me every time.

"Ah." He tilted his head, and offered a wicked grin. "It's really too bad."

"What is?" I asked.

"You will not remember anything that happened tonight." He gave me a long look, one that sparkled with regret. "And you will not remember me."